I0727207

The Unconvinced

The Unconvinced

Harrison Hickman

CONTENTS

Copyright © 2025 by Harrison Hickman
All rights reserved. No part of this book may be reproduced in any manner whatsoever without written permission except in the case of brief quotations embodied in critical articles and reviews.
First Printing, 2025

For the Musketeers

1

Part 1

Henry Jarrett
Sunday, 17 May, 2009

He had an overwhelming urge to turn back the moment he laid eyes on the place.

There was no possibility, absolutely no chance, that he would thrive here.

This was the short straw, without a doubt. Most poets landed residencies in thrilling urban projects, immersing themselves in vibrant arts venues and captivating audiences at glamorous festivals. And what had he been handed? A summer in a sleepy little village near Canterbury. His days would be filled with giving readings to clusters of the elderly, sipping tea and nibbling on cake in the quaint local café, hosting the summer fete – oh, and cutting the ribbon at the grand re-opening of the newly renovated church. Such exhilarating prospects awaited him!

In short: Henry Jarrett had been nominated for the prestigious Emerald Wordsmith Prize for his debut poetry collection, *Starling Notes*. The jury's unanimous decision had crowned him the winner... and this was his reward.

As the taxi rolled closer and the thatched roofs appeared one after another, he silently berated his own inflated imagination. What on earth had convinced him he was destined for three glorious months in L.A.?

Jarrett opened his shoulder bag and brushed his knuckles across the twenty paperback copies of *Starling Notes* his publisher had handed him—fresh ink, soft covers, and the subtle weight of nerves.

"You that poet guy?" the driver asked, glancing at him in the rearview mirror.

"Yeah, that's me," Jarrett said.

"You'll have a cracking time here—once all the tea and biscuits are gone, anyway," the driver said with a grin. "I live in the village. My daughter's a big fan of yours. Just so you don't think I'm prying."

Jarrett smiled. "No worries at all."

"You're a young bloke, if you don't mind me saying so," the driver remarked, his eyes glancing over. "You should be in London or somewhere, not stuck out here in this godforsaken backwater."

"I'm thirty-five, mate," Jarrett replied.

"Still young in my books – ha, no pun intended," the driver chuckled. "Right, I'm dropping you at the arts centre. Ridiculous place to build, if you ask me. Just because a shop shuts down and no one buys it doesn't mean you turn it into some fancy art spot."

"Well, with the financial situation the way it is..." Jarrett offered.

"Don't get me started. A bunch of tosspots in the banks have screwed everything up for the rest of us. Anyway, we're nearly there."

They entered the village, and Jarrett surveyed the narrow roads and the cream-colored buildings. It had a familiar feel – reminded him of the place he'd grown up, though he'd never mention that. Not even in his poetry.

The rain began to hammer down harder as the car rolled to a stop beneath a dark sky. Jarrett glanced up at the black sign marking his residence.

"This is you," the driver said.

They pulled up outside a door marked Amethyst Pearl Arts. A tall man in a drenched blue anorak waved at them and opened the door.

"Mr. Jarrett? Good to meet you, I'm Victor Gully. I run this majestic arts thing we've got going on here."

"Hi!" Jarrett said, shaking his hand quickly, still slightly caught off guard.

"Right, come on inside. Let's get the kettle on," Gully said, gesturing toward the entrance. He helped the driver with Jarrett's luggage before leading him through the glass doors. "I promise you, Mr. Jarrett, the weather isn't always like this. It's meant to be sunny next week."

"I just want to say, I think you're an amazing writer," Jarrett blurted, immediately regretting it. It sounded stupid, like something a fan would say.

"Oh, really?" Gully raised an eyebrow. "Which books of mine have you read?"

"Just *The Church In The Square*," Jarrett replied. "Really powerful stuff."

"I was an idealistic know-it-all when that wretched thing was published," Gully said with a laugh. "Anyway, let's get that kettle on. Tea or coffee?"

"Tea, please. With milk."

Gully opened a side door and disappeared. "Won't be long!" he called back.

The arts centre was a large, open room with minimal furniture. At one end, a smooth wooden desk sat, its leather chair waiting behind it. Blank pinboards hung on the walls, the rest of the space barren.

When Gully returned, Jarrett noticed the desk and chair. "That's for you!" Gully said, grinning. "You'll have a space to work on your next project. We've also scheduled a few open mic sessions for you this summer – assuming swine flu doesn't shut us down. I'm an optimistic man, though!"

A roll of thunder rumbled in the distance.

"Oh, damn," Gully muttered.

"Are you working on anything else?" Jarrett asked.

"Nope," Gully replied with a shrug. "This arts thing takes up all my time. But enough about me – what's your story?"

"I'm from Bradford originally," Jarrett began, "went to the local college where I started writing poetry. I got noticed and was offered a full scholarship at Reading to study creative writing. After I graduated, a publisher approached me with a contract for a collection. And here I am."

"Interesting, interesting..." Gully nodded thoughtfully. "Oh, nearly forgot. You'll want to know where you're staying."

Outside, the rain intensified, tapping hard against the windows.

It wasn't until the light had begun to die that the rainfall started to ease.

Jarrett watched the last grey streaks of storm from the dusty, cobweb-streaked window of his apartment. He sipped the remnants of his mint tea, stomach groaning in quiet protest. Mint tea always did this to him, but he knew it was hunger biting now—he hadn't eaten since lunch.

The flat was modest, but enough. Wedged above the village post office, it offered him exactly what he craved: a view into the slow rhythm of village life, and easy access to its few amenities.

His bags lay in limbo, half-unpacked—jumpers and shirts spilling like coiled snakes from unzipped mouths. The laptop was open, crouched on a plywood desk before the grimy window, a glowing blank page daring him to fill it.

Jarrett felt jittery. Unmoored. The words wouldn't come. It wasn't writer's block—it was something else. Something colder.

The rest could wait. At least his bed was made. He flung on his coat and stepped outside.

Only the gentlest drizzle lingered now, but puddles and pockets of floodwater shimmered under lamplight like traps waiting to betray the careless.

He made for the bus stop he'd glimpsed earlier, at the edge of the village. His boots sloshed as he walked. When he passed the local arts centre, he rolled his eyes—half-hoping Victor Gully might still be inside. But the place was abandoned, every window dark. He could just make out the shadowed shape of a desk through the gloom.

At the stop, there was one other figure: a wiry man hunched like a question mark, head dipped low. They exchanged a nod—brief, perfunctory, with just a hint of wariness. Jarrett leaned close to the timetable, its edges curling with age and damp.

"You heading for Canterbury?" the man asked, his voice thick with a Cockney sneer, the tone half-challenge.

"Yeah," said Jarrett.

"Three-Two-Six's the one you want. Once an hour, Sundays. Lazy sods. Should be every half hour, if you ask me."

"You sound local."

"That's 'cause I am. Hold on—Henry Jarrett, yeah? The poet?"

"That's me."

The village lit briefly as a bus crept around the bend, its headlights slicing through the damp haze. The number 326 glowed above the windscreen like a half-dead eye.

"This is us," the man said, straightening his back with a strange elegance. His face remained shadowed as he lifted a hand.

The bus was what Jarrett had expected: stale air, cracked seats, and the scent of other people's lives hanging like smoke.

A handful of passengers sat slumped and silent, as if trying to sleep through their disappointments.

"Single to Canterbury," said the man, slapping a fistful of coins onto the tray.

"Return," Jarrett said. "Not sure I've got change."

"No worries. I've got it." The man handed over more coins without hesitation.

Jarrett blinked. "Thanks. I owe you."

He took the fragile little ticket and shoved it into his front pocket – his designated ark for anything that needed saving.

They sat near the front as the bus groaned into motion.

"Forgive me," said the man. "Didn't introduce myself properly." He smiled, but there was no warmth in it. His lips thinned around the gesture, like a snake pretending to be kind. He offered a hand. "Ivan Stratton."

"Nice to meet you." Jarrett winced inwardly at the blandness of the phrase.

"You're the new poet in residence, right? I've read the notice. Shame I won't be around. Heading to London tonight, then Brazil tomorrow. Got a contract there. Event planning gig."

"Sounds exciting."

"It isn't. But it pays." Stratton laughed – sharp and hollow.

"You run your own company?"

"Something like that."

His eyes were keen, but there was something else behind them – something calculating, like a mind always measuring value, weighing angles.

"But enough about me," Stratton said. "You've got something going here. Curious what kind of chaos you'll stir up."

Jarrett gave him the usual spiel about the events and his writing. Stratton nodded along, lips twitching, but his eyes never quite settled.

"Fun and games," Stratton muttered, almost to himself.

As the bus rolled into Canterbury, the man changed. He sat stiffer, eyes fixed ahead like a hawk scanning the undergrowth.

"You okay?" Jarrett asked.

"Fine." Stratton's voice was clipped. "Just don't want to miss my stop." Then: "Ah, shit." He slammed the stop button. "Listen, my friend. Take care of yourself, yeah? Watch your back. Never know what creeps in when you're not looking." He stood, the movement too fast, almost like he'd rehearsed it. He stumbled forward as the bus halted. "Thanks, driver," he muttered, then turned back one last time.

His smile didn't reach his eyes.

Then he was gone – swallowed by the mist and the flicker of streetlights. Jarrett squinted after him, but it was as though the man had never been there at all.

"Strange bloke," Jarrett muttered to himself.

He stepped off the bus near Canterbury West, consulting a tourist sign and then making his way to the city centre.

He tried to form lines in his head, but it never worked like that. He needed a pen, silence, and a place to bleed without interruption.

The cathedral loomed in the distance, ablaze with golden light, casting judgment over the chaotic dance of nightlife below. Jarrett ducked into the first bar that looked tolerable—modern, soulless, tucked between two art shops like an afterthought.

The lighting was cold, clinical. Blue and unforgiving.

Behind the bar stood a woman – entirely dressed in black, her skin as pale as snowfall under moonlight. Her auburn hair gleamed like dying embers. She stared at him as if she'd already weighed his soul and found it wanting.

"What'll it be?" she asked, voice smooth but distant.

"Lager."

A hand with painted nails ghosted across the taps, pausing. "Which one?"

"That one."

"Four seventy."

Jarrett fumbled for his wallet, heart stuttering until he felt the leather in his back pocket.

Drink in hand, he sat and looked. That's what poets did, wasn't it? Watch the world unravel, try to trap it in language. Every argument, every stolen kiss, every bar fight – a potential metaphor.

His peers had a knack for that. They won prizes. Wrote masterpieces. Jarrett struggled to tether reality to imagination. Maybe it was his working-class roots. More likely, it was the memory of that relationship in Reading – bruises you couldn't quote in verse.

"It's a good pint," he offered. The barmaid didn't respond. Maybe she didn't hear. Maybe she did.

The door slammed. A young couple burst in, laughing too loud, eager to be seen. The boy glanced at Jarrett for half a second before turning away.

Jarrett finished his drink, checked the time. He rose and left without fanfare.

The wet chill grabbed him like a hand around the throat. He walked. No patience for another bus. He'd hail a taxi from the station. Palace Street. Yes, he was going the right way.

The city belonged to the young now. He let it. He whistled tunelessly, hands in his coat pockets. Eyes lowered. Maybe that's why he didn't see her until she was on him.

She stopped him with both hands – delicate fingers digging into the fabric of his coat.

She was exquisite.

Her dress was emerald silk, soaked and clinging like a second skin, highlighting the architecture of her body with merciless detail. Her hair – raven-dark – framed her face like ink dripping onto porcelain. Water slid down her arms and shoulders, catching the faintest shimmer of streetlight. Her eyes were wide, wild, but unfocused – as if seeing through him. As if something monstrous crouched behind his shoulders.

She laughed – a soft, broken thing.

"You alright?" Jarrett asked, voice unsteady.

She didn't answer. Just pulled him in, face close. The laughter stopped. Her lips pressed to his – brief, feverish.

And then she was gone.

She passed him without a backward glance, her footsteps heavy, echoing into the renewed rain.

Part 2

The Visitor
Tuesday, 1 April, 1980

He never liked it when it was sunny – never had, not in the slightest.

The brightness had a way of exposing things, unearthing details better left in shadow. Shuffling along in his heavy overcoat, Jerry Reed silently recited the lines he'd need for later – his habitual prelude to any meeting. He was overheating. The sun wasn't even high yet, but it was enough to stir a boil beneath the layers. Despite his years, he sweated like a schoolboy before a headmaster's scolding. The coat, a dense, grey thing with frayed cuffs, clung to him like punishment. Even the gentlest kiss of spring sunlight could make a man stew in his regrets.

"Excuse me," he said, pausing beside a middle-aged woman striding past with a canvas bag of tulips. "But could you tell me which street this is?"

"Palace Street," she replied, offering a polite smile.

"Thank you, dear. It's a beautiful city, Canterbury, isn't it?"

"It is indeed. Excuse me, I must be off."

He tipped the crown of his trilby to her as she vanished into the crowd. All around him, the city glistened in light and joy. Young couples ambled hand-in-hand, their faces alight with private laughter. A clutch of schoolchildren in matching red uniforms paraded along the pavement, herded gently by teachers with tired smiles. Shop doors creaked open with theatrical cheer: flower stalls breathed perfume onto the street, cafés exhaled steam and fresh pastry, and a bell above a newsagent rang with every arrival. It was all part of some strange, provincial ballet.

If an eagle soared low overhead, it would see a figure that didn't belong – an elderly man swaddled in a weather-inappropriate coat, a trilby shadowing his face, one hand on a polished walking stick, the other adjusting a silver pocket watch. He moved invisibly through the morning, like fog clinging to cobbles.

He never once consulted the map in his pocket. At ten o'clock precisely, he stood before the house.

It was a classic detached home, complete with a garden that refused to be tamed – ivy curled up the bricks like it had somewhere to be, and wisteria dangled lazily across the lintels. It wasn't quite the stuff of suburban brochures, but close enough to blend in.

The door opened almost immediately after his knock.

"Ah, good morning!" said a tall man with a bristled moustache and soft blue eyes. "It's Jerry Reed, right?"

"That is me indeed."

"Well, do come in!"

"Thanking yourself, sir."

Jerry stepped inside and began unpeeling his layers, the heat of the house already a balm. Butterworth took his coat and trilby, hanging them on a lone wooden stand that creaked with the weight.

"Please follow me. Can I offer you tea, coffee?"

"Coffee, please. Black."

Reed followed down a hallway that felt more like a museum corridor. Every surface was claimed – paintings jostled for wall space, ornaments battled for shelf supremacy, and books leaned into teetering towers beside dusty videotapes and thick piles of paper.

His eyes snagged on a heap of manuscripts. One sat boldly on top, its title hand-scrawled.

"'*The Church In The Square*,'" he read aloud. "By Victor Gully."

"Oh, ignore that!" Butterworth chuckled. "A mate of mine runs a publishing house. New submission rules went into effect. Authors need agents now, so in the week before the deadline, he got absolutely deluged. Legally, they still have to read them. So, he's offloading them to everyone he knows. Paid me fifty quid to give him my thoughts."

"Is Mr Gully the next great literary voice?"

"Not a chance. Every kid these days thinks he can write like Dickens just because they've read *Bleak House*."

A back door creaked open. A woman appeared, mid-step out of the garden. Her thick, wavy black hair clung to her temples with sweat and soil. Dressed in worn jeans and a moss-stained shirt, she peeled off her wellingtons with a practiced grunt.

"Hi!" she beamed.

"Jerry, this is my wife, Emily," said Butterworth. "Emily, Jerry Reed. From the paper."

"Thrilled to meet you, madam," said Reed, reaching forward with a gentlemanly nod.

"Pleasure's all mine." She removed chunky glasses and wiped them with her shirtfront. "Well, I'll leave you two—"

"Actually, I'd love your perspective as well," Reed cut in, gently. "While Mr Butterworth is the headline, it's always good to hear from the woman behind the mind."

"Oh, cheeky!" she grinned. "But sure, sounds good to me."

"Shall we do it in the kitchen?" suggested Butterworth.

"Most wonderful idea," Reed agreed.

The kitchen was a continuation of the hallway's chaos – cluttered, yes, but alive with memory. A round oak table dominated the centre, its surface scarred with heat marks and ink stains. The sink beneath the back window overflowed with crockery, and above it, a pan rack hung like a rack of armour. Beyond the glass, the garden looked wild and determined.

"Take a seat," said Butterworth. "Surprised you're not carrying a briefcase."

"Believe me, good sir," Reed said, producing a small notebook from his cardigan, "this is all I need."

"Where are my manners? The coffee! Emily, you want one?"

"Coffee sounds divine."

"That makes three!"

Cups were poured. Mugs mismatched and steaming. Reed's hands cupped his like a sacred chalice.

"William Butterworth," Reed began, setting down his cup with gentle precision, "thank you for having me. Just a few things to go through before we begin. Silly legal formalities, but the paper insists."

He cleared his throat, the notebook open but untouched, pen uncapped and idle.

"My name is Jerry Reed. I work for the Cambridgeshire Horace Gazette. You, William Butterworth, are the newly appointed Vice-Chancellor of the University of Cambridge. The proposal for this interview was sent out last week; you graciously accepted. The purpose of this conversation is to shed some light on who you are, what drives you… what lies beneath the robes and ceremony. Do you have any questions before we begin?"

"No," Butterworth said simply, his posture relaxed, hands folded across his lap.

Emily shook her head. "Ready when you are."

"Excellent." Reed offered a half-smile and scribbled something meaningless onto the page. "Professor William Butterworth – congratulations. How does it feel to hold the reins of one of the world's most prestigious academic institutions?"

"Surreal," Butterworth said with a soft laugh. "Some mornings I still wonder if I've wandered into someone else's dream. But I've always believed that leadership must be grounded in humility. I am here not only to lead – but to learn."

"You were born into academia, weren't you?"

"I was. Born in 1940, while the War tore through the sky. My parents were scholars at Oxford. It was in their presence, among musty volumes and candlelit debates, that I caught the spark. I studied Economics at Cambridge. Stayed on for the doctorate."

"Would you say Cambridge is more than just an institution to you?"

"Much more," Butterworth replied. "It is woven into the fabric of my life." He smiled at Emily. "It's where I met my wife."

"At the Fresher's Ball," she said, eyes brightening. "I remember, he was wearing a bowtie that didn't suit him at all. I stared at him the whole night."

"I was President of the Economics Society by my final year," Butterworth added, "and I was absolutely certain my future would orbit this place."

Reed's voice lowered just a fraction. "But not everything went according to plan, did it?"

The smile faded from Butterworth's face. Emily's fingers, still wrapped around her coffee mug, tensed.

"No. I made a... profoundly foolish choice. While pursuing my doctorate, I was caught selling drugs. I don't dress it up. I don't excuse it. It was reckless, and I carry the shame still."

"Many in the academic community raised strong objections to your appointment because of that."

"They did," Butterworth said quietly. "And I understand why. All I can do is show, through my actions, that I am no longer that young, arrogant fool."

"Let's turn to the present," Reed offered, letting the tension unravel slightly. "Your promises to students have drawn national attention. Tell us about them."

Butterworth leaned forward, a light returning to his eyes.

"My vision is captured in a phrase: Bridging Divides. We live in a world defined by separation. The Berlin Wall still casts its shadow, the Iron Curtain hasn't lifted. People are starving, afraid, forgotten. I want this university to become a beacon against that tide." He counted off with his fingers. "First, I am expanding female admissions. I plan to tour both the UK and overseas to personally speak with young women, encouraging them to see Cambridge as their home. Second, I'm expanding doctoral programs across all disciplines. And third, I am building partnerships with universities across the world to enhance cultural exchange."

"It's a bold vision," said Reed. "Professor Emily Butterworth, I understand you've recently received a professorship yourself. Congratulations."

"Thank you," she replied, visibly pleased. "It was... unexpected, but I'm honoured."

"This," said William, his voice rising with sudden heat, "this is what it's about! Twenty years ago, women were expected to pour tea and smile. Now they're writing policy and leading departments. That's the world I want to help shape."

Reed took a slow sip of his coffee. It had cooled. "Professors," he said, "you are both lauded figures. But unsettling rumours have surfaced. They suggest your motives might be... complicated. That your reforms may be rooted not just in vision – but in remorse."

"I've already said I regret what I did," Butterworth said, visibly weary. "The drug charge..."

"Forgive me. I'm not referring to that," said Reed. "I'm referring to your time as Governor of Milton Borstal."

Emily stiffened. Her smile vanished, a mask slipping just slightly.

"The agreement with your paper was that this wouldn't be discussed," she said sharply. "Will, you don't have to say another word."

"Please forgive me. That memo was not passed along," Reed said, tone apologetic – but not retreating. "I'm afraid I must ask."

Butterworth took a deep breath. "When I was caught, I was offered a deal. Run Milton Borstal in exchange for the charges being dropped. I governed the institution from 1965 to 1968. Emily served alongside me."

"Many believe it was your father's connections that made that arrangement possible," said Reed. "That a man from the working class might've faced jail instead of a leadership post."

"That's probably true," Butterworth admitted. "I was a product of privilege. But you don't know what it was like – working with those boys. Troubled, violent. We did what we could."

"Professor Butterworth," Reed said, gaze unwavering, "there are allegations of abuse. Abuse carried out under your direct orders."

Butterworth's voice rose. "We were understaffed. There were fights, yes – bloody ones – but we couldn't be everywhere at once."

"You misunderstand. I'm not referring to inmate violence. I'm referring to your violence. Organised. Systematic."

Emily paled.

"Last week, I interviewed a former resident," Reed continued, voice tightening. "Clifford Lake. He alleged that you instated a disciplinary system. A series of written warnings. First, second, and then... dismissal. And by dismissal, he says, you meant torture."

"Lies!" Butterworth roared, voice cracking.

"He claims you orchestrated rape sessions," Reed said, his voice now low, deliberate, the words slicing like a scalpel. "Against boys you deemed disobedient."

"You bastard!" Emily shrieked. "This interview is over. Get out of our house – now! Or I will call the police and file a complaint with your editor."

Reed stood, calm amid the chaos. He reached for his beard and, with a subtle twist, peeled it away. Latex folded, smooth and silent. Then he tugged at the base of his neck, removing the rubbery mask that had itched and irritated for hours.

The face beneath was younger, sharper, with cold blue eyes and a tight jaw. He stepped back from the table, pocketing the disguise.

"You've failed to notice something," he said. "Since we've been talking, I haven't taken a single note."

And he's there.

Standing over them, smiling.

He lets the remains of his disguise flop to the floor.

"Hi, guys. How've you been?" he says. "Been a long time, hasn't it?"

They stare, paralysed.

Emily's voice cracks first. "Clifford Lake..."

William tries to rally authority, but it's brittle. "Mr Lake, if this is some sort of sick –"

"I don't joke, Governor."

Clifford clears his throat, adjusts his shoulders like slipping into an old coat.

"Mr Butterworth, I wanted to thank you for your efforts," he begins, voice lilting into mock-corporate cheer, "but unfortunately, they are not quite up to company standards. As part of disciplinary procedures, you are now placed on a first written warning. I understand these things aren't easy. Please remember that you have access to our twenty-four-hour Hanging Gardens Medical Service."

"Emily, call the police –"

But he's already moving.

He lunges – grabs William by the hair and slams his face down onto the table. The wood thuds and cracks. A howl. A spray of teeth. Another slam. And another. The sound grows sickening – splintered cartilage, mashed pulp. The table shudders beneath the force.

Emily is screaming, frozen, unable to move.

Lake doesn't stop.

He lifts Butterworth again, and again, driving his skull into the wood like he's hammering rusted nails into old pine. Blood is everywhere now – slick, sticky, warm. The man groans once. Then just the wet sound of flesh on wood. He keeps going. Ten. Twenty. Thirty times. His arms ache. He doesn't care.

When he stops, there's nothing left that resembles thought or reason. Just a broken thing.

He breathes in.

Exhales.

And turns.

Emily is stumbling back, gasping, nearly slipping in the panic. She's at the front door, clawing at the lock.

"You'll need this," says Lake, calmly, holding up the key between thumb and forefinger.

"Please!" she howls.

He walks toward her slowly, softly, like a man approaching a deer in a clearing.

"Help me!" she shrieks. "Help! Please!"

And then he's on her.

A savage. That's what they made him. What they carved from pain and silence.

He seizes her by the throat, lifts her, slams her back against the wall. A mirror shatters. A painting crashes to the floor.

"Don't forget," he murmurs, "you're entitled to full access to our twenty-four-hour Hanging Gardens Medical Service. Just because you're on a second written warning doesn't mean dismissal. This is an opportunity to develop."

She kicks, claws, sobs.

He pushes his thumbs into her eyes. Her body thrashes.

He's struck in the shin, hard – but it doesn't register. He's trained himself to ignore pain. To compartmentalize. To wait.

And then – she goes still.

He lets go.

She falls.

Silence. The kind that aches.

It's over.

That part of his revenge – done. Finished.

Clifford Lake stepped back.

His hands, cardigan, and shirt were soaked with blood. A gentle steam rose from the warm splashes across his sleeves. He smiled. Not the smile of satisfaction, nor pride – just quiet familiarity. He'd done things like this before. Many times. He knew what to do now.

Within the hour, the corpses were tucked beneath the shrubbery at the bottom of the garden, hidden in the weeping shade of an overgrown willow. He'd scoured the kitchen floor, wiped flecks from the skirting boards, scrubbed beneath fingernails. Human detritus, gone. The bodies, dealt with. The house, quiet.

Then came the shower. Long and slow. Hot. He let the water run until the heat kissed away the tension in his shoulders. The mirror filled with steam, then slowly cleared, revealing the reflection of a man in borrowed skin.

William Butterworth's suit fit better than expected. Clifford adjusted the cuffs, straightened the tie, studied himself. Wearing the clothes of his abuser. The jacket carried a faint smell of old cologne, warm leather, and tobacco. He smirked at his reflection, then looked down at the bundle of soiled garments now stuffed into a plastic rubbish sack. That would be dealt with later. Destroyed.

He spent fifteen more minutes combing the house. Looking under beds, inside drawers, checking for missed traces. Nothing. The air had settled. Not even a creak of protest from the floorboards now. The house had accepted the change.

Satisfied, he wandered into the kitchen again, helped himself to the contents of the fridge – a few slices of ham, half a block of cheddar, leftover shepherd's pie. He ate standing up, fork in hand. When he was full, he brewed fresh coffee and poured it into a blue and white china mug with a chip in the rim.

As the aroma filled the room, he skimmed through his travel itinerary for the summer. Not long to go now. Not long at all.

Just as he reached for the door handle, his eyes caught something on the floor. The manuscript. Still there, half-trodden on, its cover bent backwards. He picked it up, ran a finger across the crease, flicked through the pages.

A cover letter was folded over the top sheet, scrawled in loopy, naive handwriting. The ink pressed hard into the paper, as if written with clenched fingers:

Dear Mr Jonathan Bateson,
My name is Victor Gully and I have enclosed my novel, The Church In The Square, *for your consideration. I know that I am only fourteen years old, but I know my book will sell really well.*

Please, please, please give me a chance. I promise that I will not let you down. I really believe in this novel. It has taken me three years to write and I am very proud of it.

Yours sincerely,
Victor Gully

Clifford stared at it a moment longer.

"Aww," he muttered. "Aww. Poor kid."

He moved into the hallway, where a brittle-looking rotary phone gleamed under the porch light like a relic of another age. Fake gold on the dial. A little crack in the handset.

He dialled the number listed at the top of the letter. When someone picked up on the other end, he dropped smoothly into the Governor's voice, slow and measured.

"Hello?" he said. "Is that the publishing house? Yes, could you put me through to Mr Bateson, please? It's about that manuscript he sent me. The one by the young chap – Gully. Look, I think Mr Bateson needs to give him a chance. I've read it and it's bloody good. You've got a real writer on your hands. A proper one. Trust me. Give this kid a shot. I don't think you'll regret it."

He hung up without waiting for a reply, then glanced down at the manuscript in his hand. Smiled again.

Because monsters, too, can keep promises.

An hour later, he was shuffling his way back through Canterbury.

Everything was working exactly as it should. Nothing out of place. No threats. That certainty filled him with such confidence that his disguise nearly slipped a couple of times. But he righted himself before it went too far. No one suspected a thing.

He was a nobody here. A nobody everywhere.

He was Clifford Lake.

No one knew he was behind the Apollo Murders. No one knew about the children and teenagers who'd met their ends at his hands. No one knew the pain he'd spread across families like a disease. And no one knew what was coming next.

He smiled – a polite, elderly gentleman's smile.

At the station, he slowed his pace even more. People brushed past him: travellers, businessmen, unemployed teenagers, office workers. All walked past him without a care.

He showed his ticket to a guard, asking which platform the London train was on.

"That one over there," came the gruff reply. "Bloody pensioner."

Lake would have snapped back, but the disguise was too important. Not because he feared being caught – just being caught too soon.

He found the train easily. Asking for directions was just an old man's habit. He sat in a quiet corner of the carriage and shut his eyes.

When he opened them again, he was in London St Pancras.

The crowd swallowed him whole and spat him back out. He walked with careful confidence. Left. Right. Left again. He found the alcove with the lockers and located number 18520. Glancing over his shoulder, he unlocked it, pulled out a large duffel bag, and slammed the door shut.

In the nearby bathroom, he changed. Ten minutes later, he emerged in a crisp wedding suit, hair neatly combed. The duffel now held the old man's gear, safely stowed back in the locker.

He whistled as he strolled through the station. Some people stared, but most barely registered him. London was used to men in strange outfits.

Out front, he joined the queue for taxis. He wasn't worried about the wait. The ceremony didn't start for two hours.

When his turn came, he offered the driver a wide smile and the address.

"Wow, a wedding in Chelsea," the cabbie remarked. "You the groom?"

"Just drive."

"Fair enough, guv."

Lake didn't speak again until they arrived.

"This is it," he said, handing over a wad of notes. "Keep the change."

A few guests milled outside the church, dressed to impress. Women in floral dresses and extravagant hats tiptoed on high heels. The men, in traditional wedding attire with boutonnières, were gently steered around by their wives and girlfriends.

Clifford Lake stood alone. He didn't need anyone else.

"Hi!" one of the women called out, waving.

"Melanie, apologies for my late arrival!" Lake called back. "Train was a bit delayed. Got here as soon as I could! How are you?"

"I'm okay." Melanie Tolson dabbed at a tear. "Bit nervous! It's my daughter's wedding, after all."

"I'm sure it'll be a wonderful day. How's Roslyn holding up?"

"You should've seen her yesterday – crying all day."

"Oh, the dear girl!" Lake touched her shoulder gently. "Might I say, you look absolutely radiant today."

"Thank you."

Two men emerged from the church carrying trays of champagne.

"Perfect," said Lake. "It's not a wedding without champagne."

"It isn't indeed."

They toasted on the church lawn. Lake felt the heat rising but wasn't burdened by latex and wigs now. He stretched his arms, flexed his fingers – freedom.

When the vicar appeared and asked guests to enter, Lake took a moment to shake hands with the groom.

"All the best, my good man. Roslyn is a fine woman, and you'll make her an excellent husband."

"Thanks," said Gus.

Lake admired him – broad-shouldered, sharp-eyed, clean-cut. The perfect match. The perfect bloody match.

"I mean it, Cliff," Gus added. "Thanks for introducing me to Roslyn."

"No need to thank me."

Inside, they took their seats. Gus and his best man, Dev, stood at the altar. Lake sat beside Melanie. He smiled as she wiped away another tear, patting her arm.

"It's a great day," he whispered. "Your baby girl's getting married."

"Thanks, Cliff. Your friendship's meant a lot to me and my husband."

"You're most welcome, Melanie."

The wedding march rang out. Lake winced. He hated that song – too full of hope. He turned to watch Roslyn, accompanied by her father and her three bridesmaid sisters, walking down the aisle.

He liked the church. Old, traditional. Stained glass. Dim light. Like a fairytale.

Roslyn's father, Russ, fought back tears as they reached the altar. He shook Gus's hand. Lake could tell, even from a distance – it was firm.

The vicar began his scripted welcome. Lake rolled his eyes.

"Your daughter looks beautiful," he said to Melanie. "You must be proud, Dr Tolson."

"Please, don't call me that – it's Melanie."

"Oh? That's odd. You used to insist on being called *Dr Tolson.*"

"Can we talk about this later? It's my daughter's moment."

"Forgive me, I just wanted to show the proper respect. You insisted on it at the borstal."

Her face froze. Recognition flickered in her eyes.

"Okay, Gus. Devlin. That's enough," said Lake.

"Thank Christ," muttered Devlin.

They dropped the posh accents like dead weight, reverting to their natural Liverpudlian tones.

"You got our money?" asked Gus.

Lake handed each of them an envelope.

"Cheers," Gus nodded, heading for the exit with Devlin.

"See you guys!" Devlin called back.

Russ stared, stunned. Roslyn began sobbing.

"What's the meaning of this?!" Russ demanded. "Cliff, we've known you for years – this is sick."

"This isn't a joke," Lake replied, peeling away the false face. "Hi, Dr Tolson. Remember me? Milton Borstal?"

"Clifford?!" Melanie gasped, trembling.

"Clifford?! I thought I didn't have a name!"

Roslyn dropped to her knees, wailing.

"Ladies and gentlemen, forgive me," Lake said to the stunned crowd. "A bit of revenge I've been planning. Roslyn, dear girl, I'm sorry. Everything's been a lie."

He knelt before Melanie.

"Gus and Dev worked for me. Your daughter believed every word when I introduced them. I remember our sessions at the borstal. You were the young prodigy, trying to convince me I was unloved, worthless. Of all the tortures in that place, yours was the worst. I fantasised about what I'd do to you. But this? This is better. You taught me how to manipulate. I learned from the best. What was it you said? *You read people like a book.* But I became the library."

He laughed, stood, and started walking.

At the church door, a shadow loomed behind him.

"You bastard," growled Ceri Britton. "You fucking bastard."

He shoved Lake, who stumbled.

"Hey, remember me? Try manipulating me."

"Mr Britton!" Lake extended a hand.

Britton slammed the door shut. "You're in deep shit, Lake."

"Oh, I missed you! Still love that Aussie accent."

"Take a swing! Go on!"

Britton was older, heavier. His red face pulsed with fury. The wedding suit barely fit. Bald head. Shaved beard. The same old screw.

"How'd you get invited?" Lake asked.

Britton punched him hard.

"Okay!" Lake shouted. "I'll confess! Take me to the police!"

"Damn right. Move."

"Yes, sir."

Britton gripped him the old way – hand on bicep, another on the neck.

"Ironic, isn't it?" Lake said as they walked. "You used to frogmarch me to your torture sessions. Now here we are, in wedding suits, doing it again."

"Shut it."

"I heard you went into whisky."

"Shut it."

"Yes, sir."

"If you touched my distillery –"

"I didn't."

"You're a filthy deviant. Always were."

A car slowed beside them. The driver leaned out. "Is everything okay?"

"Just taking a criminal to the police," Britton replied.

"Wow. Nice words," said Lake, waving.

The houses around them were neat, tidy. Picture perfect. Nothing out of place.

"Beautiful, isn't it?" Lake said. "I had a good childhood, good schooling."

"And you threw it away. Your fault."

"We're here."

A path led into a shadowy forest.

"I saw your friends, the Butterworths."

"You try robbing them?"

"No. I killed them. Smashed Billy's head open. Gouged his wife's eyes out."

Britton froze.

Lake struck – an elbow to the chin – and ran. Britton chased, bellowing.

"You're not getting away!"

Lake stopped in the clearing. Britton charged – until four masked men pounced on him.

Tape. Cable ties. Fists to the gut. Britton's terror was complete.

"Well-timed, gentlemen," Lake said. "Tell your boss he'll get the rest soon.

"Mr Britton, meet your fate. These men are from Colombia. Communist rebels. They're taking you to the jungle. Lifetime sentence, courtesy of me.

"Through the East Anglia Communist Movement. I remembered you always wanted to travel."

He grinned. "Have fun. Watch out for spiders. Bag him."

Britton vanished beneath a black sack, his muffled screams fading.

"Have a nice trip."

Lake turned to the tree he'd marked months ago. Dug at its base. Retrieved the biscuit tin.

Fake ID. Cash. Everything he needed.

One more step. One last piece.

He zipped up the tin, pissed on the tree, and walked off into the light.

Roger Miser
Wednesday, 2 April, 1980

As he always did before declaring a toast, he paused. Allowed himself a moment to reflect on a life well-lived, on a career that had spanned continents, and on a future that beckoned with ever brighter lights.

"To the festival," he said to the crowd.

"The festival," they chanted back.

He took his well-earned sip.

"Ladies and gentlemen," he said, "I cannot thank you enough for all you've done. None of this would've been possible without your help. When I was a child growing up in Yardley Wood, dreaming of travel and music, never did I think I would have this."

They applauded.

"Never did I think I'd launch the careers of so many singers and bands. Never did I think..."

More applause. He wiped away a fake tear.

"But it's not enough. This year, I'm planning to launch the careers of one hundred new artists."

The crowd clapped, but Roger Miser raised his left hand. The room fell silent.

"To do this, as you know, I'm holding a certain... festival this summer. Now, I've gone on enough about it, and I won't bore you with the religious details, but—let's give a massive thank you to the mayor of St Pierre, who's here with us today!"

Edgar Travere, newly elected, waved his left hand. His moustache twitched under the pressure of the gathering. Miser could see how out of place he was. A fish out of water. More than that—a fish plunged into a desert, utterly alone in a hostile environment.

The gathering was in Miser's Chelsea penthouse. Newly redecorated: leather furniture shipped from Los Angeles, vases from China, bookshelves from Spain, carpets from India. He could've held the event at his office, but no—he wanted it here. He wanted people to see the real him. To bond with him, here, amongst his treasures.

"Ladies and gentlemen," said Miser, "to France."

This time, he let the clapping play out like an instrument.

He drained his champagne, took another glass, mingled with the crowd, giving each guest five minutes that felt like an hour.

It was George Ashton who managed to snag him for longer. They ducked into an unoccupied, slightly dusty corner.

"Everything's finalised," George said. "Bands and singers, artists and writers—everyone's locked in. Hotel's booked too. Nice little place in the centre of St Pierre. Not New York, but it's cosy."

"I'm sure it'll be fine." Miser cleared his throat. "The festival starts officially on the first of June, but we want to be settled in well before that."

"Don't worry, I've booked it from May twentieth through to the end of August. Check-out's the first of September."

"Excellent."

Miser could tell something was bothering him.

"What's wrong?"

"Um… I don't know how to say this. Charlie's out back. In the garden. I think he wants to see you."

"Of course he does. I'll go see what he's after."

"You want me to come with you?" George asked. His whisky glass was nearly empty. He stared into it, as if hoping it would refill itself.

"Charlie's harmless. Just a pain in the neck. Go mingle. Talk up the festival. Talk me up."

Miser strode to the back door. A bouncer opened it for him.

The evening air was too cold for the season. He had no intention of descending the narrow, fragile metal staircase.

Charlie Petter stood in the shared garden, arms folded. When he saw Miser, his face lit up like a flare. A bouncer blocked his path to the stairs.

"Charlie, I'm not in the mood," Miser called down.

"Roger, Roger –"

"Mr Miser, please."

"You're holding a festival, aren't you?"

"The answer is no."

"But –"

"No, Charlie. I'm not having you plaster posters all over St Pierre. You can come to the festival, if you must, but I don't want to see a single poster."

"Please –"

"Get him out of here," Miser told the bouncer. "And make sure he doesn't sneak into any of the other apartments."

"Yes, sir."

The bouncer grabbed Charlie by the collar and started dragging him away.

Miser watched the scene disappear down the alley that led to the front of the building. He stood there a while, whisky cupped between his palms, thinking about the summer ahead.

Too much could go wrong. Bad sound equipment. Drunk musicians. No slipups this time—he couldn't afford it.

This festival was to cement his legacy. After it was done, he could retire. Spend the rest of his days getting laid. This festival wasn't about the hundred new acts. It was about him.

The Public Schoolboy
February 1965

He's too young, really, but he's on a visit to the big city.

He's awake an hour earlier than he needs to be, even for a Saturday. No alarm – he just wakes up, wide-eyed and ready.

He's out of bed in seconds, thumping down the stairs. Kettle on. Toast in the toaster. He's overexcited – that much is certain – though he's trying not to show it.

He sits at the kitchen table, feet swinging, watching the sky get lighter. When the sun finally rises, he smiles, like it's a sign.

Mum and Dad come downstairs, still half-asleep, and ask why he's up so early. He just shrugs.

He's smart for his age. Thirteen, but already ahead of the pack. Top of the class. The teachers know his name for all the right reasons. Oxford and Cambridge are already being mentioned. He's expected to captain the rugby team. He's got the presence, the confidence, the drive. When he hits his final year, he'll be Head Boy. Everyone says so. No one doubts it.

He's off to the big city to get kitted out for a suit. His cousin's wedding is next week, and everyone wants him looking sharp. It's important. There'll be photos, speeches, the whole thing.

Mum and Dad have their breakfast while he waits, picking at his toast. Mum heads upstairs to put on her makeup. Dad scrolls his phone.

When she comes back down, ready to go, they grab their coats, pick up the car keys, and head out. The city's waiting, and today, it's all about the suit.

They take the train from Canterbury into the heart of London. He's not sure how long the journey lasts – he'll probably never know – but it feels like an age and a half. He loves every minute of it. The rumble of the carriage, the steady flicker of countryside rushing past, the low murmur of other passengers – it all feels like part of something bigger.

At school, he's a stern and serious young man. Keeps his head down. Gets things done. But here, on this train, he's like a toddler: wide-eyed, grinning, fascinated with every single little thing. The world seems newer somehow.

When they arrive in the city, it hits him all at once. He's not sure where to look first, which direction to turn, which fantastical person to watch. The city moves like it's alive, everything humming, everything shifting.

Mum and Dad walk close on either side of him, weaving through crowds, never once letting go of his hands.

"We'll soon be here," says Dad, with a smile. "You'll love this…"

They pass down more streets, cross more roads. The noise builds, the colours deepen. Most boys his age would be tired by now, might start moaning about sore legs, aching feet—but not him. He's moving with purpose, hungry for more.

Dad stops him. Mum steps in behind and gently places her hands over his eyes. He lets himself be guided around a corner, not saying a word.

"Welcome," says Mum. "To Bond Street." She lifts her hands.

He blinks.

Before him: countless shops lined up like treasure chests, their windows glinting. Women sweep past in colourful, complex clothes. Sleek saloons growl along the road. Smoke hangs like gauze in the air. Men stroll in crisp suits, cigars resting between their lips. Everything moves, pulses with life. It's overwhelming—but in the best way. Like most things he sees, he knows he'll never be able to fully describe this.

Dad places a hand on his shoulder and nudges him forward.

He's heard about Bond Street at school. Boys who've been, girls who go on and on about it. Even a teacher once boasted that his entire outfit came from there. He didn't believe it at the time—but now? Maybe.

They don't walk far before Mum and Dad steer him into one of the shops.

Inside, he sees row after row of tweed ties. Dummies in black jackets stand like guards. Tables are stacked with neatly folded trousers. Racks of leather shoes catch the crystal light and sparkle. Everything is orderly. Everything smells expensive. He tries to take it all in.

Mum and Dad already know what they're after. They've been talking about it for weeks.

A tailor appears and leads him to a small raised podium in front of a full-length mirror framed in polished brass. The tailor is old, bent at the shoulders, but there's a quickness to him, a sharpness in the eyes. He produces a wooden measuring stick, smooth and worn from years of use, and gets to work.

The boy watches himself in the mirror, watches the suit come together piece by piece. Mum and Dad stand behind him, quietly admiring. He looks taller somehow, older. He's well on his way to becoming a man.

The tailor works fast, with care. He nods at the parents, tells them the suit will be ready tomorrow, delivered to their door. Paperwork and payment are handled swiftly.

"I've booked us cream tea," says Dad as they step outside. "Covent Garden," he adds.

Back out on the street, they pause. There's a brief moment of stillness as his parents look around, trying to get their bearings. Then they start walking again, slipping back into the stream of city life.

And then, suddenly – he's alone.

He blinks. Looks around. At first, he thinks it might be a joke, a bit of fun. But minutes pass. Mum and Dad don't reappear. He's alone.

He stays calm. Of course he does. At school, he has a reputation for never panicking.

All around him, high-end shops buzz with activity. Well-dressed customers drift in and out, laughing, browsing, buying. He knows he could go into any of them and ask for help. He should.

But there's one shop, just beside him. Smaller. Quieter. Not quite as fancy as the rest. It looks snug, a little cramped. He hesitates. His mind ticks over. Smaller shop means fewer customers. More time for someone to listen. Maybe even a quicker solution.

He makes his decision.

He goes in.

It's a clothes shop, alright, but not like the last one. This place is different – less polished, more thrown together. Jackets and trousers, ties and underwear, all scattered across racks and shelves without much care. It doesn't feel designed. It feels dumped.

The checkout desk sits in the middle of the room, plain and bare, save for a small stack of vinyl records, as if someone gave up halfway through tidying.

He's about to turn around – and he should – but something catches his eye. An open door at the back of the shop. Slightly ajar. He edges forward, then hesitates. His instincts are tapping on his shoulder. He walks up to the doorway, leans in, peers through.

Two people look back at him.

There's a woman in a tailored suit – smart, but lived-in – hunched over a wooden box. A cigarette dangles between her fingers, its ash long and ready to fall. Beside her stands a man, lanky, loose-limbed, with hands sunk deep in the pockets of an oversized jacket. He's absurdly thin—like a stalk, a stupidly thin stalk. The boy has never seen anyone quite like him. Stubble darkens the man's face like coal dust. His eyes look hollow. His grin is thin and wrong.

"Hi," says the man. "You okay?" His voice is coated in a thick northern accent.

"I need to call the police. I've been separated from my parents."

"Tracy, I think that's your area."

The woman snuffs her cigarette out on the floor and stands. Her movements are easy, slow. "How old are you?" she asks. Her accent is American, laid-back, a bit scratchy.

"Thirteen," he says. "My birthday is on the twenty-third of April."

"So, April this year, you'll be… fourteen?"

"Yes, that is correct."

The man lets out a loud, wet cough. The kind of cough that lives in a smoker's lungs. He recognises it immediately.

"Perfect," the man mutters.

"Absolutely," Tracy agrees. Her eyes are soft, a strange contrast—powder-blue, gentle, almost kind. Like feathers.

He doesn't like this place. It's cramped, closed-in. A courtyard, if you could call it that, surrounded by walls far too high. The bricks are stained, weather-worn. Rubbish clings to the corners. Faded cigarette butts sit scattered across the ground like dead flies. It's the first time he's ever seen somewhere that truly feels… forgotten.

"Forgive me," says the woman. "I'm Tracy Cox. I work in the shop." She laughs lightly. "Guess you can tell I'm American."

"Where from?" he asks, trying to hold himself steady.

"Upstate New York," she replies.

"Oh, interesting."

"I'm in the U.K. for a bit. Studying."

"Where do you study?"

"I think I'd better get you sorted." She smiles, placing a comforting arm around his shoulder, guiding him gently back through the shop. At the front desk, she pulls out the cashier's chair. "Please, take a seat."

He does what he's told. He watches her. There's something magnetic about her – those bright eyes, the shine in her blonde hair, the scent of perfume cut with nicotine. He can't place it. It's confusing. But he stays polite, proper.

"I need to head upstairs – that's where our phone is," she says. She opens a drawer beneath the counter, takes out a notepad and a small pen. "Could you do me a favour? Write your address for me. The police might need it."

"Yes, of course." His handwriting is neat, careful. He wants to be helpful. He always wants to be a good young man.

"Just one more thing," she adds, as he hands the note back. "Are your folks thinking about moving any time soon?"

"Not that I know of."

"That's great. Oh, silly me – what's your name?"

He tells her.

"I'll be as quick as I can," she says. "Try not to worry. I'm sure your parents aren't far." She disappears through a door behind the desk, closing it firmly behind her.

She's back quickly – almost too quickly – with a bigger smile than before.

"Just got off the phone with the cops," she says. "Turns out your folks already called in. I told them where we are. They'll be here in ten minutes."

"Tracy, thank you – thank you!"

"It's okay," she says, wrapping him in a tight hug. She kisses his forehead, and for a second, it feels like heaven.

Then the nerves creep in. He starts fidgeting. That low-level panic settles in his chest, the kind he last felt before his French exam—tight, anxious, impossible to shake.

But not long after, his parents appear outside with a policeman.

He cries. Happy tears. And like the young gentleman he's been raised to be, he makes the introductions. Tracy Cox shakes hands with his parents, shakes hands with the officer. Everyone's smiling. The moment seems to settle.

"Right," says Dad. "Cream tea? Miss Cox, you're more than welcome to join us."

"Oh, I couldn't possibly," says Tracy. "Really, I can't. I'm working until five. But you go – enjoy it."

The policeman nods once and leaves.

"Thank you so much, Tracy," says Mum.

They wave, all three of them, and step outside. But just as they're about to turn onto Bond Street, he glances back.

Tracy isn't smiling. She isn't waving. She's facing away, looking toward the rear of the shop. Toward the door that leads to the courtyard. She says something – loud enough to carry – but he can't quite make it out. Probably speaking to the man with the coal-smeared face.

It's only late that night, when he's safely in bed, tucked in, thinking back over the day—the hours rewinding in his mind like a broken tape—that he realises what she said. He may be wrong—and he probably is—but he knows, he believes, that she said: *"He's perfect."*

3

Part 3

Henry Jarrett
Monday, 18 May, 2009

He told Victor Gully everything about the woman – every single insignificant detail.

"Sounds like you had a fun night," Gully remarked. "More fun than mine, anyway." He yawned. "Bloody hell, didn't sleep at all."

"Have you seen her around?"

"No."

They were in Amethyst Pearl Arts. Gully perched on the edge of Jarrett's desk, completely unstable. Trapped in his chair, Henry Jarrett cradled a lukewarm cup of instant coffee. He stared out through the front windows. Sunlight filled the scene outside. Puddles were in the final stages of evaporating. A thin man on a bike scraped his way past. So beautifully poetic.

"Look, I just came by to see how you were doing," said Gully. "How are you settling in?"

"Well, it's my first day. I've been sitting here since nine this morning. Not one person's come in. Is this what my summer's going to be? Drinking shitty coffee all day, trying to gain inspiration for my next poetry book?"

"That's the life of a writer." Gully smirked. "Come on, cheer up."

"I'll do my best. When's my first event?"

"Not for a few weeks, I'm afraid. Don't worry, I'll have more information soon. There *is*, however, something that might interest you."

"Oh?"

"How would you feel about doing an event with a local school?"

"What?"

"Canterbury Royal Oak High School."

"What?"

"I know the writer-in-residence there. I could have a chat with him – see if there's a chance of you helping out with a workshop or something. I mean, it's not part of the residency programme, but... well..."

"You're sounding desperate."

"Do you want it or not?" Gully gave him a look.

"Okay then."

"I'll call him tonight. Let him know."

"Who is he?" asked Jarrett.

"Ellar Cameron."

"Never heard of him."

"What, really?" Gully started pacing. "He's an interesting bloke. Only had one novel published, back in '98, but he's written for TV, film, theatre, radio – you name it. I'm surprised you haven't heard of him."

"One novel published over ten years ago. Of course I haven't heard of the guy."

"Come on, he's done stuff for television –"

"I get it!" Jarrett cut in, then softened. "Sorry, didn't mean to sound confrontational. The point is – if he's so successful, what the hell's he doing as a writer-in-residence?"

"That's a strange question for *you* to ask. Look at the both of us."

"Fair. That was ignorant of me." He looked down at the blank monotony of his desk. Nothing had been written on the scrap of lined paper curling up in front of him. The pen lay beside it, untouched, like a statue inside a statue. "What's his novel called?"

"*Noke,*" said Gully. "If you want, I could have a copy sent over."

"No, it's okay. I'll head into Canterbury later. There's a bookstore there, right?"

"Yeah, a few."

"I'll get myself a copy."

"Sounds good." Gully glanced at his watch. "Listen, it's nearly one. You want to grab lunch?"

"Yeah, sure." Jarrett stood, gave a sarcastic glance at the empty paper winking up at him. "Could do with a stretch of the legs."

"You know, you should try running," said Gully, as they locked up the arts centre. Jarrett shuffled his feet, eyes fixed between his toes. "I used to know someone who liked to run first thing every morning," he continued. "Long time ago."

"Where are we going for lunch?"

"Actually, actually…" Gully backstepped into the road.

The village was quiet. Everyone at work. Kids at school. Everyone where they belonged.

"I had thought of a place nearby," Gully said, "but the food's not great. Fancy going into Canterbury?"

"Yeah, okay. That would be convenient anyway – getting that guy's book. Definitely want to make sure I read it."

"Sounds like a plan. I've got my car. This way – I parked under your flat. It's the Land Rover."

"Wow. Didn't think novelists drove Land Rovers."

"They do when necessary."

Jarrett wasn't an expert on cars. He knew they got you from one place to another, but he didn't understand the art attached to them—the male joy of gears and cylinders. Car magazines passed in a blur. Still, even he could tell Gully's model was old. Caked in dirt, it baked in the sunlight.

"Right," said Gully, climbing in. "Let's get out of here. I'm seriously bloody hungry."

On the drive, Jarrett found himself gnawed by a quiet but persistent urge to ask about the woman. He didn't fancy her – nothing like that – it was just curiosity, pure and innocent. Who was she? Why had she kissed him, of all people? Why had it felt so strangely… deliberate?

But instead of diving into all that, he chose a safer subject. "Is *Noke* a good book?" he asked Gully.

"It's quite good," Gully replied, eyes fixed on the road. "Well, maybe not everyone's cup of tea. It's under two hundred pages and very... expressive. I think the term is *postmodern*."

"But seriously, if he's written for television, radio, all that—why is he working in a school?"

"Beats me. Really, it does. But he seems to like it. And anyway, he's off soon – leaving when the school breaks up for the summer. Got some residency in Japan starting in September."

"Bloody hell."

"You like it out here?" Gully asked, glancing at him.

"Yeah, I mean... it's pretty."

Gully chuckled, leaned forward slightly on the wheel, as if to get a better grip on the road or the moment. "Sorry, mate. It's just – Ellar Cameron is going to *love* you."

"Oh, come on. He's not intimidating, is he?"

"Of course he is. Very loud. Never knows when to shut his mouth – please don't tell him I said that." Gully smiled, stretched his neck again. "He's an interesting bloke. You'll see what I mean when you read his book."

The rest of the drive passed in comfortable silence. As they rolled into Canterbury, the landscape shifted—tight streets, historic walls, flashes of honeyed stone in the sun. Gully turned into a narrow side road near the cathedral, the rooftops glinting like old coins.

"The place I'm thinking of is close," Gully said as he switched off the engine. "You like sushi?

That night, Jarrett tried to sleep. He really tried. But no matter how many times he turned over, how tightly he twisted himself into his sheets, sleep kept its distance. It wasn't the heat, nor the sticky humidity that often came as part of summer's late-night bargain – it was her.

That face. Smiling but somehow sad. Eyes lit with something wild and untouchable. The way her hair fell – not styled, not cared for, just *there*, like it belonged to another era. She was a walking contradiction: order and chaos, wound tightly together.

Who was she? Where had she been going? And, perhaps most maddening of all, why him?

Eventually, he gave up. Sleep wasn't even pretending to try anymore. He clicked on the bedside light, and the room leapt into colour and shape. Wincing at the sudden brightness, he sat up slowly. His eyes fell on the copy of *Noke* lying face-down on the floorboards, spine slightly bent from where he'd dropped it earlier.

He reached for it.

He would've preferred a hardback – something with weight, something permanent – but the man in the bookshop had told him *Noke* had only ever come out in paperback. Low print run. Cult following. The cover showed a hazy photograph of a blonde woman with her arms folded, head tilted slightly, caught somewhere between defiance and resignation.

Jarrett climbed out of bed, scooped the book up, and gave the back a lazy read, like someone practising for a late-night book review segment.

"The story of a young singer, Noke, who spends a year grappling with her sexuality, whilst discovering the truth about her humanity..."

He raised an eyebrow. Light reading, then.

Still, there was no use pretending he'd sleep. With a sigh, he threw himself back onto the bed, opened the book, and began.

Chapter 1: January is Totally Absent.

Below the title: a blank page.

"Christ," he muttered. "No wonder I haven't heard of it. Some bloody formatting error."

He flipped the page. Still blank. And then the next one, and the next. Finally...

Chapter 2: Now I Can Start.

At last, some actual words:

Sorry, I lost my confidence. Didn't have the strength to put the words down on paper. Now I can start.

It was simple. Strange. But somehow... sincere.

And within moments, Henry Jarrett was gone — lost somewhere between the lines.

Friday, 29 May, 2009

Henry Jarrett wasn't being paid for this, but it didn't matter. Too many days had passed at the arts centre staring at a blank page, waiting – almost pleading – for inspiration to come. A few hours doing something else might shake something loose.

He stood outside the gates of Canterbury Royal Oak High School, checking his watch. Victor Gully had told him to be here by ten. It was five to. He hovered near the buzzer, unsure if he should press it or just wait.

The school was... modern. Unapologetically so. Red and brown brick mashed together with sharp metal framing, like someone had built it from leftover plans of five different buildings. The gates themselves were oversized, looming protectively over a small playground littered with puddles and empty crisp packets. Beyond, the building shimmered in the morning light, its windows flashing back the sun. Jarrett had expected a campus of separate blocks; instead, it was one dense, awkward slab of a place, a single structure with no breathing room.

He caught a glimpse of movement inside — students drifting past windows, the slow shuffle of adolescent routine. A memory stirred. His own school days. He pushed it away.

A man was approaching from inside the grounds — sharply dressed, shirt tucked so neatly it almost looked vacuum-sealed.

"Henry Jarrett, is it?" the man asked, reaching the gate.

"That's me."

"I'm Kian Brearley. Deputy Headteacher." He turned and waved towards the school. The gates let out a mechanical hiss and began to open, slowly. "Saw you from the office. Thought I'd save you from hanging around in the cold."

"Appreciate it. Thanks."

As they walked across the playground, Mr Brearley started up the usual spiel – a brief history of the school, names of notable alumni, past headteachers, nothing Jarrett would remember even if he tried.

"Seems like a nice school," he offered.

"A bit chaotic at times," Brearley admitted. They passed through a set of automatic doors, into a sterile hallway that smelled faintly of polish and overcooked pasta. "Headmaster's away this week, off at some conference, so I'm running the show."

"Good students?"

Brearley gave a dry smile. "Sometimes. We keep a tight ship. Had to, ever since the old building burned down back in '69."

They stopped at Reception, the word painted in swirly cursive above a neat wooden desk. The deputy leaned in.

"Margaret, I need a visitor's pass." Then, to Jarrett: "Sorry, new safeguarding policy."

He handed Jarrett a lanyard. "Ellar's in the lunch hall at the moment. Citizenship session with Year Ten. I can walk you straight there, or get you a tea or coffee first?"

"I'm ready to get started."

"Very well. This way."

Inside, the school was the opposite of its exterior – too much space. Polished floors, high ceilings, minimalist design. New, but bland. Efficient, but soulless. Jarrett couldn't imagine writing poetry about any of it. Not even ironically.

Brearley pushed open a door marked *Lunch Hall – Orderly Behaviour, Please.*

Inside, a hundred or more students sat stiffly in rows, like a rehearsed army awaiting orders. At the front, a man paced, arms folded, voice carrying with effortless authority.

"There were some people who said Nelson Mandela was a terrorist," he said, "but of course, we know him as one of the greatest people who's ever lived. Was Martin Luther King a terrorist? Or a hero? These are the questions you have to ask yourselves. Your ideas matter."

He spotted the new arrivals and nodded briefly.

"Alright," he continued, "I want you to break into your groups and head to the tables at the back. On each table, there's an envelope with a historical figure and a card saying *Idealist* or *Terrorist*. Your job is to argue your case. Flip the assumptions. Any questions?

"Before we get started, I'd like to introduce Henry Jarrett." A few heads turned – mostly curious, mostly bored. "Henry's a poet, currently doing a summer residency nearby. He's here to help out today.

"Okay, get started — fifteen minutes. We'll reconvene after. Henry and I will be coming round if you need anything."

The room broke into motion, students dragging themselves into their groups with theatrical reluctance.

The man approached them.

"Thanks, Mr Brearley," he said, his voice dropping into something warmer, less performative.

"Not a problem. I'll see you both at lunch."

And with that, the deputy head was gone.

"I'm Ellar Cameron," said the man, holding out a hand. "Thanks for coming. I've been trying to get more links between the school and the local arts scene."

"No – thank you. You've done me a favour, honestly. Anything to get out of the centre for a while."

"Yeah, Victor mentioned a few things about that. Don't worry. Once summer hits, that place gets packed." He glanced over at a table where two students were already arguing about Malcolm X.

"What brought you here?"

"Curiosity, mostly."

Jarrett smiled. "What keeps you here?"

"Still working that one out."

A girl's head popped around the door, older than the others, waving urgently at Cameron.

"I'd better see what that's about," he said. "Why don't you float around a bit, see how they're getting on? I'll be right back."

Jarrett nodded, watching him disappear through the door. Then he turned to the room – a sea of teens trying their best not to look interested – and stepped forward.

Time to get to work.

Bizarrely, Jarrett found that he was beginning to enjoy himself just as the citizenship class was drawing to a close. The students were a great bunch – bright, committed, but just a little on the shy side. It was refreshing to see young minds engaged, even if some were clearly less than thrilled to be there.

Cameron gave them a speech on how their ideas were important, repeating the theme of their youthfulness countless times, before dismissing them.

"Let's go to the staffroom," he said to Jarrett, once the last student had gone. "Grab a cup of coffee or something."

Ellar Cameron was dressed formally, but had neglected the tie, as if trying to proclaim formality, yet rejecting any devotion to it. His casual defiance almost seemed intentional, a contradiction to his otherwise professional appearance.

He led Jarrett through the youthful rush-hour, loudly commenting on his numerous opinions of the school as they went. The corridors were filled with the murmur of students, the hustle of hurried feet – a hum of youthful energy that seemed both chaotic and somehow calming at the same time.

The staffroom was tucked away on the upper level of the school, carefully concealed at the end of a junction. No teachers were in, but Cameron worked the place as if he'd been here as a pupil himself, instantly at home.

"Would you prefer tea or coffee?" he asked. "Wait a mo, there's only coffee. Milk and sugar?"

"Just black," said Jarrett. "That'll be fine."

Cameron made them both an overdose of cheap instant, gesturing to a table right by a window. As Jarrett sat down, he noticed that the window gave an overdose of a view of Canterbury. The cathedral, the old cobbled streets, the trees casting long shadows in the sunlight – everything saved into glass.

"Have you enjoyed today?" asked Cameron.

"I have, really."

"I'm glad. You staying for lunch?"

"Yes, if that's possible."

"Oh, you're more than welcome. The lunches here are quite decent. I know school canteen food has a bad rep, but this stuff is bloody good."

"You run a good class," Jarrett said, genuinely impressed.

"Thanks. Most of the kids here I'm convinced hate my guts. They see me as a fake teacher. I think a few have read my book. You've got to be careful these days, particularly with Google. And this thing I've heard about – Twitter; it's a deathtrap."

Ellar Cameron was well-built – over forty, but still very fit. There was a clear effort in him, his sharp face, steel eyes, clenched knuckles betraying a man who had clearly worked hard at maintaining himself.

"I heard you're off to Japan this year," said Jarrett.

"Yep. Not long now. Can't wait." Cameron stood up, gathering himself. "Listen, I've got a few things I need to check on. Can I leave you up here for a bit? I'll collect you just before lunch."

Jarrett left the school just as the last of the plates were being washed. Ellar Cameron and Mr. Brearley both gave him firm, businesslike handshakes.

"It's been great to have you here," Cameron said. "Thanks for helping out today. Make sure you keep volunteering for things like this. I mean it, mate."

"Thanks," Jarrett replied, giving an absentminded, almost careless wave over his shoulder.

His thoughts? A break from the monotony of that dreadful arts centre.

He walked, each step a leap, each leap no more than a small step.

And there he was again, on Palace Street.

Sweat gathered at the back of his neck, clinging to his t-shirt.

This was the place—the place where the woman had kissed him. He could still taste her. Feel her. He scanned his surroundings. Everything seemed different in the light, but he knew it wasn't a lost cause. Nothing was. Not this. Not her.

He would find her. Yes. He would find her. Never give up, never stop the search. It was simple enough, right? Just ask a few locals, maybe check around the bars, see if anyone knew her.

And then – he'd found it. His inspiration. This search, this mission, would keep him going.

A small smile tugged at the corner of his mouth. Tiny, insignificant, but enough to draw the attention of *her*. Not *her*, not the woman he secretly fantasized about, but *her*. Jane.

She was ahead of him now, arms folded, that same squat figure, frazzled hair, and that annoying handbag that always swung too widely.

"I heard you got a residency position here," she said, her voice dripping with disdain.

"Look, I really don't want any trouble," he said, weary.

"You bet, you dick. You really are a dick!"

"I'm going home," he said firmly.

"I'm getting married next weekend!"

"Poor guy," he muttered.

Her face twisted, contorted into something vicious, something sickening. She inched forward. Each movement a millimetre closer.

"You know something, Henry? You're a dick!" she hissed. "You really are a dick!"

"Look, Jane, are you here to stalk me?"

"I'm entitled to go wherever I want. It's a free country, isn't it?"

"Jane, what happened between us was a long time ago. I've moved on." He shrugged. "Go away. Honest to God."

He shuffled past her.

"Your parents neglected you!" she called after him. "My aunt did a lecture or two at Milton Borstal in the Sixties. So many neglected kids there. You would've fitted right in."

He turned, military precision. Stared her down, eyes locking with hers.

"You know what? Fuck you, Jane!" he screamed. Innocent onlookers, drawn in like flies to meat. "You fucking emotionally abused me in that relationship. But, you know something? I fucking moved on! Studied at Reading, now I'm fucking published! And you, you despicable woman, you're fucking nothing!"

A man walked over, big and burly. Biceps bulging through his t-shirt. He held a paper coffee in one hand, using the other to create a barrier between them.

"That's enough, mate," he said, voice calm but firm. "Go home."

"This is none of your business!" snapped Jarrett.

"Mate, if you don't piss off, I'm gonna drag you away from here."

"I said, this is none of your business!"

The man shoved him in the chest, hard enough to nearly send him to the ground.

"You just assaulted me!" Jarrett shouted back.

The man calmly sipped his coffee, stared at him, unphased.

"Okay, okay," Jarrett muttered, feeling the panic rise in his chest. "I'll go."

All thoughts of the mysterious woman were gone. He walked with his head down, his chest tight, panic suffocating him. He arrived at the bus stop just as the vehicle pulled in.

"Where to, mate?" asked the driver.

"Away from here," Jarrett said. "Sorry! Rough day." The name of the village slipped off his tongue with heavy reluctance.

He considered stopping off at the arts centre, just in case any curious souls wanted to venture in there, but decided to head straight back to his flat. Too much excitement for one day.

Way too much.

The village did nothing to counter the adrenaline. Nothing could fight the past coming back.

Jane had been his abusive girlfriend in Bradford. Nothing more to say. Manipulative, cocky, sadistic. Mocking him. Slapping him. Telling him he was nothing.

He walked across the village centre, ambled his way up to his apartment. He was starting to think of the place as home. As boring and tiresome as the village was, it separated him from his past. His nightmares. Today, that trauma had found him, but he hoped it didn't know about this place.

He powered up his laptop and slumped down in front of it. Lines started to flow, like music. A poem based on the pain of the past catching up to you, of never being able to escape an abusive relationship. Of flying for the stars only to slam back to Earth.

His reverie, his inspiration, was interrupted by a light tapping on the door.

"Jane, if that's you, I'm not interested. Go away!" he called, jumping up from his chair. He strode to the door, yanking it open with the force of a statue.

He recognized the young woman standing there, but he didn't know her.

"Can I help you?" he asked, confused.

"Maybe," she said, stepping forward.

The penny dropped. The student who had interrupted the citizenship class. She could easily be mistaken for a university student – jeans and a shirt, hair hanging loose.

"Did I leave something behind at the school?"

"No," she replied. Then, without hesitation, she walked into his flat, nudging the door closed behind her.

Her face was featureless, a thoughtless apparition. She removed her clothes in a series of small movements. Tiny ones. Featureless ones. They piled up on the floor like snakeskin shadows.

"Okay, this is not funny," Jarrett stammered. "If this is some sort of prank, I'm not interested. Go home."

"I'm seventeen," she replied. "It's legal."

"Please, I think there's been a misunderstanding. Look, you need to go home."

She leaned in, kissing him on the corner of his lips. He didn't pull back. He couldn't. Everything about this was wrong, but so much had gone wrong today.

One more leap wouldn't rip the world in two.

As the barriers he'd erected crumbled, he saw her again—on Palace Street. In that dress. Desperation in her eyes. He was closer to her now.

Part 4

R oger Miser
Tuesday, 20 May, 1980

"Now it starts," Roger muttered to himself.

Memories of his childhood in Yardley Wood clung to him, stubbornly refusing to fade. There was only one flicker of brightness: his departure. He could still picture himself, a young kid sitting on the bench at Yardley Wood Station, waiting for that train – one that always seemed to take forever.

And now, he was that kid again, standing in his empty penthouse, bags packed, everything ready to go.

Where the hell was George? The man was never late, always organized down to the last detail.

Roger picked up the latest issue of one of the newest music magazines that had somehow ended up on the floor. He stared at the cover – there he was, in a tuxedo, a slim smile on his face, standing in Brooklyn with the iconic bridge behind him, arms folded, just before attending some awards ceremony in 1979. A hell of a year for him.

A sharp car horn blasted through the bricks and posh windows of the penthouse. George had pulled up outside in the Bentley. Roger watched as, believing no one was looking, George rubbed a thumb along the car's paintwork.

"You're a prat, George, but you're a decent bloke," Roger muttered.

He grabbed his luggage, knowing it should have been George doing it, but not complaining. How could he? He was as fit as a fiddle, muscular for his age. A perfect so-and-so. He dragged the leather satchels – symbols of childhood holidays he never had – through the passageway that led from the back garden of the apartment block to the front pavement.

"Sorry for running a little late!" George called out from the car. "Nightmare of a jam!"

"It's okay, let's just get going, shall we?"

George instinctively grabbed the bags and loaded them into the boot.

"Right, you got the passports?" Roger asked.

"Yes, passports, hotel reservations, money, festival documents—every single thing we need," George replied.

"That's what I want to hear. Right, we don't want to miss the ferry."

"There's nothing to worry about," George reassured him. "We've got plenty of time. The ferry doesn't leave for hours."

"Yeah, but you know what the traffic in London's like. Come on, we need to move."

"Do you think this will work, Roger?"

"What do you mean?"

"The festival. You've put so much money and effort into it. What if it doesn't work?"

"It will. George, I've spent a long time building up my career. Christ, I've built an empire. But I'm sick of it. Sick of the lonely nights, the failed relationships, the jetlag. If it weren't for all the weightlifting, I'd be dead from exhaustion. I want to retire. Get a cottage somewhere. Enjoy life. I'm done with this, George. This festival—it's my final mark on the world."

"Just as long as you're sure. You know you can always talk to me about anything."

"You're a decent man, George, really. Let's do this. Let's make the festival happen. Let's leave our mark." Roger held out his hand.

But just then, the sight of a green Jaguar pulling up to the curb made both men freeze in their tracks. Two figures stepped out, suits and ties as sharp as razor blades.

"What the hell's he doing here?" George muttered. "Roger, you haven't gotten us in debt to him, have you?"

"No! I can't think of a thing I've done!"

One of the figures grasped the back passenger door and gently pulled it open.

The man who emerged fixed his piercing gaze directly on Miser. He was thickset, still carrying a touch of extra weight, but his presence was commanding. His hair, a stark white, was slicked back with gel, giving him an air of polished authority. Gary Holmes exuded a toughness akin to lead. As he stretched, it was done with deliberate restraint, his ingrained sense of decorum evident in every movement. With a practiced flick of his fingers, he adjusted the knot of his tie before striding towards them with an air of unwavering confidence. Power, wealth, and a web of influential connections seemed to cling to him like a persistent shadow. This was a man who had carved out an empire through sheer determination, leaving a trail of hard grit, broken bones, and unwavering loyalty in his wake. Wherever Gary Holmes went, it was as if the very ground trembled beneath his feet.

"Good morning, good morning," he said, his handmade leather shoes kissing the dirt.

"It's good to see you, Mr. Holmes," Roger said, his voice laced with caution. "How can I help?"

"It won't take five minutes. Let's step inside my car." Holmes gestured toward the Jaguar with a pudgy hand, red and raw, glistening in the sun.

Roger froze. If he walked away, he'd be dead. If he went to the car, he might end up beaten.

"Mr. Holmes," Roger ventured, matching his pace. They walked side by side, like two brothers in step. "Is everything okay between us? I'm not in debt, am I?"

"I can assure you, no. You've more than paid me back over the years. No, this is something... a little different."

One of Holmes's men opened the back passenger door.

Roger stepped forward, his mind racing. The leather seats in the car were as soft and cushy as he remembered, the same ones he'd sat in years ago when he'd foolishly borrowed one hundred pounds from Holmes to start a record label. A stupid mistake, his family had told him.

Holmes slammed the door shut behind him and gave a firm nod to his men. They began backing away from the vehicle, as if giving the two men space to talk.

"Is this about France?" Roger asked, his tone tight with uncertainty.

Holmes folded his arms across his stomach. "Mr. Miser, we might have a slight problem. An old acquaintance has resurfaced. One we thought we'd gotten rid of."

"Who?"

"Do you remember Clifford Lake?"

Roger's face twitched. "What, him? Has he gone to the papers or something?"

"William and Emily Butterworth were found murdered. Brutalized in the most vicious manner."

"Murdered? Could have been anyone."

"There's more," Holmes continued, his voice low and measured. "Melanie Tolson – former psychologist at Milton Borstal – had her daughter's wedding trashed by Lake. I won't go into the details – far too messy – but it was definitely him."

"So what? What's a trashed wedding got to do with this?"

Holmes leaned in, his eyes narrowing. "Ceri Britton – former Deputy Warden of the Borstal – chased after Lake. No one has seen him since." He flicked his fingers in the air, as if dismissing the whole thing. "He vanished without a trace."

"Is there any connection to me?" Roger's voice was sharp now. "Come on, don't keep me in the dark."

Holmes' gaze locked with Roger's, his cold, dead eyes commanding the air between them. "Just remember who you're talking to," he said, a warning hidden beneath his calm demeanour. "Then he sent me a request for a loan. Fifty quid – that's all. Barely recognized the name when the letter came across my desk. My boys did some digging. Knocked on a few doors. Turns out, it's him. And here's where it connects to you: he's spending the summer near St Pierre."

"What?" Roger's heart skipped a beat.

"I don't think he's much of a threat," Holmes said, leaning back in his seat. "I trust he's after attention, but just to be safe, I'm heading down there. Taking the boys with me. We're renting a house near the town. Don't worry, we'll keep out of the way of your festival."

"Is there anything I can do to help?"

Holmes popped a cigar between his lips, the rich scent of Cuban tobacco filling the air. "Look, my purpose here today is to give you a friendly warning. Keep your eyes peeled. We'll handle the rest. Safe travels, mate." He nodded to the man outside, who promptly opened the car door.

Roger stood frozen, his mind struggling to process the information. He managed a half-hearted nod and stepped back from the vehicle, nearly stumbling. The car's engine rumbled to life, its sound smooth and powerful, like melted margarine.

George rushed over, tugging at Roger's elbow like a concerned puppy. "Are you in any trouble?" he asked, his voice full of worry. "Please, I need to know."

"No, I'm not!" Roger threw his hands up in frustration, shouting toward the sky as if the world might answer. "Well... I hope not, anyway."

The Public Schoolboy
April 1966

On the day he turns fifteen, it's a day like any other. He gets up, has breakfast, goes to school, slaps hands with his friends, and pays close attention to class, his eyes drilling into the scratches of chalk.

A year and two months have passed since his visit to Bond Street. He's changed. He's broader, more muscular—the beginnings of a handsome young man. The girls love him, chasing after him like a feather caught in a hurricane.

Academically, he's more than excelled. Physics and maths are his strong suits. He's passing his exams with no less than 90%.

It's been just over a year, but he's no longer a boy. His voice is dropping. His hair is shorter. A moustache is starting to sprout.

On the day he turns fifteen, the headmaster, Mr. Stratton, shakes his hand as he passes through the grand entrance of the school.

The public schoolboy hasn't asked for a birthday party. He just wants to spend it with his parents—wants to hear wise advice from his father, to sit in the back garden, admire the kisses of spring, fall in love with its beauty again and again. But when he gets home, he finds his friends are already there. Everyone's treated to a small glass of champagne in the freshly mown garden. A buffet table runs its length, cakes, sandwiches, and rolls beckoning hungry mouths. The teachers arrive, including Mr. Stratton—proof of how popular the public schoolboy is.

The afternoon slips into evening, and the party gradually disperses.

He helps his parents tidy up. So much food, so many half-finished drinks, so many jokes left hanging.

He knows some of his best days lie ahead – when he becomes a prefect, when he grows into the muscular school captain he's destined to be.

Picture him now: this public schoolboy with his longish hair, deep eyes, steel cheekbones, and firm, clenched hands. Imagine the potential this boy holds.

It's night now, and everything seems to fold into everything else. His parents have gone to bed, but the public schoolboy stands in the back garden, hands on his hips, listening to the sounds of the night – the scrapes and whispers of the world around him. He can never have enough of this, never quite fill the cup of memories.

He turns on his heels, locks up the house, and makes the long journey upstairs. The way he moves, the way he organizes himself – brushing his teeth, sorting his clothes for tomorrow – he's the envy of every father.

He settles into bed, the lights off straight away. The covers pull over him as he begins to drift off. He wants to dream about the fabled School Captain's Cup, but there's no time for that. He doesn't have the luxury of fantasizing about what could be.

Because he's not alone.

There's a silhouette in the corner of his room.

He launches upright, ready to cry out, but a soft hand presses against his lips.

"It's me," comes the voice, low and familiar. "Tracy Cox. You remember me? From Bond Street?"

"Tracy?" he stammers, his voice still groggy. "Tracy, what are you doing here?"

"Keep your voice down," she whispers, her breath betraying a sense of excitement, anticipation. "I'm going to have sex with you."

"What?" he barely manages, his mind racing.

"I'm going to have sex with you. Take your clothes off."

"But my parents –"

"They won't know a thing, if we're quiet."

She kisses him, and he doesn't pull away, though he's tempted to. It's the kiss he's been waiting for. Fourteen months. He feels her hands tugging at the cotton of his pyjamas. This is a moment – his moment – to live in. And he does. He kisses her back, takes the lead, and falls into the spell of it.

The night stretches into morning as he explores her and himself. He's on a journey into unknown territory, discovering things he's not meant to know yet.

She wakes him as dawn breaks, her figure outlined in the dust motes, sunlight spilling across her cheeks. An angel caught in a fleeting moment. She leans down and presses a soft kiss to his forehead.

"This Sunday," she whispers, her voice barely rising above the breath. "This Sunday, at noon, in front of your church. I'll meet you there."

He opens his mouth, tries to speak, but the words remain frozen. He blinks, once, twice – then, just like that, she's gone.

Roger Miser
Tuesday, 20 May, 1980

It was raining when they arrived, but nothing dampened their spirits. The journey from London had suffered delay after countless delay, and instead of arriving on a late summer afternoon, they alighted from the train in a brewing storm at nearly eleven o'clock at night.

He knew the station was a long distance from the town. If the rain picked up, they'd be drenched to the bone.

"Bloody hell," said George. He did a silent count of their suitcases.

The train porter did his own count on the train. Everything in order. Whistle blown. The train shifted off, crunching and groaning, disappearing into the night.

"You'd think they'd at least put a bloody phone box here, or a shelter," Miser complained. "Christ. We're going to wind up frozen."

"Hang on a minute. Isn't that a taxi over there?" George pointed to the far left of the station. Where the platform ended, a small road began, leading off into the distance. A car sat there, as blank as its driver's face.

"Well, he's been patient," remarked Miser. "Come on. I need a fucking drink."

"I'm a bit worried about Holmes," said George, as they each grabbed a bundle of bags. "If he's coming here, he's going to rip the place to pieces. You know what his thugs are like: bloodthirsty, sex-starved. They'll rape every girl in sight!"

"Gary Holmes is a traditional sort of bloke. He's a family man. Has Sunday dinner with all his kids and grandkids. Goes to church. I'm more worried about who Holmes was warning me about. I know he's not much of a threat, but... Holmes wouldn't be coming here if he didn't believe the guy was dangerous."

"It was a dreadful thing, what happened to Lake. It's affected both of us. But we had a record label to protect, we had an image to protect, and we fought for it."

He didn't remember much about the taxi ride to St Pierre. The stresses of the day were threatening to render him unconscious. He saw the lights as they entered the town, caught a couple of suspicious local eyes. Years later, he would recollect the musty sensation as they entered their hotel.

He was aware, vaguely so, of a television in the lobby. It's on full. The noise shakes the walls, vibrates the raindrops clinging to his jacket. Isn't that Ceri Britton? Miser hasn't thought of the bloke for years, but it has to be him! He's being interviewed rapidly, microphones in his face. Something about him escaping from a gang in Colombia.

Nothing else filters in. George is next to him, producing room keys.

Miser zones out, sleep coming for him.

When he's finally in bed, it's only then that he's awake.

Lake
Tuesday, 20 May, 1980

"It's nothing personal," he said for the tenth time.

She stared up at him, trembling. Fear.

"Some advice. When you get a letter saying you've won a million pounds, telling you to show up on some random street in the East End of London – say no. Better still, run a hundred miles. But you Butterworths are all the same. Thick as shit."

Pointless advice now, considering she wasn't leaving here alive.

"You killed my brother, didn't you?" she whispered.

"Yes, Kate, I did. Smashed his face off a table. Then gouged his wife's eyes out with my thumbs."

They were surrounded by dust and the ruins of dust. All of it familiar to him. Too bloody familiar.

She was trembling. From the cold and the fear. Definitely the cold. She was naked, tied to a wooden chair, three ribs broken by a crowbar.

"Don't you want to know why?" he asked. "Hmm? Why I killed your brother?"

"Was it because of the borstal?"

"Absolutely, my dear! I'd like to warmly welcome you to Milton Borstal! We're in what used to be the Chamber. It's where, if we didn't improve on Billy the Borstal's formal warnings, we'd be tortured."

The room was even more constricted than he remembered. Yet cozy, somehow.

"How are you feeling?" he asked. "Sorry about the rough ride. Not entirely easy, bundling you into a van and driving all the way up here."

"Please, let me go."

"As Governor of Milton Borstal, Mr Butterworth used to have me beaten and tortured regularly in this room. Never took part himself. Too much of a coward. Got Ceri Britton to administer the punishments."

"Please, I had nothing to do with this."

"My dear, you're Billy the Borstal's sister. You're bad blood. Your kind should be eliminated. And that's what I'm going to do. I'm going to burn you alive."

"Please!" she howled.

"No, no, no. Not this time. I'm going to fucking burn you. As your brother did to me. Kate Butterworth, I'd like to thank you for your professional conduct during this session. Please do remember that you have our Hanging Gardens Medical Service."

He lifted the petrol can, unscrewed the rusted lid, and threw it over her.

He knew the way out well enough – knew it like the back of his hand. Her screams were threatening to carry. If he wasn't careful, everyone in Milton would hear.

As he walked out, he left a trail of petrol breadcrumbs. At what had been the main entrance, he snarled and emptied the last of the fluid.

As the place burned, he walked into the night. No screams anymore. Just howls of agony.

Roger Miser
Wednesday, 21 May, 1980

He woke up from a dream in which he'd never come here.

He sat up, let himself breathe.

Downed the half-pint of water by his bed. Glanced at his watch. Just before six in the morning. He should rest a bit more.

But the curtains hid a strong, sober beauty. Sparkles of sunlight on the other side. Instinctively, he was up, tearing the fabric open.

The town of St Pierre was bathed in an orange glow, like it sat in the shadow of an open fire. Some of the inhabitants were up, ambling sluggishly through the streets.

A walk wouldn't hurt.

He was showered and shaved within fifteen minutes.

No one else was up. Not even the girl at the desk in the lobby. To his surprise, the door was open.

Didn't people steal things around here?

The town was quiet – for now. But that would change. Very soon.

Tomorrow they would come: setting up bandstands, record shops, burger stalls. A musical village layered over St Pierre. Two settlements. Two civilisations.

Everything was light sandstone. Everything.

He'd seen pictures of St Pierre, but standing here, feet on the ground, was different. A central street ran its length, interrupted by a spurting water fountain, all gleaming and new.

Proper French houses, with their cream-coloured stonework, began to quiver as the heat climbed.

Sounds filled the stagnant air: trees swishing, glass rattling, a car engine coughing awake somewhere, the shrieks of excited children.

Two stalls were being raised near the fountain. He ventured closer – fruit stalls, from what he could make out.

The women behind them, their aprons grimy and strapped tight, cast sharp, suspicious eyes at him.

He wasn't just a stranger. Some people here would see him as a threat.

This quiet, quaint little town was about to become a festival ground. Blaring music, burgers, beer.

Sordid love affairs. Cocaine. Scandal.

This was going to be his town.

The builders would arrive tomorrow. Straight to work. No time to waste.

In two days, the first musicians would start turning up.

Disco Dave among the first – always keen to make an impression.

He edged closer to the fountain. The artist in him – all record producers needed a dash of artistry, according to Herbert Buxton – studied its intricate design.

"It's lovely!" he said to one of the women. "Beautiful! You understand me? Very beautiful design!"

Only confused faces stared back.

"The patterns on the fountain!" He gestured at the stonework. "Oh, never mind."

His attention drifted almost immediately.

To his left, another road peeled off from the fountain.

At the end of it: buildings. Obscure. Out of place. Black and rectangular, glimmering in the morning heat.

A magnet to the soul.

"What's that? Those buildings over there?" he asked the women. "Hmm?"

No point waiting.

His feet were starting to sweat inside his shoes. He felt it seep through the leather.

Disgusted, he pushed forward.

St Pierre was something, that much could be said. Quaint. Cosy. Reminiscent of the little French towns kids saw in battered school tapes. That childish addiction to French culture and cuisine.

A pain hit his gut.

He stopped. Stooped. Fought it back as hard as he could.

Tears running down his face like pool balls sliding into pockets.

"Mum," he said. "Mum."

She sat in her husky chair, a damp cigarette between her lips. Wheezing.

He saw her for a moment – nothing more.

The buildings ahead were taking shape. Their blurred outlines sharpening, their shadows thickening.

Transfixed was the wrong word.

Obsessed.

Too curious.

As he neared them, it became clear: a school.

He was hunched on a bench at Yardley Wood Station, waiting for the train that would never come.

He's still there.

He'll always be there.

He's never quite escaped Yardley Wood.

Black railings block his way to the station platform. They imprison him. Trap him.

No…

They line the perimeter of the school.

Roger Miser stood still, arms folded, feet drowning in sweat.

Back now. Back to the land of the living.

The school was empty. No life stirring yet – too early.

He looked back toward the town. The women at the stalls were still staring. He gave a quick wave.

"Such a big high school for such a small town," he muttered.

The buildings were grey and peeling. Eight blocks, all rectangles, all slightly crooked, linked by a spidery web of corridors.

The playground was newly painted – hopscotch grids and football pitches – an illusion of fun.

Unappetising. Sickly. He grimaced.

He backed away and started toward the town centre.

As he neared the fountain, three men approached him. Well-dressed. Suits and ties, despite the heat. They came straight for him, stopping within spitting distance of the fountain.

"Roger Miser," one of them said, extending a brisk, blade-like hand. "I'm Eric Garson. These are my colleagues, Michael La Rue and Serge Ferris."

"Hi! Are you local councillors?"

"No, local doctors," said the one called La Rue. "We run a small surgery on the east side of the village. You're going to keep us fairly busy over the summer!"

"Well, I'm sure it won't be too bad," said Miser, giving each man a courteous nod.

Never hold eye contact too long, Roger.

They were insignificant little sods who would no doubt cause problem after problem over the next few weeks.

"I must be off," said Miser.

He breathed in deeply. Held it.

The time was now. He knew it.

His legacy – made here, in this small, dirty, insignificant town.

Not long before it was packed to the rafters with singers, music, badly tuned guitars, drunks, drugs. Not bloody long.

He was lost in France.

His flashbacks wouldn't stop.

He's back.

The train station at night. The rain falling, cascading, drowning everything. He's there with only a rucksack and frozen fingers. Waiting for a train that would never come.

He's lost in France.

But at least he's back now.

Miser pushed the remnants of a failed childhood aside and kept walking.

The Public Schoolboy
April 1966

He's an hour early. He's done something stupid – skipped Sunday service and told a lie, claiming he's sick. His parents are inside the church right now, singing hymns, while he hides behind a gravestone, waiting for this fantasy woman to show up.

Did that night really happen? Did she make love to him, or was it all in his mind?

The public schoolboy folds his arms and waits for this miserable hour to pass. When the congregation finally spills from the church, he tenses, crouches lower, and hides.

It doesn't take long for the grounds to clear. He emerges and begins to pace along the worn pathways, past the graves of people long gone. He stumbles, hesitates, and then realizes with a sinking feeling – she might not show up after all.

Noon comes and goes. She's not there. Half-past. Still nothing. One o'clock. Nothing.

Suddenly, he feels a year younger, that sweet little kid waiting in the kitchen for his parents to wake up. He was patient then. Not so much now.

A familiar breath brings him back to the present.

"I'm so sorry!" Tracy looks as though she's been running, sweat dripping down her face. She hugs him tightly, pressing her lips to his in a solid kiss.

"It's okay," he says, trying to sound reassuring.

"How are you feeling about the other night?" she asks, her voice soft.

"Oh, fine," he responds, too bloody honourable.

"You're sure you're okay about it?"

"I am."

"I really like you, Clifford. When you came into my shop last year, I kinda fell for you. But... I'm heading back to America at the end of the summer and..." She links her arm through his. "Come on, let's take a walk."

She leads him out of the church grounds. He follows like a faithful puppy, though he'll never quite realize it.

He's blind to everything except her curly hair, her cute eyes, her dainty figure next to his.

"The truth is, I think I love you," she says at one point.

They head out of the village, not down the main road but along a small dirt path that leads into the woods.

He's been to these woods many times since childhood. They hold a deep sense of comfort for him, the trees sheltering him, concealing him from the pain of growing up.

Tracy takes him deeper into the woods. She stops him by a small patch of flowers, nearly trampling them, and cups his face in her hands. She kisses him repeatedly.

"Come back to America with me," she says.

"I'd really like that." He has no idea how heavy that sentence is.

"I know you're not happy here. I can see it in your eyes. That's why I want you to come with me. We can start fresh – together, as lovers. Have our own family."

Her smile fades, and something about her expression crumbles, almost like she's falling apart.

"What's wrong?" he whispers, noticing her tears. "My dear, are you okay?"

"No!" She trembles. Tears smear her makeup. "Sorry, Clifford, I'm so sorry. It's just... there's a friend of mine who really needs my help, and I don't want to let him down. I can't... I can't go back to America unless I've gotten him out of this mess."

"Please, tell me..." In that moment, the public schoolboy feels like he's become a man, trying to care for her.

"Do you remember when you came into the shop last year, and there was that man with me?"

"Yes. Was he your boyfriend?"

"Oh, no! He's a good guy, but no, not my boyfriend. He's actually in a band. He's a drummer. Really good. They just came back from a tour in South Africa."

"That's incredible!"

She pulls herself closer to him, so close he can feel the heat of her body. His attention sharpens on every little detail – the dents in her makeup, the flecks of lipstick that have strayed from her lips.

"The thing is," she says, her lips trembling, "he's trying to leave the band."

"Why?"

"He wants to go solo, travel, that sort of thing."

"Why can't he just do that?"

"He's tied up with the contracts. He can't just walk away from them."

"Surely he can? Tracy, dear, I know so little about the music industry, but surely he can just walk away?"

"Oh, you're such a beautiful, pretty English boy, aren't you? Unfortunately, he can't. Have you ever heard of Roger Miser?"

"Nope."

"Roger Miser runs the band's record label. There are rumours he's got ties to Gary Holmes, this gangster from East London. But those are just rumours. Miser has tight control over band contracts."

"Oh, my word."

"Yes." She steps back, turns away. "There is a way out, but it's risky."

"What is it?"

"We could sign him to a new record label. If he signs as a solo artist with someone else, it could force Miser to back off."

"What record label?"

"Yours," she whispers, finally turning back to face him.

"Excuse me?"

"You heard me, English Boy. You're going to set up a record label."

"But I don't know the first thing about music, or contracts, or anything!"

"It's okay, dear. I'll take care of everything. All I need is your signature. On the fifteenth of next month, I'll pick you up, we'll head into London, meet my guy, and you'll sign the documents. Two of them. One for setting up your record label. Another to formally sign him on. Then, a month after that, your label will be dissolved. My guy goes his way, and we'll start preparing for America. What do you say?"

"I'm in."

"Excellent!" She closes the distance between them, planting a soft kiss on his cheek. "Now, why don't we start pursuing our relationship?"

Part 5

Henry Jarrett
Saturday, 30 May, 2009

He woke expecting everything to have collapsed – his career, his respect, his reputation, his freedom. But no cops were standing over him, arms folded, eyes boring into his. Nothing.

He sat up, glanced at the empty space where the girl had been, shrugged, and pulled himself out of bed.

He spent the next hour cowering—just about cowering—at his writing desk, an empty cup clutched between his palms. If it got out, even a whisper of it, that was it. Prison. Ruin. Oblivion.

The girl came back to him. Not the one from the night before. Definitely not Jane. The girl from Palace Street. The woman who had pulled him in. She felt like a dream now.

"Pack it in, mate," he muttered, flipping open one of the many notepads stacked on his cluttered desk. "Just pack it in."

But it was a rope tightening around his neck. A rough kind of justice crushing him.

He was on Palace Street again, like that bloody anorak detective. Right in the spot where she'd kissed him. Adjacent to him was a sports bar – flashy new lights, unlit for now, waiting to bring in the nightlife.

"Here we go," he muttered, stepping up and swinging his fist against the black door.

"We're closed!" a man's voice boomed from inside.

"I was just wondering if you could help me out with something. I need some information."

He heard the sound of bolts unlatching. A skinny man with an overgrown beard yanked the door open. He looked worn down, slightly neglected.

"How can I help?" the man asked.

"Seventeenth of May – were you working that night?"

"Are you a fucking journalist?"

"No! Absolutely not! I'm looking for someone. Listen, mate, it's a bit strange, but I bumped into a woman on the night of the Seventeenth of May, right outside here. Quite liked her, but didn't get her number. I know I probably sound like some desperate romantic, but I was wondering if you maybe saw us – or had her details or something."

"Mate, I'm sorry, but I can't help you." The man ran bony fingers through the forest on his face. "I was working that night, but I was behind the bar. And I think the lads outside were too pissed to notice anything. Listen, mate, I've got to get back to it. Catch you later."

"Thanks."

"No worries."

Disappointment closed in from all sides. Hands in his pockets, Jarrett pushed on. But he already knew the chances of striking lucky were slim – impossible, really – confirmed by the responses he got from local shops and cafés. No one had seen a woman in an emerald dress that night:

"Sorry, sir, I'm unaware of anyone of that description."

"Unfortunately, I haven't seen anyone like that."

"Haven't seen her, mate. Sounds like a right slapper."

"Honestly, mate, get a life."

After lunch in a hidden café, disappointment gave way to defeat. The game was up.

"You did your best, Henry," he said to himself. "You did your bloody best."

The yearning to be with her – or at least talk to her – still tugged at his chest, but he forced himself to take a step back. What he needed now was a stronger coffee and a heavy pint.

He spent some more time exploring the depths of Canterbury, though it turned quickly to aimless wandering. When he found himself back on Palace Street, a strange calm settled over him. The stress, the fear, the worry, Jane, the prick that knocked him over – all gone.

Time to relax. Time to breathe.

He had the world at his fingertips: poetry, literary events, awards ceremonies. Everything he needed.

"Hey, mate!" a voice called out. "Mate!"

Jarrett spun around. For a second, he saw Jane, ready to mock him. Or that musclehead, fists clenched.

"Hi!" he stuttered.

It was the man from the sports bar. He was wheezing, sweat pouring down his face and trickling into his shirt.

"Sorry, saw you walking past," the man said, panting. "Wanted to catch you. Listen, mate, there's someone I know—a private detective, of sorts. After you left, I gave him a quick ring. He's up for helping you out. No charge. Here's his contact."

He held out a small slip of paper.

"Nice." Jarrett's fingers trembled as he took it.

"No worries, mate. Good luck with your search. Right, better get back to the bar. You have a good day, yeah?"

It wasn't a real business card. No fancy lettering. Just a scrap of paper with a mobile number scratched in near-empty pen.

Jarrett pulled out his phone and keyed in the number.

What should he say? Just introduce himself? Jump right in?

"Yeah?" a gruff voice answered. American.

"Hi, is this the private investigator?"

"Yeah, that's me."

"My name is Henry Jarrett."

"Oh, yeah – Ron just phoned me about you. Listen, buddy, I'll text you my address. Can you come by tomorrow?"

"Yeah, absolutely."

"Cool. About half two in the afternoon?"

"Yeah, sure. Absolutely."

"Right, man. I'll send it tonight. And hey – don't tell anyone. I keep my business discreet."

"Sure."

The line went dead.

Jarrett stood alone in the crowd. He turned to face the spot where he'd met the woman in the green dress. More than a meeting – a kiss without meaning. But he had to find that meaning. Wherever it took him.

That's what he started telling Victor Gully when they met for dinner at The Lake Arms, the only pub in the village. Beneath a dusty coat of arms, in front of the disused fireplace, and behind their respective pints of ale, Henry Jarrett laid it all out.

"Honestly, mate, it doesn't sound like a good idea," Gully said once he'd finished. "Bit dodgy, if I'm honest."

"I feel like I have to do it." Jarrett dug his fork into a cottage pie he wasn't ready to eat. His tongue clung to the roof of his mouth.

The Lake Arms was too warm, borderline humid. Both of them sat in t-shirts and jeans, summer bearing down like a heat lamp. They looked like teenage loiterers – dripping, brows damp with moisture.

"You've got something next Wednesday," Gully said. "A group of old dears doing a poetry workshop with you."

"Fun times."

"It's an all-day thing. Honestly, Henry, you need to focus on what you're actually here for. Not gallivanting around Kent after some woman you kissed once. Come on, man, have some sense."

"I'm just curious –"

"Curiosity's a killer, mate. Trust me." Gully took a long pull from his pint, then returned to his roast. "That bloke text you yet?"

Jarrett pulled out his phone. "Not yet."

"I suspect it's some kind of practical joke. You've got to be careful with this stuff. Especially now with the internet bleeding into everything."

"I'll be careful."

"Up to you. Do what you want. But I'm advising against it."

"Tell me more about this old people's event, then."

Gully perked up slightly. He chewed a few mouthfuls, sipped his beer, and launched in:

"Basically, it's the local seniors' club. They're coming to the centre for the day to... I don't know, *work on their imaginations. Express themselves. Turn their feelings into poetry* or whatever. Personally? Waste of bloody time. A bunch of old dears writing verse – it's an absolute joke. I know that's ageist, but it's true. You'll be running it. Come up with some inspirational prompts, that kind of thing. Nine to five, all day. There's a caterer from Canterbury doing lunch – that'll be the highlight, trust me. Anyway. Rant over."

"I'll give it my best shot."

"I know you will."

"Anyway..." Jarrett raised his pint. "To a good summer."

"Here, here," Gully said without looking up.

They focused on their food after that, occasionally muttering something about a writer or poet or something else literary.

As they were placing their dessert orders, Jarrett felt a vibration in his pocket.

Sunday, 31 May, 2009

He set off in the early hours, after a soft pastry and a rushed instant coffee. Hours later, via a muddle of trains and buses, he arrived at his destination.

The address led him to a warehouse in Thamesmead, wedged between two crumbling council estates. He showed up just after noon. Better early than late, he supposed. After grabbing a sandwich from a grimy off-licence, he walked loops around the area. He pretended to be collecting ideas for his next poetry collection, jotting a few lines in his notebook, but after the fifth lap past the warehouse, even he couldn't kid himself. It was pointless.

Eventually, Two-Thirty arrived, and he stood squarely in front of the building.

The warehouse was small, squat, and forgotten. Rust peeled from its corrugated skin. A metal shutter sealed its front like a clenched jaw, streaked with unreadable graffiti and soot stains. Broken bottles glittered in the weeds nearby. A pigeon fluttered out from the roof gutter, startling him.

Just as he raised his hand to knock on the metal, he heard the scrape of chains. The shutter began to rise with a groan, dust and grime falling from the track.

A man stood on the other side. Slightly resembled the barman from the sports bar, but this one was tidier – beard trimmed, hair gelled down flat, spectacles perched delicately on the ridge of his nose.

"Henry Jarrett?" the man asked.

"Yeah, that's me."

"Come on in."

He stepped through the threshold.

"I really appreciate this," Jarrett began. "I mean, I know –"

"Hold on. Just bear with me," the man interrupted.

The shutter screeched and rattled behind them, slowly descending. Chains groaned like old bones.

Inside, the warehouse was cavernous but mostly empty. Cold grey walls, rows of exposed pipework, the faint buzz of a single overhead light. In one corner, a modest stack of wooden crates sat like abandoned luggage. The floor was concrete, littered with gravel and blackened gum, dust swirling underfoot. No desk. No chairs. No sign of business.

"You do all your stuff from here?" Jarrett asked, glancing around.

"I'll go through things with you as soon as this damn thing's shut," the man replied. "Oh, name's Elijah."

Then, movement – small, sudden. A few figures slipped under the closing shutter just before it sealed with a hard metallic thud. Quick, like rats.

Jarrett froze. "What –?"

Three men. Big. Built like doormen. Tattooed arms, heavy boots. They moved with quiet precision, spreading out around him.

"There's one thing in this world I can't stand," Elijah said calmly, "and that's men who sexually harass women."

"Mate, I think there's been a misunderstanding –"

A punch silenced him. One of the tattooed men gripped him by the neck and drove a fist into his stomach. The pain didn't register – only shock. He crumpled, flat on his back, eyes blinking up at the naked bulb above.

Elijah stepped into view. "Men like you disgust me. Preying on women. Stalking them. Your days are done."

The other men loomed.

"Please!" Jarrett gasped. "Please, guys –"

A boot stamped down on his right hand. He heard his fingers snap – each one, individually – before the pain slammed in. Then more boots, more blows. Ribs. Knees. Jaw. A barrage.

They didn't stop.

The light above trembled as the warehouse swallowed every sound but Jarrett's bones breaking.

6 |

Part 6

The Public Schoolboy
May 1966

She picks him up right outside the church. Not a minute late. Seven A.M. on the dot.

"Still trying to get the hang of all these English roads!" she shouts as they cross the village boundary. "You damn English, with your fancy gear changes!"

They're driving fast – too fast – tearing through the countryside. Not quite burning rubber, but definitely enough to make hearts race.

To the public schoolboy, it's a glimpse of how fast life can shift. Not that he understands the mechanics of how it all unfolds.

"Thanks for this," she says. "I really appreciate you doing this for me – and for him."

She places a gloved hand gently over his. Fragile.

"You and I, in America – we'll be great. Clifford, you're amazing. A truly amazing young man. I want you."

"I want you too, Tracy, my dear lady."

"Oh, you're such a cute English guy!"

"You're such a wonderful woman."

"You're too kind. Now you'll have to be quiet for a bit – let me focus on the road."

"Where are we going in London?"

It's a small warehouse in Thamesmead, spanking new and polished to a shine. Wedged between two grimy construction sites, it belongs to a world the public schoolboy refuses to know. He's covered places like this in geography – undesirable, forgotten. To him, it might as well be another planet.

Tracy pulls up in front of its massive metal door. *Grand. Open. Proud.* That's how the public schoolboy sees things. Maybe because he's never had to live this way. She steps out, pats his elbow reassuringly, and marches to the door, banging her fist against the steel.

Something inside groans. A vicious screech – metal on metal – like one of those wild creatures from a nature documentary, the kind he used to watch as a boy. Slowly, the door lifts, inch by inch.

He steps out cautiously, feet dragging. He imagines Mr Stratton's voice ringing in his ears: *"Walk like a man!"*

There are things in this world he knows he shouldn't touch – shouldn't even understand. A man waits inside. He's seen him before. Over a year ago. The man gives him a curt nod and hands a clipboard to Tracy.

"Clifford Lake, you remember Jefferson Reed, don't you? One of the best drummers ever. You're doing a great thing here today, Clifford – a wonderful thing." She jabs the clipboard into his chest.

Why is she being so cold?

She pulls out a fountain pen, warns it might leak, and passes it to him like she's peeling off a layer of skin.

He doesn't hesitate. Doesn't think. Absentmindedly, he signs.

He's thinking about cherry trees. About England's green and pleasant land. About meadows and garden parties. About the girl from school with the dark hair that hung just right. About becoming a man. About Tracy Cox. About what life might be. About what it's been. About the trophies with his name etched into them. About dreams. And about everything he'll never have.

"Okay, cool. We're done." Tracy snatches back the clipboard and hands it over to the man.

Jefferson Reed looks fresher now – if that's the word – than he did behind the Bond Street shop. He skims the paperwork and gives Tracy a small, knowing wink.

She slings an arm around the public schoolboy's shoulders and leads him out.

"It's all done!" she says. "All done!"

Back in the car, she kisses his cheek – soft, tender. And all he feels are birds and bees and cute little butterflies.

On the drive back, she talks nonstop. About them. Their future. All the plans. She's thanking him from the bottom of her heart.

"Oh, my lord, Clifford, you've really saved him!" she says again and again, like one of those tapes the headmaster plays in assembly – always stuck, always repeating, never changing.

"When do we leave for America?" he asks.

"You're an amazing guy, Clifford! I think the world of you!"

"When do we leave for America?" He hates repeating himself. Hates it more than anything.

"Clifford, I'm so sorry – I meant to tell you earlier... there's been a situation."

"What situation?"

"I'm so, so sorry."

"Tracy, tell me. Please."

He already knows. He feels it. The loss curling in. The creeping horror of disappointment. The brutal truth settling in his chest like ice. It's over. All of it. Gone.

"Me and him – we've been talking. We've decided to go to America together," she says. "I'm so sorry. Jefferson and I... we're in love."

"But why can't I come? Please – I want to go. I *really* want to go!"

Her face twists. The smile becomes a sneer. It's shocking.

"Oh, Clifford," she whispers, "I couldn't fancy a snobbish little cunt like you. Look at you."

"Tracy, my darling –"

"Could you stop calling me that? *Please?*"

Her voice sharpens with every breath. Anger building, as if she doesn't know how to stop.

He feels it—loneliness blooming like a bruise. He'll never admit it, but it's there.

He worries she'll dump him in the next town. But no. She drives him all the way home. Right to the front door.

"Honestly, you weirdo. Fuck off," she says. "Get out of my fucking car."

He's crying now, babbling like a spoiled child. Fumbling with the seatbelt. Tugging the door handle like it might bite him. For a second, he feels a hand on his shoulder – and dares to hope she's been joking. But then: a shove. Hard. He hits the pavement.

"Do me a favour and shut my door, won't you?"

He's crawling. Hands and wrists cut open on the gravel. Blood seeps into the cracks in the concrete. His blood. He's never seen it before – his *own* blood.

"I said, shut my fucking door."

She towers over him. A giant blotting out the sky.

"T–T–"

"Stop stammering, boy. Shut my door."

On his elbows. No choice. He has to. His legs feel like rubber. His vision's swimming. He's thirteen again. That timid child, lost in London.

With everything he has, he lashes out. It isn't enough.

"Not good enough!" she spits. "Fucking do it. Come on, you stupid little boy. *Do it!*"

"Please!"

"Oh, fuck you." She slams the door shut. "Get those cuts looked at."

He sobs. Wails. Somewhere inside, a small part of him still hopes this is a prank. A cruel joke. And that any second now, she'll come back.

Even as the car fades away.

Even as silence falls like feather bricks.

He still hopes.

And so it continues.

The days pass like seconds, like moments.

He dreams of her, unable to let go.

The wounds on his hands and wrists heal, but the pain she's left him – the jagged tear in his heart – will never fully heal.

He makes it through his exams. He thinks he's done well, but her face is everywhere.

He's a lovesick loner, hiding in the back of the classroom. He becomes a shadow of himself, and then, a true shadow.

In the afternoons, when school lets out, he wanders the old city of Canterbury. Through its gardens. Through its narrow streets. He moves through it all, trying weakly to cut away the feeling of her. Sometimes, he catches glimpses of her smile – but it's always from behind.

When he sleeps – in the bed they shared – he reaches out for her.

Gradually, the realization settles in: she's not coming back. Accepting it feels like accepting a thousand lashes, but he starts to make peace with it. Slowly. It gets easier, lighter on his heart. Chinks of light begin to break through.

He starts smiling again. It's like lifting the moon, but his laughter begins to return. Healing will be hard. He knows that. He finally tells his friends what happened, and they throw their arms around him. Companionship, friendship – these things begin to stitch up the wound.

He starts accepting that it was a foolish mistake, a careless blunder on his part. He thinks ahead to his future. He wants to travel.

On the last day of the Summer Term, he's summoned to the headmaster's office. The room feels heavy – oak bookshelves lined with old books, a polished desk that reflects the light from the high windows. A portrait of some old alumnus hangs on the wall, staring down like he knows something Clifford doesn't.

Mr. Stratton sits behind the desk, cape on, glasses resting on his nose, all set for the closing assembly. He doesn't smile when Clifford walks in. The air is thick with something Clifford can't quite name.

Two policemen stand to the side, looking as stern as Stratton, their dark uniforms standing out in the otherwise quiet room. They don't move.

"I'm very sorry, Clifford," Mr. Stratton says, his voice cold. "But, alas, there's nothing I can do."

"What –?"

The policemen step forward, each taking one of his arms. Their grips are firm and unyielding.

One of them speaks, his voice rough: "Clifford Lake, you are under arrest on suspicion of rape."

Roger Miser

Friday, 23 May, 1980

It was late evening when he finally had the chance to relax.

Stretching out in his hotel room, he lifted the third glass of shoddy French lager to his lips and let out a short laugh.

"It's been a tough couple of days, Roger, mate," he muttered to himself. Not that he'd actually done anything.

Since eight o'clock yesterday morning, he'd been watching builders and contractors set up bandstands, tents, anything to keep the crowds happy. All that observing in the heat had left him tired.

Just then, George walked in. He didn't knock. Didn't need to. They'd known each other long enough to skip such formalities.

"They'll be here soon," George said.

"Fun, fun, fun," was Roger Miser's response. "Fun, fun, glorious fun. What time?"

"Nine."

"Well, I'll finish this beer, then head to the station."

"You're going to the station?" George raised an eyebrow, sounding surprised.

"Well, this is a big summer for me. I should at least give some of the people a welcome."

"You don't have to."

"I feel I do. After all, I'm retiring soon. This is my send-off."

"I wish you wouldn't use that word." George opened the fridge, grabbed the last bottle of cheap lager, and rested it on the windowsill. With a hard slap of his hand, the cap popped off.

"It's the truth, George. I'm not lying to myself anymore. I am stepping back. Done my bit. This festival, this summer – it's my last hurrah."

"If you say so. If you say so."

"And this thing with Clifford Lake…"

"Roger!" George took a long drink, then slammed the bottle down on top of the fridge, the metallic clink ringing out in the small room. "Roger, come on. What happened, it's in the past. You need to let it go. I've put it behind me."

"That's exactly why I'm leaving the music business. I need to let shit like that go."

"What are we doing for dinner tonight?"

"The hotel's got a restaurant out the back, hasn't it?" said Miser.

"Yeah. Shall I book us a table?"

"Book the whole restaurant. Give them whatever they want. The new arrivals – I'm buying them a slap-up meal."

"It's not because you've got a crush on that singer, is it?" George laughed. "She's a bit young for you, mate."

"Age is relative. Oh, Christ, I just realized who else will be on that train! Charlie Petter!"

"Everybody loves Charlie." It was a catchphrase in British music – and had George nailed it perfectly.

"Absolutely. Everybody loves Charlie."

The two men finished their beers in silence and headed downstairs. Miser watched as George, with his usual air of authority, went about commanding the hotel's flamboyant owner (who clearly missed the heyday of his own flamboyance) to give them the restaurant that night.

They set off for the station, no jackets, no frills – just shirts, trousers, and sunshades. Two men at their respective pinnacles of life. The summer evening dropped its heat like a lead ball, leaving a cool shadow hanging over them. By the time they arrived, they were rubbing away the chill that had built up on their arms.

"Should be here any minute now," George said.

"Don't hold your breath. French trains aren't the most reliable..."

No sooner had Miser spoken, a rumbling echoed in the distance, followed by the shriek of metal on metal. The train barrelled into the sleepy town, slicing through the calm like a knife. With one final screech of its brakes and a juddering halt, it decapitated the quiet and replaced it with... well, who knows what.

The doors flung open, and the passengers spilled out, some of them almost falling. Guitars, oversized suitcases, six-packs of beer, slippery sunshades, golden blonde hair, colourful streamers, and every kind of weed imaginable. Some shouted, others panicked, a few flashed smiles at Roger and George.

"Well, well, well," George remarked. "What the hell are we going to do with this lot?"

Some were invited, others were chancing it, hoping for a spot at one of the many events.

The conductor appeared, shoving two men in pink wigs out of the way, blowing his whistle and glaring at a few others before climbing back on board. The train jerked back into motion, and Miser watched it go, feeling as if his sanity were riding away on it.

"Ladies and gentlemen!" George's voice rang out, sharp as thunder. "If I could have your attention, please! It's great to have you here! My name's George Ashton – though I think you all know who I am. Welcome to St Pierre, and I know we're going to have a fantastic summer ahead. Now, you all know – at least I bloody hope you do – Roger Miser. As a special welcome treat, we've booked out the hotel restaurant and we're giving you all dinner tonight."

There had to be at least a hundred people there. How on earth were they going to fit them all in the hotel restaurant? And where the hell were they all staying?

Miser didn't have a moment to spare for trifles, for threading through the bustling throng came Charlie Petter himself. Even among others, Charlie always seemed even smaller – his oversized blue t-shirt draped loosely over his frame and his baggy green shorts swaying with each step. His flat cap, tossed carelessly on the left side of his head like a misaligned army beret, only added to his eccentric allure. His grin was broad and genuine, a burst of warmth amidst the lively chaos.

"Hi!" Charlie bellowed, his voice cutting through the murmur of the crowd as he caught sight of Miser. "It's so good to see you!"

"Good to see you too, Charlie," Miser replied with a nod, his tone mixing cordiality with a hint of amused resignation.

"I met this man on the train!" Charlie proclaimed, his eyes alight with excitement. "He says he knows you!"

Almost as if summoned by those very words, a suave, self-assured figure in a sharply tailored business suit stepped forward. The man's presence was magnetizing; his faded sunglasses hinted at countless untold adventures, and his quiet confidence filled the narrow space between the crowd and Miser.

"Oh, Christ," Muttered Miser, his voice low and laden with disbelief. "Christ!"

"Shit," George chimed in, his tone a blend of surprise and recognition. "Is that who I think it is?"

"Disco Dave," the figure announced with a cool, almost theatrical flair. "That's what I call myself. I won the Manchester Indigo Disco Competition in Nineteen-Seventy-Five."

"Bring it out, Charlie – let's show them what I've got," he urged with a charismatic grin.

Without hesitation, Charlie produced a speaker nearly as tall as his leg, setting it down with a thud that might have seemed too clumsy if not for the endearing, habitual nature of his movements. For a few moments, the self-styled celebrity hovered uncertainly, a trembling tape clutched in his fingers. "Ready?" he called out, inserting the tape with a hurried flourish.

"Always," came Disco Dave's steady reply.

In an instant, the opening notes of Stayin' Alive erupted into life, blasting through the space with infectious energy.

Disco Dave, the former champion of disco, launched into a mesmerizing display of acrobatic dance. He moved with rapid precision—shaking out his legs, spinning in wild circles, and picking up the tempo with each beat of the iconic song.

His voice mingled with the music as he belted out the lyrics, his arms cutting through the air with theatrical flair. At first, the crowd's laughter bubbled up in amused disbelief, but soon that mirth transformed into resounding cheers, birthing a collective encouragement. Some onlookers even began to mimic his exuberant moves. As the final note dwindled, he capped off his performance with a dazzling backflip that drew howls and applause from the enraptured audience. With a mischievous bow, he strolled over to Miser.

"Good to see you, mate," Disco Dave greeted warmly, extending a hand in camaraderie.

"Good to see you too," Miser replied, though he opted not to return the handshake, his expression hinting at guarded contemplation.

Then, with an effusive flourish aimed at the gathering, Disco Dave shouted, "My name's Disco Dave, and I am the man of the moment!"

A ripple of laughter, mostly from the girls, swept through the crowd—whether at him or with him, Miser couldn't quite tell.

Soon, the merry band, with Roger Miser and George Ashton leading their impromptu expedition, began their jaunt toward town. It was as if they were reenacting the daring adventures of days gone by, meandering through tangled shrubbery, crumbling roads, and winding, hand-drawn footpaths that whispered secrets of a wild past.

For Miser, every moment was fleeting and precious – a transient burst of life that he savoured, aware that this summer marked a final exuberance before the shadows crept in.

He felt the impending weight of a future filled with haunting sadness – a burning dread searing through the mind and heart like the relentless heat of a sun tearing through the horizon. But right now, in the brilliant immediacy of the present, he allowed himself a simple, unburdened joy.

They ambled forward beneath the memory of a fading sunset, like intrepid travellers or even audacious invaders, reclaiming every precious moment.

Striding ahead, Miser declared with unrestrained enthusiasm, "Right, we're here! We're bloody here!"

Inside the restaurant, he joined George, Disco Dave, Charlie Petter, and a few others, settling into their seats. Almost theatrically, the hotel manager burst into the scene – his presence a whirlwind of dramatic French exclamations as he hurled curses at the head waiter, even delivering an exuberant French kiss to his wife. The manager's face was etched with alarm, his expression silently echoing the very question that had gnawed at Miser's mind. Over eighty desperate, fame-hungry musicians hovered nearby, their eyes glimmering with anticipation of being fed and watered. Amid the simmering tension, the head waiter's gaze shone with a mysterious, knowing light as he murmured a stream of expletives. Speaking a bit of French himself, Miser caught the vague suggestion in the waiter's tone – a promise of something shifting in the air, as enigmatic and charged as the moment itself.

Tables and chairs from the restaurant – and extra ones from storage and even the head waiter's house – were dragged out and arranged along the road outside the hotel. The hungry, travel-weary musicians took their seats like pilgrims at a sacred meal. Roger Miser and George Ashton gave each other a congratulatory pat on the back. Miser could taste success.

And so, that's how the evening went.

Over a hundred musicians wined and dined on posh, semi-posh, and cobbled-together tables. Time fluttered by. Miser scanned every face, every sparkle of laughter, every pretty girl.

If he hadn't glanced up at just that moment, he would have missed her. A near slip of his wineglass – his fingers catching the stem in time – caused him to look up. And there she was. Straw-coloured hair. Moving through the crowd with the grace of someone not trying to be noticed. Not one of the musicians – her pace was too casual for that. She didn't see him. She passed right by. But he saw her.

"Bloody hell, mate, you okay?" George slurred slightly, clearly tipsy. "Wow, she's fit. You gonna ask her out?"

"I might," said Disco Dave, standing up with too much energy.

"Sit down!" barked Miser. "I do not want you doing another one of your routines!"

"Oh, come on!"

"You just behave yourself. You're a guest here."

But Miser felt the anger melt away. What was there to be bitter about tonight? He turned, eyes trailing her retreating figure, and felt that stupid, familiar sting: wishing he'd said something – anything – before it was too late.

The Public Schoolboy
October 1966

"Two years," says the judge. "Two years. Enough time for you to have a proper think about what you did."

The public schoolboy – not a public schoolboy anymore – whimpers. He'd imagined this moment before, even fantasised about it in a strange, twisted way: a misunderstood figure, an innocent caught in the storm of justice, torn apart by barristers and flashbulbs. But the real thing is different. Worse. It isn't some grand courtroom with mahogany panels and dignified silence – it's a damp, echoing basement room in the bowels of a hotel. An experimental youth court, part of some new government initiative. Lake heard a copper muttering about it earlier.

Now, he's part of the experiment.

The judge, though robed and wigged, is perched behind a scratched wooden table with one leg slightly shorter than the others, giving it a tired tilt. Lake sits on a grey plastic chair. Two heavyset officers flank him, arms crossed, faces made of granite.

"Take him away," says the judge, barely looking up as he shuffles a stack of papers.

Lake is hauled to his feet. He stumbles as he's yanked forward, wrists gripped too tightly. As they drag him out of the basement and into the hotel's golden-lit lobby, the contrast stings. Plush carpets. Marble counters. The kind of place with bellboys and polished suitcases. He stayed here once with his parents, shortly after the visit to Bond Street. Now it's hell. People glance at him, pause briefly, then move on. They don't recognise him, and worse – they don't care. To them, he's nothing more than a dirty smudge on the hotel floor.

"Watch your filthy fucking fingers don't touch these vehicles," one of the coppers spits, as they shove him across the car park. "Get moving, you little bitch. Move."

A bus pulls up, coughing thick black smoke into the air. From a distance, it looks tired – rust bubbling at the seams, its paintwork grimy and dull. The driver, short and squat with a belly like a dropped sack of potatoes, steps off and pushes his glasses further up his greasy nose.

"Clifford Lake?" he says, scanning his clipboard with an oily finger. "Right. Let's go."

"Please!" Lake yells. "Please!"

"Get in, you little nonce," one of the cops growls.

Lake kicks, writhes, howls for the suited men and women drifting into the hotel. They ignore him. Polite blankness, like he's part of the scenery. He could scream into their faces and they'd still pass him by.

"I swear to God," mutters the driver, "they've got to stop putting these courtrooms in bloody hotels." He flashes a grin at Lake. "Don't worry. We treat little nonces exactly how they deserve."

The cops lift him, no grace, no care, and toss him onto the first step of the bus. Inside, it reeks of sweat, piss, and something chemical. Other boys – rougher, louder, older – line the rows. Their cuffs clink like cutlery in a drawer. Lake feels their eyes, hungry, interested, amused.

"How ya doin', sweetheart?" a bulky lad with tiny teeth calls out, smirking. "Nice of you to join us."

Lake's never ridden a bus before. The rows of cracked leather seats, the scratched poles, the mesh cages – it's all how he imagined, only grimmer. A cop cuffs him to a seat, slaps him across the face, and leaves him to sink into his own skin.

The driver does a quick headcount, then climbs into his sealed-off cab. A click echoes through the bus – years from now, Lake will realise it was the cab locking. The driver didn't trust them. Not one bit.

Behind the cab, in a seat that faced backwards, sits a guard with a nightstick resting across his lap. He's got the eyes of a man who enjoys watching things fall apart.

The bus jerks into motion.

Lake stares out the window. Outside, the world is ticking on as usual. Men with briefcases, couples sharing coffees, families dragging suitcases. Everything normal. Everything gone.

Taunts fly in from the other seats. Snickers, murmurs, crude guesses about what he's in for. But Lake doesn't respond. He curls up like a dying animal. His confidence, once so polished and showy, is gone. Now he's just a boy in a school shirt that doesn't quite fit anymore.

London's bustle fades. Suburbs take over. Then countryside. Fields. Silence.

When the sign for Milton appears – that cursed brown sign welcoming visitors to history and charm – he whimpers. Laughter erupts behind him.

"Please!" he cries. "I didn't do anything!"

"Shut your little hole," the driver barks.

"Little nonce." "Gonna break his fucking fingers." "He's not gonna last a week."

Later, the driver pulls into a motorway service station. "Don't fucking move."

The guard stands and looms, blocking the aisle. Lake watches through the open door as the driver fills up the tank, glancing at his watch and scratching his belly.

"I need a piss," someone mutters.

"Shut your gob," says the guard, red-faced, unshaven.

Then, a flash of colour – a child in a bright red coat bounds up the steps of the bus, all cheer and bounce, crumbs around his mouth.

"My name's Charlie!" he says proudly. "Charlie Petter!" He waves a half-eaten sandwich. "Would you like a marmite sandwich?"

"Help me!" Lake screams, lurching forward, chains clinking.

Charlie tilts his head. "Marmite sandwich?"

"Please! Help me!"

"Marmite?"

Before anything else happens, a woman in matching scarlet appears, flustered and breathless.

"I'm so sorry," she says quickly. "Charlie's not normally like this." She scoops him up with an embarrassed smile. "You can't just run off like that."

"Please!" Lake begs. "Please, my dear woman! Help me!"

The driver's hand lands on her shoulder. "Ignore him. He's a vicious criminal. On his way to borstal."

"Well, I do hope it knocks some sense into him," she says, and walks off with her son.

Lake watches them go, the red of their coats like two flames disappearing into fog. The driver slams the bus door shut and turns back. This time, the hit across the face stings so much he can't even scream.

"You try that again, you little shit," the driver growls, "and I'll make you regret it."

The engine growls back to life, fiercer now, like it's angry too.

"You keep an eye on that little shit!" the driver calls to the guard. "He so much as coughs, smash him."

Lake turns to the window. There's nowhere else left to look. Outside, the world rolls by: kids licking ice creams, dogs on leads, mums unloading shopping.

Then, that sign again: *Welcome to Milton.*

The driver grins. "Soon be here! Bet you're excited, eh? Returning tourists and little bumboys heading to borstal."

The bus pushes on. Inside, the air is filled with sweat and fear. Outside, life carries on like none of this is happening.

"Poppycock!" his father said, the second the headmaster finished speaking. "He would never do that. Not my Clifford."

The headmaster, seated neatly on the edge of the sofa, gave a regretful nod. "I'm sorry, sir, but it's a police matter now."

Clifford was in the corner of the room. Two policemen flanked him, each with a heavy hand clamped on his shoulder. He was too shocked to speak.

He never found out which girl had accused him. Never saw a name. Never heard a voice. If he'd gone the normal route – a trial by jury – it would've been different. But a week later, Mr Stratton returned, arriving at the family home just after dusk with what he called a "chink of light."

They gathered in the living room. His father sat stiffly in the leather armchair; his mother perched on the edge of the ottoman. Clifford stood. The headmaster looked between them all and then at Clifford.

"There is a new justice procedure being trialled," Stratton said. "It's experimental, for youthful offenders. No jury. No public courtroom. It takes place in private. If found guilty, the punishment would be... milder. A custodial sentence, yes, but not prison. Not criminal records. But –" he adjusted his glasses "– you won't be allowed to know who made the accusation."

His father made the choice before Clifford could speak.

The rest faded. His memory of that evening, of the weeks that followed, frayed and unstitched itself. What stayed was the dwindling hope – Tracy might still come back. She might walk through the door and say it was all a mistake.

The bus passes through Milton to the other side. Lake sees a row of greyish buildings – ghouls in the sunlight. They turn off the main road down an extremely narrow junction. The tarmac gives way to stones and dirt. Behind him, the lads whoop and cheer.

In front of the borstal sits a large square of tarmac, like a giant playground. The building beyond is hulking and grey, its brickwork stained with age and damp. Rows of narrow windows glare like slit eyes, some barred, others boarded. Rust streaks down the gutters. A guard tower looms over one corner, unmanned but menacing. The air smells of smoke and something chemical. Several men are gathered in a tight huddle, waiting. As the bus stops, they're immediately on it, ripping open the door and charging in like a pack of wolves.

"Get your lazy fucking arses up!" one of them screams. "Fucking move it, you cunts! Get up!"

Lake's dragged to his feet by the scruff of his neck.

"Please!" he shouts to no one in particular.

"No one fucking cares, you little bastard."

A deep voice booms: "Right, you shits, get in line! Single file!"

It's an Australian accent. Lake knows this from his many geography lessons. Geography had been one of his favourites.

The Australian man is stocky, somewhat overweight, but his eyes and cheeks burn with anger and hatred.

"Right," he growls, "now you're in single file, I can fucking talk. My name's Ceri Britton. I'm Chief Warder. You are nothing but the worst scum on Earth – especially you, Mr Lake. Believe me, sunshine, you're gonna wish you'd kept your zip up that day. We're heading inside now, nice and slow, and you're going to meet the Governor. You treat him with the utmost respect. Any funny business, and I'll be smashing kneecaps."

"Move!" another warder barks. "Move, move, move!"

Lake walks. Shuffles. Barely blinks, as the daylight disappears and the borstal walls swallow him whole.

The corridor reminds him of school, but the stench of chlorine replaces the smell of floor polish.

"Move, you little fuckers!" another warder shouts. "Fucking move it!"

They're herded into a room smaller than the boys' changing facilities back at school. Lake can barely see anything, but he feels a vicious thudding beneath his ribs.

Ceri Britton has him by the collar, slamming him against the wall.

"Line up!" Britton barks. "Good! Now shut your little holes. You'll go in one at a time to meet the Governor for assessment. I hear a whisper, I'll start cracking bones. Right – you, Lake. You're first."

He drags Lake out and down the corridor.

"In here."

The chlorine stench vanishes. The whirr of a fan and the click of a typewriter give the room the feel of his father's office. A man and a woman sit behind a desk, heads down. The woman's in a nurse's uniform – at least, he assumes so. He's never really seen one before.

"Mr Butterworth, I have Clifford Lake," says Britton.

The man looks up. He's fit – athletic – with neatly trimmed facial hair. Surprisingly young. No tie. A rolled-up blue shirt that fits perfectly.

"Mr Lake, welcome to Milton Borstal," he says, his accent close to Lake's own – a piece of home. "I'm William Butterworth, the Governor. This is Dr Melanie Tolson, our psychologist. Mr Lake, you've been convicted of an extremely serious offence. But we run a constructive programme here – focused on redevelopment. I suggest you engage with it fully."

He glances behind him at a woman hammering keys on a typewriter.

"Come over here a second," he says.

She rises – also in a medical uniform, but clearly uncomfortable in it.

"What is it?" she asks.

She's pretty, Lake thinks. Maybe she'll save him. Sneak him out in her car. Take him home.

"Mr Lake, this is Emily Butterworth, my wife – and Matron."

The Governor stifles a yawn.

"You'll be assigned to Dormitory C. It's typically used for long-term inmates, but I think it'll be good for you. Please be assured, Mr Lake, we're here to support you."

Dr Tolson begins to speak. "It's incredibly important that you engage with the programmes on offer, Mr Lake. We have educational and work-based opportunities for development."

"We also operate a warning system," the Governor continues. "Fail to meet our standards and you'll receive a First Written Warning. After several days, if nothing improves, a Second. Beyond that, you'll face what we call Dismissal – a disciplinary hearing. But I'm confident we won't reach that point."

"We also offer our Hanging Gardens Medical Service," says Emily. "It's available twenty-four hours a day."

"You're a lucky kid," Britton growls. "Count yourself blessed."

"Right," Emily says, glancing at her husband. "We have other inmates to process."

"Actually," Butterworth replies, "I thought we'd begin Mr Lake's development programme immediately. Dr Tolson, if you would be so kind..."

She stands, holding a waste bag. Her knuckles are white from gripping it. She empties it in front of Lake.

Trophies. Certificates. His.

"Over the summer," the Governor says, "we were in contact with your school. They kindly sent us your sport and academic awards."

"Thank you, sir," Lake whispers. "They'll help me settle in."

Butterworth licks his top lip.

"As part of our programme, we ask inmates to distance themselves from their previous lives. For you, that means starting from scratch. I'd like you to burn your certificates. And carve your name off the trophies."

"Sir, I can't do that!" Lake babbles.

"You will."

The Governor walks to the desk, rummages in a box, and retrieves a matchbox in one hand, a hammer and chisel in the other. He passes them to Britton and sits.

"I suggest you start with the trophies. Then move on to the certificates. Don't even think about trying anything. Any damage to staff or property will have serious consequences."

"Get on the floor," Britton orders. "Come on, you lazy cunt, get down."

Lake kneels. Tries to.

"He's shaking, poor boy," says Emily.

"I'll take care of that."

Lake's ears ring. He slumps down.

"Please," he pleads. "Please don't hit me, Mr Britton!"

Britton drops the hammer and chisel beside him – worn tools, tired from decades of violence.

Lake's fingers tremble, but he manages to pick them up. He selects his 100m trophy – his first one. He was twelve. A winter's day. Mr Stratton's proud handshake.

He positions the chisel above his name and taps with the hammer.

"Harder, boy! Harder!" Britton yells. "Chop it right out!"

He hits again. Misses. Cracks his thumbnail. Winces.

"Keep fucking going, you little shit."

Tears burst with each strike, but eventually his name gouges out. He moves to the next one – his 300m trophy. He hits harder, with muscle. The metal cracks. His name splinters.

When he finishes, a matchbox drops by his hand.

"Burn the rest, please," the Governor instructs. "One at a time."

He tries not to look. Not to see the pride he's about to set alight. It's strange – how his confidence builds with each flick of a match. The scent of burning paper and ink stings his nose, claws at his throat.

When he's done, Britton drags him up.

"I think it's time Mr Lake was shown to Dormitory C," says the Governor. "At present, we have no bedding or uniform for you, but these should be issued in the next few days. Mr Britton, take him away."

Again, he's dragged—grubby fingers in his hair, his feet barely touching the floor.

He begs. Pleads.

"In Australia," Britton snarls, "we know how to deal with little perverts like you. We cut their fucking balls off. In here."

He jams a key into a lock and wrenches open the door. Lake tumbles in, falls to his knees.

The door slams shut behind him. He leaps up, bangs on the tiny window.

"Please! Please!" he screams. "Mr Britton! Mr Britton!"

Footsteps approach behind him.

Twenty or so lads. Big lads. Arms folded. All in filthy grey borstal uniforms.

"Look at this little shithead," says one.

"Heard he's a nonce," taunts another.

"Raped a girl. Sick bastard," sneers a third.

"Leave him to me," says a fourth. He elbows past the others. Enormous – fat hanging over his waistband. His face beads with sweat. Lips wet and spongy. He sticks out a plump hand and grabs Lake's collar, hauling him upright.

"Please," Lake says. "Please, don't hurt me."

"I won't hurt you," the fat one says. "My name's Fabrice Ortelli. And I'm going to look after you. How about we have a snuggle in my bunk for a bit?"

Roger Miser
Sunday, 25 May, 1980

Since arriving, Roger Miser had grown fond of the evenings. They reminded him of the life that could have been, had he not turned to music, had he not boarded the train at Yardley Wood, had he stayed put, had he avoided risk.

As the day collapsed into dusk, he allowed himself an extra moment on the hotel's doorstep, soaking in the surroundings.

Over the weekend, more musicians had arrived. Most by train, but some on foot, some by bus. A few had driven here, but with nowhere to park, the cars lay idle along various roads, their tires rotting away under the unforgiving sun.

The majority of the musicians hadn't been invited; they were there to chase fame, hoping to somehow pierce the heart of it. Poor souls, in every sense of the word: their tents dotted fields, even spilling into someone's front garden. From this distance, he could hear guitars strumming softly, the sound drifting from behind mounds of fabric, reverberating across the town like a slow, intimate kiss. He couldn't see it from here, but there was a field to the east of St Pierre where the un-invited had gathered. Already, it was a disgusting mess: piss, shit, and rotting food filled the space.

Miser spent the next hour walking around town, inspect-ing the stages and sound systems. Everything was in place. Nothing was missing.

On his way back, he passed the front garden with the tent still pitched. Some ignorant soul. Should he? He probably had better.

"I'd get out of there, mate," he said, his voice dripping with mockery. "You know what these French are like..."

A woman's head popped through the tent flap. White skin, black lips, wide eyes. Punk. She pulled herself out.

"I'm Patsy Monroe," she said, extending a narrow hand.

"Roger Miser," he replied.

"I know who you are. Everyone knows who you are. It's an honour."

"Are you with a band, or are you flying solo?"

"Solo singer," Patsy Monroe replied, her neck stretching, almost like a bird's.

"What made you decide to come to my festival then? It's a dog-eat-dog environment, you know that?"

"What, you think a girl can't handle herself?"

"How old are you?" Miser asked.

"Eighteen."

"Eighteen, huh?" He raised an eyebrow, studying her. "That's very young to be coming here, all by yourself. Listen, I think I can get you a spot on one of those stages."

Patsy Monroe's eyes flickered, maybe a little in disbelief. Her hair was too short to give away any emotion.

"My hotel's this way," Miser said, gesturing for her to follow.

Roger Miser lay on the bed, arms stretched wide. The dainty figure of Patsy Monroe was next to him, face down. He was too tired to cuddle her, but he relished in the luxury of not having to.

He lifted a cold beer to his lips and took a slow sip.

Perfect end to a hard week.

He yawned, trying not to fall asleep, reminding himself that he still had the main course to come.

"You were amazing," he whispered over to her.

"Mm," she murmured back.

The paradise of the moment was shattered by the distant rumbling of engines. Miser had spent enough time around a certain type of person to recognize the hum of a Jag.

"Oh, fuck." He rolled out of bed, frantically dressing. He no doubt looked like shit. "Stay here," he told the girl.

He bolted downstairs, tucking in his shirt and straightening himself up. He was still far from perfect, but it would have to do.

Gary Holmes's motorcade had arrived. Five cars, all Jags. Men dressed in the finest suits stepped out, looking fit and fierce. A few of them had pistols at their sides. Their polished shoes clicked sharply on the tarmac. They were at the very peak of their game.

And then, the old dog himself stepped out, sweat glistening under the sun. Miser approached, extending his hand.

"Lovely place," Holmes said, eyeing the hotel. "Absolutely lovely. I reckon I'll be quite happy here. Very happy."

"Did you have a good trip?"

"Fairly good, fairly good. Drove down to Dover, then took the ferry over. Stayed in Paris for the night, then had a nice slow drive this morning after a Sunday service." Holmes pulled out a cigar, striking a match. "Lovely. Just lovely."

He took a long drag and blew out a thick cloud of smoke.

"Now, I promise you, you'll hardly notice we're here."

Miser knew better than to challenge Holmes's words. "Where's the place you're staying? It's nearby, isn't it?"

"A short distance outside of town, about a mile. Nice little cottage. We're fortifying it, making sure it's battle-ready. I'm not the kind of man who takes any chances."

"How is your family, Mr. Holmes?"

"They're very well, thank you."

Gary Holmes stepped back, signalling to his men. They began moving back to the vehicles, but one stayed behind, standing at attention in perfect, rehearsed obedience.

"I'd better be off," Holmes said, his voice growing distant. "I wish you a lovely evening."

The last man opened the door for Gary Holmes, and the mob boss climbed in, still smoking his cigar, his weight shifting as he settled.

Miser waited several minutes after the cars had gone before returning to the girl.

Around him, there was only emptiness. The birds in the trees, the scent of grass spilling from the fields, the soft snoring from the cottages – everything still. He felt his stomach clench, and his eyes watered as the dread, cold and hollow, slowly filled him.

Part 7

Victor Gully
Friday, 26 June, 2009

"He was a great man, a humble man, and an honourable man," was how Victor Gully ended the eulogy. "Though I barely knew him, he struck me as a man of deep integrity, and that is how we should remember him."

The gathering gave him a modest round of applause. He stepped down from the pulpit and returned to his seat, sighing as he did so – then immediately cursed himself for letting his fed-up, grouchy self slip through. He was emotional, though not about Henry Jarrett. Still, he had to play the part.

As the priest returned to the pulpit, the congregation fell into murmuring silence. Gully recognised a few writers from festivals past – faces he hadn't seen in years. Most of them probably couldn't stand Jarrett, but funeral wakes had always been prime ground for networking and free sandwiches. As his old friend Herbert Buxton – if "friend" was the right word

– once said: *"A writer's funeral is a small-scale writer's conference."*

The priest launched into a prayer.

Gully looked down at the programme. A smiling photo of Henry Jarrett in the Maldives – taken just after a poetry reading – beamed up from the front page. A fitting tribute, all things considered.

At the front, several tearful relatives huddled together. Probably upset about the train fare to London, Gully thought—then immediately regretted the cruelty of it. After all, poor Henry had died violently. His body parts scattered across Canterbury. The police had long since given up trying to find the person responsible.

For the rest of the service, Gully kept his head bowed. The real emotion was creeping in now—not for Jarrett, but for Susan. This was the same church where her funeral had been held. The grief stabbed through him, sharper than expected.

As the crowd filtered out, Gully spotted Ellar Cameron – for once in a proper suit and tie. The former prodigy was deep in conversation with an elderly couple, nodding with committed intensity. But when he saw Gully, he offered them a respectful farewell and crossed over.

"Very good service, I thought," he said. "Very authentic. And may I say, your words were beautiful. I only met Henry a couple of times, but I really liked him. You summed him up well."

"Thanks for coming."

"Not a problem," Cameron said.

"Where's the wake being held?"

"Pub just down the road. Walking distance."

They trailed behind the main procession, a few steps back. Cameron seemed... jittery. He kept glancing this way and that, like he wasn't sure whether he should be seen. Whether that was nerves or performance, Gully couldn't tell. Cameron had always been something of an enigma.

"Lovely day, isn't it?" Gully offered.

"It is. Meant to be even sunnier tomorrow. Though I doubt Gordon Brown's enjoying the good weather – not with this expenses thing going on. Poor guy."

"I don't feel sorry for him."

"Awful business all round," Cameron said, clearing his throat. "Anyway, not really the time, is it? We should be talking about Henry. Great guy. Uniquely suited to that residency. Who's taking over?"

"Yours truly. No one else for it."

"I think you'll do well. You're an inspiration." He gave Gully's elbow a light pat. "*The Church in the Square* was a major influence on *Noke*."

"I've always wondered why that book of mine did so well. My others have... sort of dissolved. But that one stuck. I dunno."

They left the church grounds, stepping into a tired residential street. A man in a browned vest slumped in his front garden, watching them with deep, dragging puffs of a wilting cigarette. Gully raised an eyebrow as they passed.

"What are you working on at the moment?" asked Cameron.

"Oh, nothing major. Just pulling some notes together. You?"

"Just finished a first draft. Been working on it for five years. Multi-period novel – Ancient Rome to the far future."

"Sounds ambitious."

"Well, it's something to do. Hopefully it'll be my break-through."

"Wasn't *Noke* your breakthrough?" asked Gully. "Sorry, probably a personal question."

"No, it's fine." Cameron paused. "Honestly, it just wasn't... Oh. Here we are."

The Ilford Crown stood at the top of the street – mahogany exterior, cobwebbed windows, and a weary kind of grandeur. A group of young drinkers loitered outside, their sunglasses catching the fierce sunlight. Bickering and laughter drifted through the propped-open door.

"Let's get a pint," said Cameron. "We should stop talking about work. A man's died, and his family's grieving. That should be the focus."

"You're right."

They ducked under the ivy-covered stone arch. Gully caught sight of the food table: sandwiches, crisps, rolls, all arranged in quiet little heaps. It was tempting, that spread – tempting enough to forget, at least briefly, his grief. He peeled a paper plate from the pile and built himself a meagre lunch.

Questions came thick and fast: "How did you know Henry?" "Were you two close?" "I know you! You're Victor Gully, aren't you? *The Church in the Square* – I read that in school. Really powerful stuff." "I was so sorry to hear about Henry. Lovely guy. Were you good friends?"

He had resolved not to drink. That crumbled within fifteen minutes. By the time he noticed, he was on his third pint.

The place had its charm, but the ceiling was too low for his liking. Beams of split wood threatened to crack his skull if he moved wrong.

Cameron came over, wiping his fingers on a napkin. "I'm off," he said. "Good to catch up."

"Likewise." Gully shook his hand.

The author of the "incredible, imaginative" *Noke* made for the exit, stopping to swipe an extra sausage roll on the way out.

Gully ordered another drink and returned to the mingling. But soon he felt clumsy, disoriented, and thoroughly bored. He left as soon as the glass was empty.

The afternoon was quiet, vacant, nothing to be excited about. The kind of afternoon where time folded in on itself. Plenty of space to think, too much space to stew in pressure.

The residency was his now. Amethyst Pearl Arts had refused to consider anyone else. And all the funding was being cut. They were letting him host events at the centre, but everything else – except for the Dover trip, which had been locked in months ago – was cancelled.

On the train ride back, he tried to pull together some ideas for activities at the centre. Family workshops. Local poetry nights. A zine-making afternoon. Nothing stuck. His brain felt damp and unhelpful, like a sponge left in the sink too long. Inspiration was out of reach, beyond the clouds.

When he got to Canterbury West, he was annoyed to find the taxi rank empty. Not even a stray Uber. He started walking towards the centre of town.

The heat was unbearable. Summer had smashed through the door and settled in for the long haul. Sweat trickled down the back of his neck. He yanked off his tie, slung the jacket over his shoulder, dipped his head low as he weaved through crowds of afternoon drinkers. Pints in hand, peals of laughter echoing from sunlit tables. He wanted to join them, more than anything.

On Palace Street, he stopped. Glanced left. A bar with its doors flung wide, bodies spilling out onto the pavement like a summer landslide. Hadn't Henry mentioned a bar like this? The place with the woman in the emerald dress? He went in.

The inside was dark and stifling, like stepping into a greenhouse that served booze. Music throbbed from hidden speakers. On the TVs, boxers clattered into each other in digital slow motion. Gully pushed through a knot of muscly lads shouting at the screen. Their eyes grazed him – middle-aged, overdressed, too tired for the scene. He felt their unspoken judgment settle on his back like dust.

The bartender was a wiry figure, borderline skeletal, with a scraggly beard that gave him most of his substance. He moved with a sort of startled energy, all elbows and angles.

"What can I get you?" he asked, wiping condensation off the bar.

"Whatever beer's going."

"I know just the one. You've been to a funeral, I can tell."

"Obvious, right?"

"Yep. Bear with me."

Gully took in the room again. It seemed a good enough place for a drink, but everything was turned up too high – the bass, the lights, the voices. It reminded him of the sports bar in Calgary where he'd once done a reading. He grimaced. That time he'd tried to hit on the barmaid. Terrible idea. Didn't end well.

"Here you are, mate," said the barman, handing over a cold, frothing pint.

"I've only got a tenner. Don't have any loose change."

"It's on the house, mate."

"I can't..."

"It's fine. Honestly, you look like you need it."

Gully took the pint, nodded his thanks. "Can I ask you something?"

"Sure, mate." The barman leaned in, curious.

"A friend of mine was murdered a few weeks ago. That's the funeral I was at. I heard he came in here that day. I just wondered if you'd seen anything."

"Ah, I'm sorry to hear that." The man straightened slightly. "Was that Henry Jarrett by any chance?"

"Yeah. You knew him?"

"Didn't know him, no. But the police came round. Asked a bunch of questions. I didn't see anything. Sorry, mate."

Gully exhaled. "No, thank you. Sorry to bother you."

"Not a problem." The barman tugged at his beard. "Was he a close friend?"

"Not especially. We worked together. But what happened to him was awful. I feel like I owe it to him – to find out the truth."

The barman nodded, slow and thoughtful. "If you want the honest barman's opinion, I'd walk away. Life's too short. Go and live it, properly."

"Maybe you're right."

"Good man." He flashed a crooked, toothy grin. "Anyway, I'd better keep the beer flowing before I get lynched. Enjoy the pint."

Outside again, head swimming, the words repeated like a scratched record: *Go and live life to its fullest.*

He knew the guy was right. But on Palace Street, with the sun throwing gold across the pavement and the echo of Jarrett's stories behind him, curiosity and obsession began to bubble into something darker.

"Victor, mate, don't do it. Don't," he muttered to himself.

It sounded like something out of the fantasy novel he'd always meant to write – but the search for the woman in the emerald dress was officially on.

8

Part 8

L ake
October 1966

Fabrice Ortelli lets him go as the sound of bootsteps echoes down the hall.

"Get the fuck up!" a voice booms.

Clifford Lake tries to wriggle free of the fat kid, but he doesn't need to. The slimy, greasy, sweaty arms release him. He's barefoot – his shoes were stolen overnight. He tiptoes across the floor, stepping into something soft: a smear of ketchup. He gags.

"I think the new boy's put off by our midnight feasts!" one of the lads yells. He's a small, shrewd little kid, dirty in every sense.

The door crashes open. A skinny man with dark eyes yawns as he steps in. "Right, you lot," he sniffs, "get the fuck outside. One line. You must be Clifford Lake, our new guest. I can't wait to get stuck into you. Name's Morton Jerkov. You'll get to know me real well."

The boys start filing out. Lake tries to blend in, but he's shoved to the back. As he tiptoes past the screw, he feels fingers brush against his left thigh.

"Dirty little slut."

"Please," Lake cries. "I'm innocent."

"Keep your filthy mouth shut, you little bitch, or I'll smash your teeth down your throat."

He tries not to shake – knows it'll show weakness – but he's trembling. Every inch of him.

There's screaming and shouting in the corridor as warders push the boys into a single line down the centre. Lake finds a place in the queue, surprised that no one tells him to move.

"Listen up!" It's Britton; he stands alone at the end of the corridor, arms folded. He doesn't seem to notice Lake. "You know the drill. File down, turn left, enter the mess hall in complete silence. Any fucking around, and you'll go without your breakfast. Right, lads, move it!"

To Lake's relief, no one howls at him. Britton doesn't even notice him: his twitching eyes and bushy eyebrows are locked on the back of the line. As he passes through the cloud of vile deodorant, he does his best to avoid drawing the man's attention.

Like ants, the boys trickle to the left and down a narrow passageway. The scent of musty food and the screeching of cutlery bring back distant memories of school trips.

His vision falters as he enters the dining hall. The queue slows to a crawl. He tries to block out the sight of boys shovelling slop onto plastic plates. It's a conveyor system; he sees every component. Each boy enters empty-handed, and each one exits with a lump of grey grime and a glass of juice. Some of them take their seats at three long tables stretching the length of the hall. Six warders watch over the scene at strategic points.

He's too scared to think, too scared even to realize he's scared.

A hand lands on his shoulder. Lake smells the lemon deodorant.

"Did you think I'd missed you?" says Britton. "I'd never forget to say good morning."

"I'm really scared!" Lake cries. "I want to go home!"

"This is your home now! And we know how to make our boys feel right at home…"

Britton points to one of the dining tables. A plate with a steaming Full English Breakfast lies between two pieces of silver cutlery. A silk napkin has been neatly folded, placed on the stool. It's alien in this place.

"A posh country boy deserves a fine breakfast to start his day." Britton leads Lake over. "I'm not going to feed you the shit the other boys have to eat. There's just one problem. We don't do fresh food." He pulls up the napkin, shoves Lake down, and drapes the cloth over his legs. "Barefoot? Fucking hell! Don't worry, you'll get your uniform in a bit."

Lake knows something's wrong with the food. Stuff's crawling around in it.

"Proper organic food," says Britton. "It's alive."

"I can't!"

"You can, and you fucking will."

Lake glances behind him, right into Britton's greasy eyes. The Australian's lips curl; saliva drips down his chin. He grabs Lake by the scalp and twists his head around. Lake is inches away from the bacon crawling with maggots. He gags.

"Don't you fucking do that!" Britton yells. "Don't you fucking dare! This is beautiful food, and you're going to eat every last bit of it. You'd better get used to this, because this is your breakfast every fucking day you're here. Now stop fucking crying, and eat!"

November 1966

Clifford Lake knows he's seriously ill. His stomach is burning. Twice last night, he threw up, narrowly avoiding Fabrice Ortelli. He knows the cause – it's obvious. For a month, he's been fed nothing but mouldy bread, fermented milk, rotting vegetables, and maggot-infested Full English Breakfasts to start each day.

It's a cold, bitter day. There's no heating at Milton Borstal, and the air feels like glass. Lake cowers and rubs his arms, but Morton Jerkov smacks him hard on the ear.

"Enough of that, Lake."

"I'm so cold... Please, sir, please."

"Shut your little cakehole."

They're standing outside the room where he was taken on his first day. Jerkov pounds his fist on the door and doesn't wait for a response before throwing it open and shoving Lake inside.

Governor Butterworth is sitting behind his desk, rapidly scribbling notes. He smiles when he sees Lake. "Good morning, Mr. Lake. I trust you're settling in okay? I wanted to have a quick meeting with you to discuss your performance so far."

"Please, sir, I'm really ill."

"Shut your mouth!" Jerkov roars. "You don't interrupt the Governor! You understand, you little shit?!"

The Governor seems to ignore the outburst. "Now, Mr. Lake, I've been reviewing your progress on the programmes you've been partaking in, and unfortunately, you haven't met the standards required at Milton Borstal. This means, regretfully, you're being placed on your First Written Warning. Please be assured, however, that this is a supportive measure. Do you have any comments you'd like to make?"

"Please, sir, I'm sick," Lake begs. "I've only eaten rotten food since I got here. I'm sick, I'm really sick."

"Mr. Lake, I want to thank you for your professional responses. I realize these things are never easy. Please remember that you have access to our Hanging Gardens Medical Service, which is available throughout the day."

"Please..."

"Mr. Jerkov, could you take Lake away please?"

"Yes, sir." Jerkov seizes Lake by the shoulder. "Right, let's go."

But Lake doesn't take a single step. He vomits, splutters, and collapses. Jerkov's still trying to move him.

"Shit," the screw mutters. "Oh, shit."

Lake throws up again. He can taste the blood, can see it, can feel it against his cheek.

"Get him out of here," the Governor orders. "Oh, Christ, call an ambulance."

A cool hand on his forehead rouses him. A kind face smiles at him, pale blue eyes offering a sense of calm. He feels warmth – more warmth than he's felt in weeks. For a moment, he convinces himself he's in his own bedroom, that the past few months were just a bad dream. But reality soon settles in as the gentle face begins to speak.

"Don't try to talk," the voice says. "You'll be okay."

The accent is French – soft, yet thick.

"Please," Lake whispers. It's a word he knows all too well, a word that will soon become like family to him.

"Please, rest."

"Who are you?"

"My name is Serge Ferris. I'm a doctor. You're safe now. You've had severe food poisoning. You're in Cambridge Primrose Hospital. You're being looked after."

"Don't send me back there. Please, don't send me back to Milton Borstal. They beat me. They feed me mouldy food. I'm dying. Please, save me."

The doctor's face tightens. He looks around, his gaze frantic. "I'm sorry, I can't," he whispers. "What do you want me to do? I've just qualified. This is my first job. I have a young family. I'm sorry, monsieur, but I cannot risk it."

"Please."

"I can't."

Two days later, Lake is back at the borstal. All hope is gone now.

Maybe Tracy Cox is still out there – maybe she'll come to save him. Oh, how he longs for her to rescue him! Even as Ceri Britton grips him by the collar and smacks him in the jaw, he still holds on to the thought of her. He knows she'll come for him.

He's taken back to the Governor, who doesn't even glance up as he's shoved inside. Matron Butterworth and Dr. Tolson sit beside him.

"Mr. Lake, unfortunately, your performance continues to fall short of the standards required at Milton Borstal," Governor Butterworth says. "As such, you are being issued with a Second Written Warning. Please understand that this is a supportive measure, and you will have access to our Hanging Gardens Medical Service at all times."

"Right, this way," Britton says. "You're in for it now."

"I beg you!" Lake cries. "Mercy! Let me go!"

"No chance."

The next morning, he's hauled into the office again by Britton and Jerkov, where he's informed that he's being dismissed. A hood is jammed over his head, and he's dragged off. He hears another door slam open as the warders half-drag, half-carry him through. A chill crawls over him.

"Shut the door, Jerkov," Britton orders.

"Welcome to hell," Jerkov mutters.

Lake's uniform is torn open. His legs are swept from under him.

"Kneel," Jerkov barks.

"A hundred should do it," Britton says. "Go on, Jerkov, fucking give it to him."

He becomes ill again quicker than he realizes. Within days, he's holding back the urge to throw up, nearly choking himself several times to avoid vomit spilling over Fabrice Ortelli or the desk in the Education Centre.

Thoughts of Tracy Cox comfort him, but they fade from his mind faster than his emotions. Soon, she's just a speck, a shadow. All gone.

The borstal is nothing but routine – routine and more routine. The mornings begin with a breakfast that's nothing short of a nightmare.

Mouldy sandwiches for lunch – each bite feels like chewing on wet cardboard and decay. The bread is stale, disintegrating at the edges, crumbling with each bite. The filling? A slimy, unidentifiable meat paste, like something that had been left out too long and was scraped off the counter with all the care of someone just wanting to be done with it.

And then dinner. Putrid soup. It looks like water that's been drained from a dishpan, with floating chunks of congealed fat and gelatinous, off-coloured lumps of vegetables. The smell of rotting cabbage and stale broth fills the air, so thick it coats the back of his throat before he even takes a spoonful. It's a liquid nightmare, lukewarm and revolting, the kind of thing no human should be forced to eat, let alone believe is food.

He's told that he's lucky he's getting this kind of service. He should feel privileged.

Winter arrives, and a relentless cycle of Written Warnings and Dismissals begins. He's lashed, punched, forced to lick out the toilets, cuddled by Fabrice Ortelli, and made to walk naked in the snow.

The days blur together. He doesn't even notice when the New Year arrives.

Once, he's beaten so badly during a Dismissal that he's sent to the hospital for two weeks. The French doctor is gone. When he asks about him, one of the nurses tells him that Serge has finished his contract and returned to France.

When he returns to the borstal, he's handed what's called a Second Dismissal. He expects another beating, so he feels a strange sense of relief when he's simply ordered to eat liquidized food waste for three days straight.

Summer arrives.

The Governor treats the boys to a seaside excursion, but Lake isn't allowed to go—too many Written Warnings and Dismissals. Instead, he's left alone in the Education Centre to catch up on work.

He's not used to solitude. It feels alien.

A visitor arrives to deliver a talk on International Law. All the boys attend – except Lake, who's been signed off sick by the Matron. But the Governor insists: he must come anyway.

In a feverish haze, the memory burns itself into Lake's mind. A plump, self-assured South African woman stands before them, wrapped in a loud patterned scarf, her voice sharp and theatrical as she launches into a speech about the importance of nations working together – peace, law, democracy.

She's too young for this, Lake thinks.

What the hell is she doing here, feeding them this crap?

But it's how she ends that sets something off in him.

"I am a radical woman," she says, beaming. "I own that, and I'm proud of it. Thank you so much for listening."

"Thank you," the Governor replies. "I think a large round of applause is in order."

Lake doesn't clap. He's too weak. Too angry.

The Governor gives a thin, polite smile as the applause fades.

"Diedre, thank you so much for coming. Boys, Diedre has generously signed a copy of her book for each of you. After dinner, you'll remain in the hall to collect yours. The cost will be deducted from your wages – but I'm sure you'll all agree, this is a kind gesture."

Groans and curses erupt from the inmates.

"Shut your mouths!" Britton barks.

Days, weeks, months blur together.

Each moment slides into the next.

Summer ends. Before he realises it, a year has passed since his arrival. There's no ceremony, no recognition – just an extra rasher of rotting bacon.

Another winter comes. He drifts through it like a ghost, pulled along by something he can't name.

He survives, though he doesn't know how.

The following year, he loses consciousness altogether.

He no longer sees – he only feels.

Two years after his arrival, at three o'clock in the afternoon, Ceri Britton and Morton Jerkov enter the dormitory, their faces drawn with solemn expressions.

"Your sentence is complete," Britton says. "Please come with us."

Fabrice Ortelli looks shattered. Heartbroken. Lake strokes his face and apologises for leaving.

"One last cuddle," Ortelli sobs. "Please…"

"No – we've got to make a fucking move," Britton snaps. He grabs Lake's arm, though he doesn't need to. There's no resistance left.

The Governor doesn't come to see him off. Neither does Dr Tolson or the Matron. No goodbyes. Nothing.

It's bitterly cold for October, but Lake knows: two years of rotting food have left him defenceless to even the faintest chill.

He's not allowed to collapse. Britton and Jerkov each grip an arm, dragging him forward.

"Where's the bus?" Lake manages to ask.

"You're not going on a bus."

It's a van – like the one the school caretaker used to drive. A vile green thing, paint peeling, wheels rusting. The back doors gape open, a wide, waiting mouth.

"Get in, you little shit," Britton says.

When the doors open again, it's night.

"Look, should we be doing this?" is the first thing Jerkov says.

Both men wear woolly hats with torches stitched in, beams slicing the darkness. The light is blinding. Lake shields his face, but pain slips through his fingers.

"Butterworth's orders," Britton replies. "His parents topped themselves from the shame, school wants nothing to do with him – he reckons a disappearing act suits everyone. Right – fucking grab his legs."

Lake tries to fight. But there's nothing to fight with. He's gone – body, will, everything.

"Take your clothes off," the Australian orders. "Do it now."

He's done this before. Too many times. He strips, hands over the rags.

Hills roll in every direction like clenched fists. The stars blaze above him – fierce, brilliant, stolen from him too long. They're on a forgotten road, rough and crumbling. Stones bite into the soles of his feet.

"Welcome to the breezy Yorkshire Dales," Britton announces. "Hope you're happy here. It's been an absolute privilege looking after you. Hope you enjoyed your stay."

Both men give a short wave and return to the van. Jerkov takes the wheel, dragging on the stub of a cigarette. The engine roars. They pull a clumsy U-turn and vanish down the road.

At first, Lake doesn't feel the cold. He walks as fast as he can. But then the shivering starts, and he knows – this is it.

He stumbles often in the dark, nearly falling each time, but catches himself – until he can't anymore.

He drops, with as much dignity as he can manage. He's earned this sleep. He's ready.

Something touches his hand.

He looks up, but sees nothing.

A voice – soft, quieter than anything he's heard in months – whispers:

"It's okay. It's okay, dear boy. You're safe now."

9

Part 9

R oger Miser
Sunday, 1 June, 1980

"The town is yours, but treat it with respect," declared Miser, his voice resonant with authority. He raised his glass of priceless champagne, the golden bubbles glistening under the soft lights, as if toasting to a future filled with promise. His long, elegant neck stretched out like that of a regal ostrich, signalling his approval. "For years, I have harboured dreams of this moment, a vision that has dwelled in the deepest chambers of my heart, and now it has materialized into reality. This summer, I will be selecting one hundred bands and singers, one hundred of you fortunate souls!" The audience erupted into a tsunami of applause, waves of sound crashing over him as he stood, nearly engulfed by the sheer enthusiasm of the crowd. "Do your absolute best, give it your all! That's all I ask," he implored, his eyes gleaming with expectation and hope.

He was mildly drunk – not that anyone noticed. Not that anyone would care.

He gave his thanks to the mayor and councillors of St Pierre, along with its good residents, then backed off the stage.

The first band stepped up. Just a warm-up act: a three-piece folk group from Guildford. They took the stage with nervous smiles and, after a few false starts, began to play. Miser hated folk music – it always made him want to throw up his lunch.

But the scene was something else. The main street of St Pierre was alive: stalls and makeshift bars lined the road, wannabe musicians mingled with tourists, laughter rising with the dusk. Two young strangers were already snogging on someone's garden wall. Another couple was splitting up right in the middle of the crowd – the girl delivered what had to be the weakest bitch slap in recorded history.

Fun and chaos. Old and young, together.

Roger Miser felt full. Full of something like joy – drug-fu-elled, maybe, but joy all the same.

He walked through the crowd, faces bright around him, cheers rising.

George emerged from between two absurdly large, bearded men. "Excellent speech," he said, a little out of breath.

"I need a beer," said Miser. "Come on, George. Let's get a cold one. I'm dying here."

Someone was shouting his name. He turned to see Dr Garson waving at him, borderline hysterical.

"It's good to see you!" Miser yelled. The music had grown louder – Jesus, maybe the band was actually good. "How've you been?"

"Okay, I suppose."

"Your colleagues here too?"

"No, they're at home. Actually, I came to ask – you'd be welcome at mine for dinner. Dr La Rue and Dr Ferris are coming. We'd be honoured to have you join us."

"That's very kind, but I've got plans tonight, as you can see. Leave your contact details at my hotel and we'll sort something out."

"Of course. I understand."

But Miser had no interest in wasting the first night of his festival talking about stethoscopes and case reports. There were drinks to be had, connections to make, memories to burn into the streets.

"This is already a triumph," he said to George, leading him deeper into the noise and light. "Look at them – they're transfixed."

Beers in hand, Roger and George watched the last of the day's bands finish their set.

There were five stages set up across St Pierre and a sixth one two miles south, spaced wide to avoid clashing noise. For today, only the central bandstand was in use. Built smack in the heart of the main street, the builders had nicknamed it "Central Applause" – a name that had stuck.

Miser watched as the final group onstage packed up their gear, the applause already fading.

"Waste of space, if you ask me," George muttered, jerking a thumb toward the stage. "Wouldn't give 'em another shot."

Evening was slipping in. Overhead, strings of multi-coloured lights blinked into life, zigzagging between buildings like electric bunting. A warm breeze carried the scent of sizzling barbecue – charred meat, spiced veg, a faint sweetness of grilled pineapple. Everything shimmered slightly, a soft haze settling over the street as the sunlight drained away.

The festival looked like a postcard from somewhere far warmer and more exotic than Yorkshire.

"You've done it," said George. "Roger, you've bloody done it."

"Tell that to me come September."

Then, a disturbance – a ripple in the crowd, punctuated by groans and startled laughter. The smoky aroma of meat was joined by something more artificial, acrid.

"Oh, shit," muttered Miser, spotting the unmistakable flash of white trousers and open shirt. Disco Dave had begun his routine again. From the sound system, Charlie Petter's voice boomed out with desperate cheer.

It was *Saturday Night Fever*. Miser hated the film – found it nauseating – and seeing Dave's exaggerated pelvic thrusts made it worse. Petter clapped wildly, desperate for the crowd's attention.

"Any chance we can boot those two out?" George grumbled.

"Not a chance. Would be a PR disaster." Miser sighed. "Come on. Let's get back to the hotel."

"Agreed."

They turned from the chaos and slipped into the flow of the crowd. Familiar faces popped up between bursts of laughter and choruses of music – musicians Miser had known for years, others he barely remembered. Most would disappear in time, forgotten as quickly as they'd come.

But one face caught his attention. Someone he trusted. Someone who, once, had seemed destined for something glittering.

"Colson Lane!" Miser called, grinning. "Good to see you made it!"

The legendary folk singer turned, a haggard look beneath his boyish face. Bags hung under his eyes like bruises.

"You just get here? Train problems?"

"Nope," said Lane. "Got in yesterday. I'm on my way home."

"Excuse me?"

"You heard me. Heading home."

"But why? Is there an issue with your slot? I can promise you, you're one of the acts I absolutely plan to push. Trust me." Miser heard the pleading in his voice and didn't care.

"I'm going home because I have two young sons. A family."

"I don't get it." Miser gave a shaky laugh.

"I don't like this business," Lane said, brushing hair from his eyes. "Never really did. I want out."

"What?" Miser stared. "Colson, you've got promise. This – this festival – it could be everything."

Colson Lane stood lanky and still. With his wiry frame and boyish face, he always carried a kind of casual authority, like he was the ideal everyone else wanted to be.

"My wife and sons are everything," Lane snapped. "Thanks for the opportunity."

"But, Colson –"

"I don't want to miss my train. Take care."

Miser made to follow him – but someone gripped his elbow.

Three men. Well-dressed, their sharp suits at odds with the carnival air. They carried themselves with an unsettling calm. Each one was armed.

"How can I help?" said Miser.

"Mr Holmes would like you to join him for dinner," said the one in front, voice dry as dust. "He insists."

"When?"

"Now. We have the car waiting."

The speaker was tall, gaunt, bird-like. Hooked nose, sharp chin, sunken eyes. Bruce Ryall. Miser recognised him immediately – Holmes's right hand, with a reputation that ran dark.

"Am I to come as well?" George asked, cautiously.

"No." Ryall's stare turned cold. "Go and enjoy the festivities, Mr Ashton. You deserve it. Roger – come with us."

The car was parked just off the main drag, tucked into a narrow side street. Miser raised an eyebrow. One of Gary Holmes's prized Jags sat there, glistening under a streetlamp – completely unguarded. That alone was shocking. Even in a town as quaint and civilised as St Pierre, surely Holmes wouldn't leave his crown jewels out in the open? Holmes cherished a lot of things – his money, his reputation – but nothing topped his obsessive love for his fleet of Jaguars.

Bruce Ryall stepped forward and opened the rear door. "Please, do get in," he said.

Miser glared at him. "You watch your tone, Ryall. Don't ever forget why Holmes recruited you."

Ryall flashed a sharp grin. "Well, I'm one of his chief enforcers now. I'll rip your limbs off if you're not careful."

"I believe you," Miser replied, slipping into the back seat. "Come on, then. Let's get going."

The interior was thick with the scent of cinnamon aftershave – the firm's unmistakable signature. Ryall took the wheel. Miser wasn't entirely confident in his driving; the man had likely gotten his licence by slipping a test examiner fifty quid. That would explain why it took Ryall three or four miserable attempts just to get the Jag into gear.

Eventually, they pulled off. The car jerked forward and started the short journey west, away from the heart of the town. Miser watched through the tinted windows as the soft festival lights of St Pierre fell away behind them. The drive took about ten minutes. They followed a winding narrow road into the outskirts before veering off onto a narrow, gravelled track.

Branches overhung the path, clawing at the windows like skeletal fingers. At the entrance to this wooded lane stood two more of Holmes's men, each holding a pump-action shotgun. Miser recognised them instantly – Little Dave Perkins and Big Dave Rogers. Vicious bastards, both of them. As the car rolled past, Big Dave offered him a crooked sneer.

The track ended at a small clearing, surrounded on all sides by towering trees. In the middle of the space sat an old cottage, its rustic charm now buried beneath layers of paranoia. Armed guards patrolled its perimeter, their shotguns slung across thick arms.

Miser stepped out of the car. The air felt colder here – sharper. He instinctively rubbed his arms. The cottage itself might once have been a peaceful retreat for poets or lovers, but now it looked like a converted fallout shelter. Security cameras blinked lifelessly from every wall. Rusting metal plates had been bolted over the stonework. The original door was long gone; in its place stood a thick slab of steel fitted with a digital combination lock.

To the left, Miser spotted a neat row of Jags parked with surgical precision. They were staggered, probably for a quick escape. Typical Holmes – always one step ahead, always planning for the worst.

Then, the steel door creaked open, and Gary Holmes emerged.

He wore a garish purple smoking jacket, a cigar wedged between his teeth. In his other hand, he nursed a crystal glass of scotch.

"Good evening, good evening," Holmes said, arms outstretched like a host greeting an old friend. "I hope you had a nice day, Rog."

"It was indeed, thanks. Good start to the festival."

"Excellent, excellent. I like it when an investment pays off."

"How are you settling in?"

"Very well, actually," said Holmes. "Please, come on in, son. Got a lovely bottle of French red waiting for us."

"Appreciate it," Miser replied.

Holmes led the way. "I was determined to give the place a homely feeling," he said, ushering him inside.

The interior didn't match the exterior's grim severity. At first glance, it had the trappings of a countryside getaway – wooden beams, cosy carpets – but each room Miser peeked into was filled with firearms, crates of ammunition, and military-grade gear. The hallway stretched straight through the house, ending in another reinforced door. Furniture had been stripped out, judging by the heavy indents in the carpet.

Holmes gestured right, guiding him into a dining room.

Soft classical music floated from a turntable in the corner, just low enough for conversation. "I keep all weapons out of where we sit and eat," Holmes explained, "as well as the lounge. We'll go in there for a scotch after."

Two enforcers entered. Holmes handed one his empty glass, the other his cigar stub.

"Bring the bottle in," he ordered. "We're ready for starters."

"Should be ten minutes, sir," one replied.

The dining room was lavish in a way that felt completely at odds with the rest of the house. A silvery silk cloth covered the table. Twin candelabras rose from its centre like skeletal trees. The table was massive – far too grand for a place like this – and dominated the room. Each place setting was meticulous: fine cutlery, wafer-thin placemats, wine glasses with intricate designs.

Holmes shrugged off his jacket, revealing an Italian suit and a crimson tie. Gold cufflinks flashed under the candle-light.

"Be seated, Rog," he said as the bottle arrived. The glasses were filled with smooth, deep red wine.

"Did you let it breathe?" Holmes asked.

"I did, sir."

"Good man. Straighten that tie before you come back." Holmes dismissed him with a flick of the hand, then raised his glass. "To good health, Rog."

"To good health, Mr Holmes."

"Gary, please. We've known each other long enough. I consider you my most valuable investment."

"If I may ask," said Miser, "why the sudden invite? Is this about him?"

Holmes shook his head. "No, this is just a friendly dinner. A catchup. There's been no sight of Clifford Lake. My boys have combed the town and surrounding countryside. Nothing. Trust me, I'm not letting my guard down. But tonight's just about us."

"Well, it's good to catch up. You should come dine at the hotel sometime. They do a solid French Onion Soup."

"No doubt. But with Lake out there, I'm not taking any chances. Once he's caught, we'll have that slap-up meal."

"How's Tessa? Is she here with you?"

"Nope," said Holmes, sipping his wine. "She's back in London. Gus and Gerry are watching over her with half my firm. I'm not taking risks – not with someone like Lake. But she's well. Back into knitting. First time I met her, she was working on a scarf for her sister. Funny how those little things stay with you."

"One of my star performers walked out on me today," Miser said, draining his glass. "Colson Lane. Complete and utter pillock…"

"Don't get angry. Trust me, Rog." Holmes refilled their glasses. "You let anger cloud your judgement, things go sideways."

"I wouldn't allow that."

"I know you're a straight-faced kind of bloke." Holmes barked a laugh. "Anyway. Enough of that. How's the business?"

Miser sighed. "I'm getting tired of it, if I'm honest. This festival – this is my legacy. My last kiss to the world of music. I want to select a hundred acts from the whole lineup."

"Sounds like you've got it all worked out."

"I just don't want the Lake stuff hanging over it. If he's here, I know he'll do something."

"He won't get the chance. My boys will handle it."

"How's your firm?"

"Busy. Giving Gus and Gerry more responsibility. When I pop my clogs, they're taking over. I want them ready."

A knock on the door. The young enforcer returned, silver tray in hand, wobbling slightly as he carried in two steaming bowls of French Onion Soup. He placed them down and gave a short nod to Holmes before retreating.

"This is delicious," Miser said automatically, spooning the stuff with effort. He hated French Onion Soup, but he'd never say so to Holmes. The man was fanatical about French cuisine.

They dined for nearly an hour, drinking steadily and chatting about the old days. Afterwards, Holmes led him into the lounge.

Two deep leather armchairs sat facing a soot-dusted fireplace. Between them, a small wooden table held a beautiful decanter of whisky and four glasses. Bookshelves lined one wall, stuffed with ancient volumes and the heads of old philosophers. A plush suede sofa ran along the opposite side.

It was tight. Oppressive, almost.

Holmes slipped back into his smoking jacket, handed over a glass of whisky, and lit two cigars.

"Lovely, lovely," he said, puffing contentedly. "Can't beat this. Lovely."

Miser narrowed his eyes. He had seen this moment before – this exact scene.

She haunts him like a ghost.

She's always there – strumming her guitar, cigarette dangling from her lips. Short blonde hair, messy as hell.

What year was it? 1975? Maybe.

He was drunk. Some festival, somewhere. The kind of date that doesn't deserve remembering.

She's staring straight into his eyes, offering him everything – promising a future, a family, a house with steady walls and warmlight.

And he?

Too stupid.

Too proud.

Too bloody ashamed.

He tells her no. Says he wants his next girlfriend to be a trophy – someone who makes him look like he matters.

"I'm sorry…"

"Lovely little town this," said Holmes. "I think you did a good job selecting it."

Both men were dissolved in clouds of smoke, trapped in their armchairs, their conversation sinking into the hazy fog.

"How are things with you, generally?" Miser asked, breaking the silence.

"Same old, same old. A few new deals to sort out, but nothing exciting. Taking this bastard out is my highest priority." Holmes gave a wry smirk. "Oh, you'll never guess, Rog. Do you know who I ran into the other day? Bloody Philip Leighton!"

"What's he up to?" Miser groaned.

"I know you two don't exactly see eye-to-eye."

"It's a long story."

"Well, anyway, Philip's pretty much running the company now after that unfortunate mix-up in New York."

"Yeah, I heard. How's Philip taking it?"

Holmes rubbed his chin, stubbing his cigar out in the ceramic ashtray. "He's doing as well as a man can do, Rog." He swallowed the last of his whisky. "It's getting late. One of the boys will give you a lift back to town."

"No, it's okay. I could use a walk."

Still high on whisky fumes, Roger Miser took his time heading back to St Pierre. A meal with Gary Holmes always had a dizzying effect, no matter what was on the menu. He remembered the road back only in fragments, a snaking path to the town that blurred in his mind.

The party was still in full swing when he returned, but it was beginning to spiral out of control. Drunken shouts and arguments spilled into the night. The closer he got, the more offensive the words became, the music industry's worst terms hanging in the air like smoke.

He found himself thinking about Colson Lane's whereabouts. Probably halfway home by now, that utter backstabbing bastard. After everything he, Miser, had done for him?

"Fucking traitor," he muttered under his breath.

But if Lane wanted to sod off, that was his choice.

"You look a little lost," a soft voice interrupted.

"Excuse me?" Miser asked, surprised.

A calm face gazed at him, her features soft and unfamiliar but hauntingly recognizable. Even in the darkness, she was bathed in some unearthly light, an aura of obsession and dirty fantasies surrounding her.

"What are you doing out here?" she asked.

"I'm taking a stroll."

"Watch yourself. The roads get dangerous at night. Cars don't always observe the speed limit."

"Thanks for the advice."

Then it hit him – the recognition, the memory. The hammer to his chin, like the punch he'd once taken from Gerd Snaijer, the drummer he'd had kicked out of a band at George's insistence.

It was her. The night of the meal outside the hotel. She had passed by, not noticing him, or anyone else. Had Miser been too transfixed, distracted like a lovestruck teenager? Christ, she was beautiful. Unthinkably so. Even up close, in the shadows, he could make out the different shades in her straw-coloured hair, the freckles on her cheeks, and her deep, pale eyes.

"You look like you need help," she said, her voice carrying a mild French accent with a strong undertone of American twang.

"Oh no, I'm fine. Just a long day."

"You're Roger Miser, aren't you?"

"Yep," he replied sheepishly.

"There's a lot of talk about you from the locals. You've caused quite a stir, ripping up their town for the summer."

"Well, it's had the blessing of the mayor."

"I've no doubt. You seem like the kind of guy who follows all the correct channels." She smiled briefly. "Anyway, I'd better go. I'll catch you in town sometime, Roger."

"Take care."

Only when he was back in the chaos of the party, surrounded by desperate musicians hoping to make a name for themselves, did he realize his mistake. Why the hell hadn't he asked her name?

Thursday, 5 June, 1980

Days later, a group of the youngest musicians attending the festival ambushed him in the street, wide-eyed and grinning, demanding his autograph. Normally, he shrugged off attention like this, but today, for reasons he didn't care to examine, he was feeling generous. He gave them what they wanted.

When they asked for a photo, he initially refused. But after a rapid-fire chorus of "please" – stacked on top of each other like a crescendo – he relented with a sigh.

He hesitated over the location, glancing around, until one of them suggested the woods nearby. A short walk under the glaring sun brought them into the shade of tall, slender trees. The air grew cooler. The canopy swayed slightly, dappling the ground with shifting light. A few birds murmured overhead, and the distant hum of the festival faded behind them. The place had the hush of somewhere forgotten, comfortably so.

"Who's going to take the photo?" he asked.

As if on cue, a man appeared at the edge of the clearing, stepping between the trunks. Definitely a local – his thick beard, stooped posture, and worn, leathery face spoke of someone who hadn't left this town in decades. Miser waved him over, raising the camera one of the kids had handed him.

"Of course," said the man, with a voice crisp and precise – Oxford English, bizarrely enough. Miser didn't question it.

He sat down cross-legged on the leaf-strewn ground. The young musicians – full of future and nerve – crowded in behind him.

"Say cheers for Jerry Reed," the man said. A flash. He returned the camera with a nod and disappeared back into the trees, whistling softly, as if nothing had happened.

"Thanks!" Miser called after him, but either the man didn't hear or he chose not to.

Miser stood, brushing dirt and leaves from his trousers.

"Thank you, Roger," the kids said in unison, more or less.

"Not a problem," he replied. "Actually, one small favour – when you get it developed, could you send a copy to the hotel? Something for the manager."

They nodded and drifted off, scattering like seeds on the wind. Roger Miser turned back toward the noise of the festival, returning to the slow work of sealing his legacy. The musicians walked in the opposite direction, just beginning theirs.

It was a beautiful day – warm, golden, suspended in possibility. A day for legends. A day for triumphs.

Part 10

Victor Gully
Sunday, 28 June, 2009

Not exactly a resounding success.

Victor Gully stood and watched as the last of the semi-retired crowd trickled out of the arts venue. Fifty people were supposed to attend. Thirty-two had cancelled. Four more hadn't bothered to show up. He stood there, disgruntled and bitter, quietly resolving to take his frustrations to the pub later.

He looked down at the cold remains of his instant coffee, now sitting thick and lifeless in the bottom of the Styrofoam cup. It had seemed creamy, almost promising, at the start of the event. Now it looked diseased. He dumped it in the bin.

Over at the desk, he powered up his laptop. No internet out here – not even the whisper of a signal – but a tabloid left crumpled on the table offered a short-lived distraction. *Michael Jackson Dead*, the headline blared. The world, apparently, was stunned. Accusations were flying like darts in a pub.

Gully sighed, crumpled the paper further, and dropped it in after the coffee.

He opened up his latest project: a blank page.

No point pretending otherwise – he needed a new book, and fast. *Saving The Pale Mountain* had tanked. A 500-page, globe-spanning literary thriller? What was he thinking? Readers didn't have the patience for something that ambitious anymore. Maybe they never had.

He tapped out a few fragments of half-formed ideas, the document still looking painfully empty. Still, twenty minutes of solid work. Could've been worse.

And then – she was there.

She was always there. Wherever he went, somehow, she found a way in: standing across the road during his morning run, lingering near the selection boxes at the supermarket, and now, staring at him from the screen. Her tearful, hollow eyes met his.

His stomach turned.

That night. He'd never forget it. The pain crackled through him, jagged and relentless. He was still there in his mind, sitting in one of those stupid little chairs, about to make small talk with Herbert Buxton about some vapid literary theory. And then Rowan Colt – silent, sudden – burst in like a gunshot. The knife rose and fell again and again. Susan didn't stand a chance. The blood came fast, soaking into the carpet like spilled ink. A grotesque blot nobody could clean.

He snapped the laptop shut and stood. Coat on. One destination.

The pub.

He settled in with a cool pint, tucked into a corner of The Lake Arms that the regulars tended to ignore. His table – wedged awkwardly between the front wall and the brick flank of a long-disused chimney – was too large for one person. He tried to look modest, to blend in, but he could feel the stares pinballing off him.

He already knew he'd be spending a lot of time here. The emerald woman was driving him to drink – no use pretending otherwise. For the past two days, she'd been digging into him like a splinter under the skin, cutting into his soul. He didn't even know what she looked like – hadn't seen her clearly, not once – but he was obsessed.

A group of four men in muddied work overalls burst in, trailing laughter and barbed profanity behind them. Their boots slapped wetly against the floor.

Gully took a long drink of his bitter, then bent to retrieve his A4 notebook from his rucksack. The latest in a long line – soon it, too, would be filled with illegible fragments and discarded thoughts. He poised his pen over the first page, managed only the date.

"Great," he muttered to himself.

The pub's energy was swelling by the minute. Conversations got louder, more animated. Sunday evening was rounding off the weekend in a proper haze of beer and bravado. The workmen had already drained their first round; the youngest of the bunch – a shy-looking kid, barely past eighteen – was bullied into getting the next.

Gully tightened his grip on the pen and forced out a sentence. Or part of one. Not much, but enough to convince himself the evening hadn't been a complete waste.

He was just about to return the notebook to his bag when he felt it – that creeping sense of company he hadn't invited.

"Mind if we sit here?" one of the workmen asked.

Before Gully could answer, they dropped themselves around the table, their lagers thudding onto the wood like declarations of territory.

"What you doin'?" one of them asked, eyeing the notebook. "Why you got that in a place like this?"

"Oh, just some personal stuff," Gully replied. "Nothing major."

"This isn't the place for it."

"You're right," Gully said, folding the notebook shut. "That's why I'm putting it away."

The young one – barely old enough to shave – flicked his eyes toward him. "Mate, why you acting weird? Tosspot. Honestly, you should leave."

"If you guys want the table, that's cool," Gully said, rising carefully. "I'll find another spot."

"No, trust me," one of the others muttered, low and cold. "You should leave."

He nodded and tiptoed toward the door, the sound of sniggers brushing at his back like flies. The air in the pub had changed; it was poisonous now. People stared at him like he was some malformed creature, something crawled out from under a child's bed.

Outside, the cool night hit him like a slap. And then came the sensation again – that hot, sick surge of trauma. The same punch to the gut he'd felt watching Susan die. Everything was tilting. Nothing felt real.

He took a few shallow breaths, tried to still the trembling. He didn't want to remember. Didn't want to see her torn open on the floor again.

Tried, and failed, to push her brokenness out of his mind.

With the police investigation dead in the water, there was no longer any reason to keep Henry Jarrett's apartment sealed off. It had been handed over to Victor Gully – he was, after all, the writer-in-residence.

He was in it now, slouched in a chair, genuinely depressed and half pretending to be.

A cup of tea sat cooling in his hands as he stared through the window. Summer rain had begun to spit lazily at the glass, droplets crawling down like they weren't in much of a hurry to reach the bottom.

"What's happening to you, Victor?" he muttered aloud.

An embarrassment. That's what he was. Pushed around by those workmen like some helpless schoolboy. Bullied, dismissed – utterly pathetic.

He flipped open the laptop and threw himself into two hours of work: planning upcoming events, signing off forms, composing half-hearted emails to people who needed to feel important. Someone had to remind the arts centre to clear the gutters. The glamorous machinery of a writer's residency.

Later, before bed, he idly surfed the web. The usual syrupy panic about swine flu clogged up the headlines. He checked a few local news sites, half hoping there might be a mention of the project. No such luck.

Bored, he searched his own name.

The latest one-star reviews were up. Angry, disappointed, almost spiteful readers tore into him. Once, their scorn made him furious. Now, it was just another part of the noise. He chuckled bitterly at one particularly dramatic takedown.

He was about to shut everything down when an impulse stopped him.

One more search: *woman emerald dress.*

A wall of links to clothing stores. Green silk. Summer chiffon. He added *Canterbury.*

A single new result popped up: a link to a local paper from Sevenoaks.

The headline grabbed him like a hand around the throat: *Woman Robs Café; Owners Ruined.*

He clicked.

The article was short, barely two paragraphs, but there it was – a blurred CCTV still, frozen in motion and brimming with suggestion.

"I can't believe it," he breathed. "Bloody hell."

A woman in a green dress was strolling down a narrow street, her face turned away. In her left hand, a sagging carrier bag – presumably filled with the stolen goods. The image was grainy, anonymous. But to Gully, it was her.

He smirked at the screen. Then he laughed. Actually laughed.

He was too curious, far too curious about her. But the desire was rooting itself deeper with every nervous exhale.

She was real. And he needed to know more.

Monday, 29 June, 2009

The train screeched to a halt at Sevenoaks Station, jerking Victor Gully awake. He rubbed his eyes and dragged himself off the carriage.

It was ten o'clock, and the tail end of rush hour was giving its final, raucous performance. A brash businessman elbowed him as he walked past, and Gully shot him a sharp, annoyed yell.

Outside the station, he unfolded the map from his notebook. The café wasn't far – just a brisk, punishing walk.

He got lost twice, but after twenty minutes, he found it. His heart sank when he saw the front of the building. How the hell had he not recognized it from the news article? A tear crept down his left cheek.

He'd been here before – four and a half years ago, interviewing Scarlet on the fifteenth anniversary of her band. This was where one of the greatest music groups in history had been born, right here, amidst the coffee cups and cakes. The birthplace of some of the best music ever made. But to him, it was a cradle of pain.

He walked inside. Not much had changed since 2005 – same open, airy feel – but there was a fresh coat of green paint on the walls. The chairs and tables were as stiff and unmoving as stone statues. No one else was in.

"Sorry to hear about what happened," he said to the man behind the counter.

The young man shrugged, his face as pale as paper. Thin as a rail, with overgrown hair and tired blue eyes, he looked too young to be working here.

The glass display still held its usual array of cakes and pastries. Gully felt a rumble in his stomach as he glanced over them but forced himself to settle for an espresso.

"Sit down, and I'll bring it over," the kid told him.

Gully chose a table at the back of the café. A dog-eared, laminated menu lay sideways. He skimmed it. Fish and chips, lasagna, roast mutton – far more than the pitiful sandwiches on offer in 2005.

"Did they find out who it was?" Gully asked.

"You mean the thief? No, no idea. Some well-dressed tart. Police are investigating."

"She was spotted in Canterbury."

The boy brought over the espresso, setting it down with a force that betrayed his anger. "Mate, are you a private investigator?"

"No! Sorry, I didn't explain. I'm a writer –"

"Oh, I should've known. A fucking journalist."

"No, fiction. My name's Victor Gully."

"Oh yeah, I know the name. *The Church in the Square*, right?"

"Yeah."

"I need to make a few calls, place an order. But hey, if you could share what you know, that'd be great."

"Sure," Gully replied, grateful for the small window of co-operation.

The young man moved to the counter. Gully flipped through his notes. He hadn't made much progress with his investigation. In fact, he needed more than a break – he needed a bloody miracle. He knocked back the espresso in one go, his fingers drumming absently on the table. He glanced at the boy, who was now on the phone, speaking in a tense whisper.

Gully stood to use the bathroom. The stickman on the wall – a crude drawing, arms outstretched – seemed to mock him. Something brushed against his back, sharp and cold.

"Turn around, slowly," a female voice commanded.

He froze. A woman with wavy, ginger hair stood behind him, a flick-knife held in a fencing pose, the tip aimed squarely at his chin.

"What the fuck?!" Gully gasped, his heart slamming in his chest.

"You've been roundly screwed," said the boy from the counter, his voice flat.

"Wait... you're the ones who robbed this place, aren't you?"

"Nope," the woman replied. "The owners are away on holiday. We're running things for them this summer. Some lady burgled the place – no idea who she was – but, see, Amias and I are thieves too. We're mugging you, rich-boy. Take out your wallet, empty it of cash. Now."

Gully had no choice. His stomach churned with humiliation. He pulled out his wallet and began peeling the bills from it.

"Drop it on the floor," the boy said.

Gully let the notes fall, the paper swishing softly to the ground.

"You may leave," the woman said. "Don't worry, we're not interested in your credit cards. We're not that cruel."

Gully raised his hands in surrender, backing toward the door. Behind him, they chuckled, the sound like nails on a chalkboard. "Loser." "Prick." "Softy."

Out on the street, Gully broke into a run, not stopping even when his lungs screamed for air. His chest ached, breath ragged and shallow. His ego had been bruised again – more than bruised, really.

Enough was enough.

Enough of the exhaustion, the fear, the terror. The hunt for the woman in the emerald dress had given him nothing but heartache and stress. There were other things to focus on. He had a residency to manage. And an ego to resurrect.

Part 11

R oger Miser
Saturday, 14 June, 1980 – Sunday, 15 June, 1980

He dared himself – finally – to approach her.

Pushing through the tide of hopeful musicians, Roger Miser kept his eyes locked on her. She was tantalisingly beautiful. Something about her straw-coloured hair reeled him in.

She didn't belong here, not really. Despite the sweltering heat, she wore a leather waistcoat over a thick brown shirt, a greying tartan dress falling to her ankles. Yet not a bead of sweat. She looked like she'd stepped straight out of wartime France.

"Hi!" he called.

"Well, hello," she replied.

"I'm sorry about the other night. I was in a rush. I wasn't quite myself."

"It's quite all right." Her pale eyes caught the sunlight like diamonds. "How are things going?"

"Brilliant," he said. "The festival's in full swing. Everyone seems to be enjoying themselves."

"Are *you* enjoying yourself?"

"It's not supposed to be about enjoyment."

A group with an array of drums barged past them. Miser thought he recognised one of the performers. He nearly called out, but reminded himself of what was right here in front of him.

"I'm Claudine," she said, holding out a hand.

Miser took it. Her skin was rough, like a farmer's palms.

"Well, you know who I am."

"How could I not? The great Roger Miser."

"What do you think?" he asked, jerking his thumbs over his shoulder.

"Of what?"

"The festival."

"I think it's... okay. Not really my scene, but... it's okay."

"It's good to finally put a name to the face."

"It is. I'm assuming you'll be asking for my number?" She gave him a knowing look.

"Am I allowed?"

"I'll tell you what," she said. "I'll drop my number and address at your hotel later. You should come for dinner sometime."

"I'd like that very much." He grinned, pleased with himself.

"You'll be meeting my father as well. He lives with me." Claudine stepped in closer.

There was something unsettling now about the detail in her face – the calm eyes framed by the wild straw hair. A contradiction.

"What, you think I'm easy?" she whispered. "I'm not that easy. You've got to earn me. My father will make you."

Nobody made Roger Miser do anything. He was the one who gave orders. But here, his response came out thin and dry. "I look forward to meeting him."

"Have a lovely day, Roger," said Claudine, and disappeared into the crowd. He watched as she melted away among the summer's hopefuls.

There was a commotion behind him. Miser turned to see Charlie Petter being shoved by two large, burly men. In Petter's left arm was a roll of billposters, in his right a tin of glue. The two men were brothers – twins from Limerick, drummers in some band launched in '74. Miser couldn't remember the name. Two years ago, they'd won an award, but that was their one and only success. They hadn't even applied to come here—or had they?

Charlie was backing away, apologising over and over.

"What's going on here?" said Miser, grabbing Petter by the collar. "What did I say about this nonsense?" He dragged him away from the twins and gave him a slap – not enough to hurt, just enough to pause him.

"Mr Miser, I was only putting a few bills up," Charlie whimpered. "Just a few posters, Mr Miser."

"I don't give a shit," said Miser. He turned and mouthed a silent apology to the two Irishmen. "What was he doing?"

"He tried to glue those fucking posters on our tent!" one of them roared. "Fucking pussy!"

"I'm really sorry," Miser said. "I'll handle this."

"You'd better," the other one growled.

"Charlie, you can't just do that!" Miser led him away from the crowd. In front of a small patch of shrubbery, he laid down the law.

"Charlie, you can't go around glueing things to people's tents. You just can't. I didn't even want you here. You're an amazing little man, my friend – but, and I hate saying this, you don't have a backbone. Charlie... pack up. Go home."

He left him there, crying in front of the flowers.

Back at the hotel, Miser flopped onto his bed. He was restless. Siestas never worked for him – never had.

For two hours, he lay on his side, watching the alarm clock tick. Bored and irritated, he got up and went for a walk.

On impulse, he swung by Patsy Monroe's tent. Empty. She had a big performance coming up tonight – one of the headline acts. He found her eventually, on the north edge of town, slumped by a tree with a guitar across her knees. She was strumming random notes, humming, whistling.

When she saw him, she paused—then kept playing, this time shaping a tune. He let her go on, but not for long.

Later, in the waning glow of the afternoon sun, he cradled her soft head in the crook of his arm. The quiet was short-lived — she had to leave for her set. Of course, he went with her, gave her a warm introduction, then they were back in bed.

When he woke up, she wasn't there.

No note. No goodbye kiss. She had simply vanished.

A loud banging rattled the door.

"It's George! Roger, you need to come with me... quick!"

"What's happened?"

Christ – something had happened to Patsy. Shit.

Miser threw his clothes on. Yesterday's shirt still had damp patches. No time to care.

George looked pale, his face brimming with shock. "It's Charlie," he stammered.

"What – what about him? Is he okay?"

"Roger, you need to come. Right now."

"I'm ready."

George led him out of the hotel, picking up speed in the lobby. Out on the street, he broke into a slow run. Miser followed as close as he could. Something in the air smelled wrong – sickly, chemical, like burnt tyres.

Musicians were setting up for the day, but Miser didn't glance their way. When something worried him, the rest of the world vanished.

Flashing police lights in the distance sent his heart scrambling. The field east of town – the one filled with all the tents, the uninvited.

"Shit," he muttered. "Shit, shit, shit."

They broke into a sprint.

Only two police cars had pulled up at the roadside, but officers were scattered across the camp, taking statements from dazed, smoke-streaked witnesses. A grey haze had settled, clinging to every surface, creeping into every fold of skin.

At the far end of the field, the blackened shell of a tent smouldered, coughing its final wisps into the sky.

"Was Charlie in there?!" Miser shouted. "George, was he in there?"

People stared at him. Dark looks. Shocked looks. Disbelieving ones.

"It was those two Irish guys," George said.

"Christ – they *burned* him to death?!"

"No. Quite the opposite. Charlie set *their* tent on fire. Last night. He's been taken to the police station."

"He wouldn't do that!"

George's voice darkened, slower now. "Did you say anything to him, Roger? Did you?"

"I told him to go home. Told him to pack his bags."

"Did you tell him he didn't have a backbone?"

"Oh, fuck!" Miser shouted as another police siren sliced through the air.

A tight huddle of very young women were crying beside one of the tents. Weren't they supposed to be performing tonight?

Nearby, a man dressed in too many layers – some sorry imitation of a country singer – sat on a loose rock, shaking, spitting into the dirt.

"He put these up around town." George handed him a crumpled slip of paper. One of Petter's billposters, smeared with thick, drunken handwriting:

I have a backbone.

"I didn't think he'd take it like that," Miser muttered. "Fucking stupid little toerag... Where's Disco Dave?"

"Giving a statement to the police." George looked him dead in the eye. "And speaking of that – we need to draft *your* statement. The media'll be all over this soon."

Lake

He watched it closely from a distance, smiling to himself.

In his Jerry Reed disguise, he allowed a small chuckle to escape. He didn't like the outfit – it made him feel old – but it was the most effective one he had. He could witness the distress on Roger Miser's face without a flicker of worry about being recognised. Who gave a shit about a shuffling old man?

The plan had worked perfectly. Jerry Reed had approached Charlie Petter on the street and slyly suggested he post those flyers around the campsite. Then he'd tipped off the Irish brothers, letting them know Petter was the culprit. Like clockwork, they'd gone after him.

He'd followed Miser from a distance, watched him pull Petter aside and deliver those choice words. The magic word *backbone* – perfect for those... confessions.

Last night, he'd set fire to the tent himself, wearing the same pathetic clothes Petter always wore, then planted the rest of the posters for good measure.

Oh, poor Charlie Petter! All the evidence against him, neatly arranged. A lifetime behind bars now awaited. And, naturally, Clifford Lake would make sure the right officials were paid to keep Petter off the guillotine.

This was payback. The stupid little twerp who had once boarded a bus and offered him a Marmite sandwich was now going to suffer like Lake had.

A lifetime of being poked, prodded, punished.

Revenge – pure and simple.

Part 12

L^{ake}   **October, 1968**

He tries to move, but he's not allowed to. A cool hand rests gently on his forehead, steadying him.

"Stay still," comes the command.

A blurred face swims into view, but there's no strength left in him.

He wakes again, but he can't tell if it's the next day or the next decade.

He feels something at his lips – metal. A salty taste floods his tongue. It's familiar, yet... unusual. He recognizes it, he knows it well. Something he used to have on the occasional weekend: French onion soup.

His eyes strain, his ears throb.

Slowly, agonizingly, he swallows more soup, bit by bit, giving up on hiding his distaste for normal food.

"Who are you?" he manages to ask, almost failing to speak.

"Mike," the man answers. "Now you rest."

"How are you feeling?"

This time, the voice is closer than anything.

He jerks upright, body tensing, ready to cower.

He's under silk covers in a four-poster bed. The room feels ancient, like an old headmaster's study – dimly lit by a roaring fireplace in the corner. Shelves lined with aged tomes and manuscripts. Grand, patterned curtains pulled back to reveal hills stretching beyond the window.

"Where am I?" Lake demands. "Where am I?"

"The Yorkshire Dales. In my humble home."

The man sits on the edge of the bed. He's old, his grey beard fanning out beneath his face like a tangled brush. His skin is wrinkled, but his muscular arms betray his age. His pale eyes study Lake with quiet intensity.

"I found you in my front garden," the man continues. "You've been here for five days. Care to tell me what happened?"

Lake can feel the mattress tremble as the man shifts his weight.

"It's nothing," he mutters. "I was out for a walk and got lost. I'll leave today."

The man raises an eyebrow. "Out walking stark naked, were you? Sorry, pal, I don't believe you."

"Please, sir –"

"Don't believe you," the man cuts him off. "And call me Michael. That's my name – Michael Wool."

"I've heard that name before."

"We'll talk later. Get some rest."

Lake tries again, his voice weak: "You're that martial arts man, aren't you?"

"That I am." Michael pauses at the door, glancing back. "Rest. You're still not well."

The next day, Lake is able to eat solid food.

Unsure of what to make of the Full English breakfast propped on his lap, he's initially reluctant. He hasn't had breakfast in bed in years; it's a forbidden luxury to him. But the saucer of coffee, made from freshly ground beans, and slices of white toast covered in butter stir something inside him. His stomach growls with hunger. The problem is, he's used to eating rotten food. Gradually, he musters the courage to take a bite of the bacon. A cascade effect follows, and before he knows it, he's devouring the rest of the meal, eating like an animal. Never has he felt so good! Tears cling to his eyelashes as his throat clogs with fat and grief.

"Are you going to tell me what's happened?"

Lake hadn't noticed Michael Wool standing in the corner, almost camouflaged against the lime-green wallpaper. The man has his arms folded, his lips pulled back, silently watching him.

"It was…" Lake hesitates, unsure of how to start. But there's no point in hiding now. He tells him everything, from the day he met Tracy to the moment he was dumped in the Dales. He goes through it all methodically, as though giving a report rather than reliving the traumatic tale. Michael Wool shows no emotion, staying in the same posture, unmoving. When Lake finishes, the man remains a statue for a few moments, then finally shifts off the wall.

"Finish your coffee," he tells Lake. "I'll be back in an hour."

The man returns well over an hour later. He brings sandwiches and fruit juice, along with a stream of apologies. Pulling a chair up next to the bed, he sits down.

"I'm truly sorry for what you went through," he tells Lake. "I am truly, deeply sorry."

"Thank you." That's all Clifford Lake can manage.

"I've been thinking about it. Made a few notes in my study. This Tracy Cox you mentioned – when you first met her in that shop on Bond Street, did anything strike you as odd? Anything unusual in what she said or did?"

"It's been so long."

"Try."

"Well... she asked me how old I was. Yes, that's what she wanted to know. How old I was."

"Anything else? She must have asked more than that." Michael Wool's voice is both gentle and insistent. "Think," he says. "Think deep."

Lake tries, but nothing surfaces.

"I'm sorry – I'm asking too much," Wool says. "Rest for now. I'll come back later."

"Wait – hold on. She asked for my address, too. And if my parents were planning to move. I think she said it was in case the police asked."

"And this man who was in the shop with her – just to confirm, he's the same guy who was at the warehouse in Thamesmead?"

"Yeah. His name was Jefferson Reed."

"Eat your lunch. I'll be back in a bit, and we'll talk more."

When Michael Wool returns later, he's carrying a pile of clothes.

"Belonged to my son," he says. "They should fit you. Get dressed and meet me out in the corridor."

Being given clothes feels foreign to Lake. He lifts the white shirt – pristine and stiff like it's never been worn. The brown trousers, oil-black socks, and ocean-grey leather shoes seem like artifacts pulled from the ground.

Other than trips to the attached bathroom, he hasn't stood much. He's wobbly at first but steadies himself and dresses. Then he walks – his first real walk in so long – to the door. It's opened for him. Michael places a hand gently on his shoulder.

"I'm feeling much better," Lake says.

"Good. Let's head downstairs."

The corridor feels like something out of a long-forgotten school. Paintings and plundered treasures line the stone walls. A dusty turntable sits beneath a pile of records. Lake squints to read the labels, but Michael nudges him along.

"How big is this place?" Lake asks.

"It's pretty big. Over two hundred rooms, more than a thousand acres of land. I bought it fifteen years ago, right after my last fight. Used to belong to a duke or something."

"When I was at school, we used to talk about you all the time. Your karate matches in Japan – we reenacted them."

Michael Wool grins. "You did, huh? Well, I'm glad I haven't completely faded from memory…"

They reach a grand staircase made of marble steps that gleam like still water under soft, filtered light. Each step is bordered by dark, polished wooden panels, the bannisters carved with swirling patterns of ivy and mythical beasts. Time has worn the edges just enough to give them a story. A chandelier, ornate and teardrop-shaped, hangs from a braided cord, its crystals catching the light and throwing fractured rainbows across the walls. Lake traces the line up to a vaulted ceiling another floor above – pale with age, dust-speckled, and painted with a faded mural of stormy clouds and winged figures. It looks bitterly fragile and delicate, like a breath might bring it all down.

"Beautiful, isn't it?" Michael says. "This is the beating heart of the house. Three floors, all connected by this staircase."

"It is beautiful. We had one kind of like it at school."

"Let's talk more about that. There's a smaller lounge downstairs we can use."

The room is tight, barely able to contain the three sofas and countless side tables. Every surface is buried under books. Heaps of them spill across the floor – any attempt at order clearly abandoned.

"Sorry – I know it's a bit chaotic in here," Michael says. "But I make do. Please, have a seat." He brushes off a cushion and waves Lake over. "Go on, sit."

Lake sits, but tension settles over him. Michael stands in front of him, arms folded, then sinks into the opposite sofa with a long, hissed breath.

"It's clear to me you were set up," he says. "No easy way to put it."

"But Tracy couldn't have done this," Lake says. "No way. She's... beautiful, gentle –"

"She practically threw you out of the car. You've got to face the facts. Line up the pieces. It's the only way to find the truth. And as far as I can tell, Tracy Cox set the whole thing up."

"Why are you helping me?"

"I'm a sixty-year-old former martial arts champion. My time's passed. Now, I want to help others. If I can help you get justice, that's enough for me." Michael shrugs. "You deserve to be happy."

"But how am I supposed to find Tracy Cox?"

"She's probably settled back in the U.S. by now. But there might be one person who can help – your old headmaster."

"What?" Lake blinks.

"Trust me. I think he knows."

"That doesn't make sense."

"Nothing about this makes sense. But you need to confront him. Get to the truth."

"I can't do that."

"You're not ready – not yet." Michael leans forward, elbows on his knees.

Lake glances past him, briefly, at a heavy tome with a peeling spine.

"I'm going to teach you to fight," says Michael.

The next day, Lake is dragged from sleep in the early hours.

"What?" he mutters.

"Put this on."

"What?"

"This uniform."

In the blackness of the winter morning, Lake sees his rescuer standing in what looks like a karate uniform. Is it a karate uniform? It's hard to tell.

"Put this on," Michael Wool repeats. "Now." He points to the pile of white cloth dumped on top of Lake.

Lake runs his hands over the fabric. He makes out a jacket like the one Michael is wearing, and a pair of trousers. Somehow, despite the oppressive darkness, he manages to put them on.

"Follow me."

Michael's voice has shifted – no longer caring or grandfatherly. It's sharp now, almost violent.

"Where are we going?"

"The last classroom you'll ever step in."

It's mid-December, and snow has swallowed what little dignity the outside world had left. Every one of the mansion's five fireplaces is lit, but the cold still bites deep.

Lake and Michael finish their final sparring session of the day in the Classroom – a filthy, disused room on the east side of the house. It once served as the servants' quarters, but Michael has filled it with trophies and memorabilia from his career. They bow to each other and step back.

"You're coming on well," says Michael. "Can't believe how fast you're progressing."

"Revenge is what's pulling me through. What I'm going to do to the headmaster..."

"You need to pause. Don't let your emotions boil over. If you face him like this, you'll kill him. And then what? You've got to slow down."

"I will. I promise."

Lake's Christmas passes in a frozen blur of training and meditation, broken only on Christmas Eve and Day, when Michael cooks a feast for them both. They gorge themselves in the dining room, laughing and joking like best friends.

Lake excels – he knows it. It's as if he was built for this. Born for it.

As 1968 ends, he spends New Year's Eve in a punishing three-hour karate session. When a live radio broadcast from New York counts down to the new year, Lake sits nursing a bruised cheek.

Days fall into a rhythm of physical training and reading. Michael insists both are essential – balance the body and the mind. Lake dives into the classics, from Ancient Greece to the Victorian era. Each story draws him in deeper, until he wonders if he'll ever make it back out.

In February, he beats Michael for the first time, knocking him to the floor with a split lip. Michael crawls away like a wounded zebra while Lake stands, victorious.

Winter melts away. Spring arrives in a blaze of sunshine. Their sessions move outdoors. They ditch the uniforms. They fight in the mud, feet sticking and unsticking. Lake keeps winning. His strength soars. His body thickens with muscle.

"Less than a year, and you're stronger than I've ever been," Michael says in April. "Can't believe it."

By May, Lake has become the teacher. He still looks up to Michael – still respects him. He'll always be the sensei.

He admires Michael. Loves him like a father.

Near the end of the month, Michael says, "You're a son to me."

"Thank you," is all Lake can say.

"It's my birthday soon. The twenty-fifth. I'm throwing a party at the house. A lot of important people are coming. It would mean a lot if you were there."

"I'll be there, Michael. I promise."

"Good."

They've just finished training. The sun's dipped, and the wind is picking up. Michael rubs his arms. Lake stares at the mansion. From halfway up the slope they've been training on, it looks like a thumbprint on the land.

"I have a request," Michael says, voice dropping. "Would you stand with me at the door to greet the guests?"

"Of course!"

"Would you serve the wine?"

"I don't understand."

"When we're dining... would you serve us wine? It would mean a lot."

"I'd love to."

"Thank you, Clifford."

Michael gives him a tuxedo.

"It belonged to my son," he says, helping Lake into it. "Fits you well."

They stand before the large oval mirror in Lake's room. Michael's hands rest on his shoulders.

"You're stronger than you think."

Lake sees it. Thick with muscle. Toned. Sharp-eyed. He barely recognizes himself.

"We should greet our guests," says Michael.

They head down to the grand entrance porch – Lake's favourite part of the mansion. Marble floors, carved stone faces, miniature statues of forgotten heroes. It feeds the medieval fantasies of his boyhood.

Michael has told him, You're the son I never had, so many times that it's starting to grate.

"You'll love these people," whispers Michael. "Wonderful souls." His grey hair is slicked back with Brylcreem. He's ready.

"I've checked the table," says Lake. "Everything's set."

"Just need our guests."

An hour passes. Still nothing. No headlights. No voices. Just silence.

"Must be a road closure," says Lake.

"But they delivered the food earlier. There's only one road here."

"Maybe a crash."

"Ah, it's no use!" Michael snaps. "Christ's sake! I sent the invitations myself! They all confirmed!"

"I'm sure it'll be okay."

Another hour. Still nothing.

"Well, they've decided not to come." Michael rips off his bowtie and hurls it to the ground. "Fuck it, I'm getting drunk."

"I'm so sorry. I wish there was something I could do."

"Help yourself to the food. It's all paid for." He storms back inside.

Lake stays on the porch another two hours before giving up. He finds Michael passed out in the lounge, slumped in an armchair. Two empty wine bottles and a stained glass lie at his feet. In one hand, he clutches an iron key on a silvery chain.

Lake eases it from his fingers. The man doesn't stir.

He's curious. Maybe too curious. But he has to know. He's seen Michael carry this key everywhere. He's sure it unlocks the study – one of the few rooms off-limits.

It's my private, personal space.

At the door, Lake hesitates. He was raised better than this. But those days are gone. He slides the key in and turns. The echo of the lock snapping open makes him wince.

The room is windowless, stale. He finds a light switch and flips it. Harsh white light spills over the room. It's not what he expected. No fireplace. No armchairs. No cozy décor. It feels clinical. Cold. Like a nurse's office.

At the far end: a metal desk and plastic chair. Shelves line the walls, crammed with trophies.

"You certainly have a collection," he mutters.

But as he inspects them, he sees they're all blank.

One trophy sits on the desk. This one has writing.

Michael Wool. First Place. Southern Australia Karate Championships. November 1969.

"What the hell?"

To the right, another door. He opens it – unlocked. He fumbles for a light switch and slams it on.

Machines. Conveyer belts. Pistons. Displays. Bits of trophies. Piles of gold, silver, bronze sheets.

It hits him – the machines make trophies.

On a workbench, a small device with a fine needle. Nearby, a dust-covered trophy.

He holds it up, then looks at the device. It's an engraver.

"Christ," breathes Lake. "It can't be..."

He stumbles through the workshop, sickened.

Another door. He throws it open.

"No, no, no!" he howls.

He's seen this room before – in a news clipping at school. Michael Wool, famous kick, knockout blow to Hogarth Kern, legendary Australian champ.

It's a fighting arena. Spectator seats. A white mat marked with Japanese symbols.

Without thinking, Lake slips off his shoes.

"No! This isn't happening!"

A photography setup. Camera, tripod, lighting, reflectors.

Horrified, he retraces his steps. On the study desk, an envelope – opened.

No more good manners. He pulls out the letter.

Please find enclosed the bill of fifty pounds for our services. Billy's Acting and Costume School.

He reads it again. And again. But there's nothing else to learn.

He shuts off the lights, locks up, and returns to the lounge. Michael is still snoring. Lake slips the chain back into his hand.

The next morning, he sits opposite Michael, waiting calmly for him to wake.

Lake is already breakfasted, alert – enraged – but holds back, refusing to lash out until Michael opens his eyes.

"Sorry about last night," Michael croaks, licking his lips. His feet knock over empty wine bottles, and he curses under his breath. "Were you okay?"

"Why?"

"What do you mean?"

"Why did you lie to me?"

"What are you talking about?"

"I went into your study last night."

Michael's face crumples into panic.

"You've been kind to me," says Lake. "You saved my life, and I'll always be grateful – but you owe me an explanation for what I saw."

"Oh Clifford, I'm so sorry –"

"I don't care about sorry. I want the truth."

"I'm sorry."

"Just tell me the fucking truth!"

"I lied! I fucking lied! I'm sorry!"

"Stop saying sorry."

The once-mighty Michael Wool shrinks into his chair, eyes streaming. He can barely speak – words catching in his throat like glass shards.

"I've always been a coward!" he sobs. "I faked everything! The black belts, the trophies, the success!"

"Why? Why?"

"The fame! The glory! Oh, Clifford, I'm so sorry!"

"Shut up!" Lake's face twists into a snarl.

"Wha –"

"I've relit the fire..."

"What?"

Lake reveals the poker he's kept hidden behind his leg. He watches the so-called black belt freeze – eyes wide, terror and guilt colliding. He swings. Once. Twice. Both kneecaps crushed.

Michael howls. Lake doesn't pause. He drags him across the carpet, a streak of blood marking the path, and shoves his face into the fire. He holds it there – flesh sizzling, the stench making him gag – until the screams become muffled whimpers, until the tuxedo fuses to melting skin. Even then, he waits.

When it's done, he resists the urge to cry out. Why should he pity a fraud?

"Congratulations on your promotion to black belt," he mutters. "Congratulations, you backstabbing cunt. You filthy cunt. *You cunt. Cunt.*"

It takes him several days to clean the house, but he doesn't worry about being discovered. No one comes. No one cares.

He drags the body outside and burns it on the driveway. Then he sweeps the charred remains into the grass.

What troubles him is *what comes next*. He can't stay here. He needs to return to the world. He needs answers.

For two weeks, he trains, patrols the grounds – *his little kingdom* – and plots his return. What will he say to his old headmaster? What question could possibly unlock the truth?

Sir, could you tell me who was behind sending me to borstal?

One night, with nothing on the telly, he goes back into the study. He combs through every room. In the workshop, he finds more bills from Billy's Acting and Costume School. In the studio, he perches on the stage, imagining the match – Michael Wool versus a hired actor. A play dressed up as history.

He's about to give up when he notices the faint outline of another door.

This new room is smaller than any he's entered. Unlike the rest of the house, it's clean, ordered. An oak desk and a red leather chair give the space a stern, authoritarian feel. Built into the walls are seven safes with combination locks. Above the desk, a narrow shelf crammed with notebooks and paper.

He rifles through them.

Journals – confessions from a fake. His *first* karate match at sixteen (a win, of course). The day he "earned" his black belt. Falling in love. Losing his wife. Glory, grief, retirement from a career that never existed.

A man so enamoured with his own legend, he must have believed it.

On the final page of the last diary, Lake finds a series of numbers. He tries them. One by one, the safes unlock with mechanical precision.

Inside: wads of cash, stacked high in every currency. Fake identification documents from around the world.

Everything. The whole world. Right here.

The summer flies by. His plan to uncover the truth curdles into cold-blooded revenge. He envisions mutilating Bill Butterworth and his wife, ruthlessly torturing Ceri Britton and the other borstal staff. Only logic restrains him: he must pay a visit to Mr Stratton first.

There is one day – he'll want to forget it, bury it in concrete – when he loses control. Rage and hatred boil over. He ends up facedown in the living room, tears and saliva soaking into the carpet. When he lifts his head, a watery image flickers on the television. Neil Armstrong announces one giant leap for mankind.

"Man has walked on the moon," Lake murmurs.

The next day, he disappears into the hills.

A week later, he returns.

Destroying the clothes from his expedition is a meticulous task, but he's confident there's nothing linking him to the three girls he's killed over the past seven days.

That night, he watches a news report and smirks when a policeman dubs the murders the "Apollo Murders." But Lake is genuinely surprised when the name sticks. He's not caught. He's too smart for that.

He lies low, waiting for the dust to settle.

He trains relentlessly and teaches himself to drive using one of Michael's many cars. It comes naturally to him. He doesn't venture more than half a mile from the house – not until he's certain the investigation has run cold.

Strength builds on strength. He becomes a precise, lethal weapon.

On the one-year anniversary of his arrival, he allows himself a glass of wine and an evening off.

He's a man now. The youthful, fresh-faced beauty is gone. In brief flashes of the TV screen between scenes, he glimpses a new face – ragged, carved by time.

On 15th November, he makes his move.

In the early hours, he loads his gear into Michael's prized Bentley and sets off. He's calmer than expected. Focused. Ready.

It takes three days to reach Canterbury.

He finds himself with a full morning and afternoon to kill. As he wanders the city, he spots places where he once pined for Tracy. Shame creeps in. He's ashamed of how pathetic he was – how consumed by emotion when he should've just enjoyed what he had before it was ripped away.

He treats himself to a pub lunch – a luxury he's never known – and strolls through the older parts of the city like a tourist. It's been a long, long time.

As five o'clock approaches, he returns to the guest house. A lukewarm cup of tea steadies his nerves. Deep breaths. He's got this.

He dresses in black and slings his equipment bag over his left shoulder.

In the bitter cold, he walks the streets toward his old school. Memories cling to every brick. His gloved fingers curl around the railings as he stares at the stone walls, stained glass, and echoes of old voices.

Then the front door bursts open.

It's him.

Mr Stratton, briefcase in hand, marches out. Lake locks eyes on him as he heads for the gate, whistling cheerfully.

Lake follows – at a distance.

He remembers where Mr Stratton lives. Smiling at the memory of playing Knock Down Ginger on his doorstep at thirteen, he forces himself to stay focused, trailing twenty paces behind.

The ruse doesn't last long. Stratton still lives in that shabby little cottage near the school – the thatched roof sagging, garden wild, plants sickly. Still humming, he reaches his front door, pulls out his key, singing as he enters.

Lake is right behind him.

Stratton turns – just as a cloth covers his nose and mouth.

"There we are," says Lake. "Nice and easy.

Lake's already smiling as Mr Stratton opens his eyes. He's hung him from the ceiling by his wrists, cut away his clothes with surgical scissors. God, his body is so repulsive, just like the garden.

They're in his living room, which Lake has turned into an empty chamber. Furniture, school trophies, and photographs – everything removed, except for a table where he's placed his equipment and a chair he's sitting in. Six candles, positioned at precise intervals, cast a suffocating glow across the room.

"Good evening, sir," says Lake.

"What is this?" Mr Stratton can hardly speak. His voice croaks, bitter and struggling.

"You don't remember me, do you?"

"I don't keep the school money here, if that's what you're after. You'll have to go to the school itself."

"It's not the money I'm after. It's you. You really don't remember me, do you?" asks Lake.

"I've caned a lot of boys in my time. If you're after revenge, just get on with it."

"Oh, I'm after revenge, but... Are you seriously telling me you don't recognise me?"

"Did you fail your exams or something?"

"Well, I didn't have a chance to do my exams, because I was in borstal."

Mr Stratton forces a snarl. His eyes widen.

"Ah yes, now you're remembering..." Lake stands up, puts his face right before Stratton's. "It's Clifford Lake. You've probably forgotten, haven't you?"

"Was borstal fun?"

Lake clasps Stratton's ears and twists, causing him to yelp. "Don't be so fucking cocky," he hisses. "Now, I'm going to give you a chance." He releases his grip. "Tell me everything. Who was behind this?"

"Why do you want to know?"

"So I can pay them back."

"Clifford, I'm truly sorry for what happened." Stratton's voice starts to quiver.

"If you're sorry, then tell me who was behind this." He rotates Stratton's ears again.

"Please!" howls Stratton. "I can't say his name, he'd kill me."

"Who?!"

"Please!"

"Who?! Tell me, you bag of shit!"

"Gary Holmes!"

"Who is he?"

"He's a gangster! He told me to set you up!"

Lake removes his hands. "Right, now you're going to tell me everything. From the very beginning. I want to know names, dates, locations – everything. If I think you're leaving anything out, I'll cut your dick off. You understand?"

"Yes. I'll tell everything."

"Then do it! No time like the present, as you used to say."

"May, Nineteen-Sixty-Six. I think it was the Twenty-Third. I'm not sure. My diaries have everything in it."

"Where are your diaries?"

"In my study – the one I have here."

"Right. Go on with your story." Lake sits back down in the chair.

"I was walking out of the school, when a group of men approached me. One of them identified himself as Gary Holmes. He told me that I was to have you framed for rape, and he'd give me a thousand pounds for it. Clifford, the school needed the money. I did it for the school! Please believe me!"

"I don't give a shit. Is that it? Why did this Gary Holmes want to have me framed for rape?" shouts Lake.

"I noted it all down! I swear! Holmes was this really traditional sort of bloke. He's a gangster in the East End of London. Sat me down over a bottle of wine and told me. Please, oh please! Don't hurt me!"

"What did Holmes say?" bellows Lake.

"I felt really bad after you were arrested, I really did, so I noted it down. I really did! Honest!"

Lake slams his fists against the arms of the chair. "What the fuck did Holmes say?"

"One of his close friends was Roger Miser. Owns a record label. It was something about you signing on a member of one of his bands. Miser asked Gary Holmes to do something about it."

The sweet smile of Tracy Cox haunts him. That fucking, treacherous cunt. No surprise. "Why was Holmes telling you all of this? If he's a gangster, he'd be much more careful."

"Holmes thought that it was best for me to know the full details, so I didn't make any mistakes. He threatened to have my school torched if I told anyone."

"How did you set the accusation up?"

"Gary Holmes did. He paid a few coppers to get a girl to tell them you'd raped her. Please, Clifford, I didn't know you were going to borstal!"

"For two years, I was beaten and fed rotting food."

Mr Stratton starts crying openly. Wailing, coughing, shaking. "Oh, I'm so sorry! I'm so, so, so sorry! I didn't know! I felt really bad about it afterwards!"

"It's okay." Lake knows he will get nothing more from him. "Everything is in the notebooks?"

"Yes! Oh, I swear!"

"Then I have no more questions."

"Please let me go! I'll never tell anyone about this, I swear! I swear!"

"Oh, Mr Stratton, I'm not letting you go anywhere. Now, I accept that you feel remorseful for what you did, but you still went along with it..." Lake goes to the table and lifts his new toy up. It's a short rod with strands of barbed wire hanging from the end. "I know you're a religious man, Mr Stratton. I remember all those lectures you used to give us on the crucifixion. I've been a good little boy and done my homework, and I've prepared a real-life reenactment for you!"

"No! Please!"

"Before you ask, I've soundproofed the room. Have a look at your lovely new wallpaper!"

"I have two-thousand pounds, in cash, in my safe! All yours!" Stratton is whimpering, trembling.

All around them, the room has taken on a stillness. Lake moves the chair to the side, rolls up his sleeves, and shakes the rod to ensure that nothing is tangled.

"When I'm finished with this, I'll bring you to your back garden. There's a cross out there for you. You'll love it!" Lake exclaims. "It's handmade, very much like the real thing. You'll carry it to the bottom of your garden. I had a look out there earlier – it's quite a distance to the bottom. You'll carry the cross like Jesus did and then I'll nail you to it. Now, according to the bible, Jesus was scourged at the pillar. I'll start with the front of you, and then move to the back. Don't worry, I won't leave anything out. So, Mr Stratton, shall we get started?"

As dawn breaks, Lake admires his handiwork. His old headmaster hangs from the cross, nails through his ankles, legs, arms, hands, and a few fingers. He's barely recognisable: most of his skin has been cut away with the whip. A crown of barbed wire has been rammed onto his head, tearing into the scalp.

Lake sips coffee and munches on a warm croissant. He almost feels sorry for Mr Stratton, but there's no pity to be shared anymore. Only anger, vengeance, and retribution have any meaning.

He goes back inside, to the study. Rummaging through the diaries is a task that proves more difficult than expected, but he finds the one for 1966 without any major trouble. There's an old leather chair behind the desk, bits of it peeling off like bark. He sits down and starts leafing through.

Bloody hell, Mr Stratton made copious amounts of notes about absolutely nothing! The boring ins and outs of daily school life – pride and arrogance stuffed into a single packet. Things change on May 23rd. Everything is as he said. He came out of the school, was approached by a group of men, one of whom identified himself as Gary Holmes.

Mr. Holmes drove me a short distance away and asked, no, firmly requested that I sit inside his car. He said he had a task for me. His exact words were something along the lines of: "I know you have a boy at your school, Clifford Lake. He's caused my mate, Roger Miser, a bit of trouble. I'll keep this short. I want to get Clifford Lake out of the picture, if you know what I mean..."

I told him I couldn't possibly kill him.

"I'm not asking you to kill him," he replied. "I wouldn't ask a decent man like you to do that. But I do have a couple of coppers and a detective in the area. I'm going to pay them to frame Lake for a crime. Rape."

I tried to reason with him, saying Clifford Lake would never be suspected of something like that. He's a good, hardworking boy, always focused on his studies.

Holmes's response was something I can't quite remember, but it was along the lines of: "There are no limits to what I can do, Mr. Stratton. Now, all you have to do is be the dutiful headmaster you are. Call Lake into your office at the right time, and the boys in blue will arrest him. I can assure you, he won't go to prison. There's this new youth justice program I have connections to. He'll be tried and sentenced there. At most, he'll be doing some light labour around London."

I agreed to help. What choice did I have? Holmes had his men right there, standing by the car door. I've never been a fighter, and I'm certainly no hero. He invited me to one of his restaurants the next day to discuss the details further.

I can't help but feel the weight of this day, the stark contrast between waking up with God in my heart and now, feeling myself descend into madness.

Lake skips ahead to the next entry, May 24th.

His car arrived at the school gates around six in the evening, long after the last teacher had left. I was relieved no one noticed. The journey to London was quicker than I expected, although I had thought Gary Holmes would be driving me himself. Instead, it was one of his... associates, for lack of a better word.

The restaurant – if you can even call it that – was in a dilapidated area of East London, a place I pray none of the boys from this school ever end up in. Holmes had apparently closed it for the evening so we could dine together. I must admit, the food was exquisite. Only the finest wine, steak with creamy potatoes and asparagus – far beyond anything I could afford as a teacher.

Holmes told me everything. When I questioned his motives, he claimed he believed in complete transparency. "An honourable, decent man like yourself, I don't believe in deceiving. I was raised in the shadow of the docklands," he explained.

We dined for two hours, sipping wine and indulging in food I never dreamed I'd have the luxury of tasting. Despite his ruthless nature, Holmes proved to be quite charming. Afterward, he drove me back to Canterbury and wished me a peaceful night.

He told me everything, or at least, I believe he did. As I noted earlier, my memory of his words isn't perfect, but here's what I can summarize:

Jefferson Reed was part of a band signed to Roger Miser's label. Apparently, Reed wanted to leave but couldn't persuade Miser to release him from the contract. Instead, he signed with a new record label run by Clifford Lake.

I was shocked to hear Clifford had set up a label; he never seemed the type, and truth be told, I don't think he cares a thing about music.

But I digress. By the time Miser found out, Reed had fled to the United States. There was also a woman named Tracy Cox involved somehow, though it's unclear exactly how. Miser's anger, though, is directed at Lake. It's revenge. Holmes calls it "removing a problem," but I know better. I've taught long enough to recognize every kind of emotion, and this is about something deeper than business.

The question I'm left with is: what do I do now? Holmes has promised me money, as well as support for the school. If I sacrifice one innocent life, I could elevate this school to greatness. I know what I must do.

I pray for forgiveness. Oh Lord, I hope I'll be forgiven for this.

It's December now, and Clifford Lake sits alone in the mansion, watching the snow drift silently outside. The fire crackles in the hearth, its warmth doing little to ease the chill of the empty space around him.

He cradles a glass of whisky in his hand, his gaze fixed on the roaring flames. The solitude is absolute – no family, no friends, not a single soul to call upon. But it doesn't bother him. He has what he needs, and that's enough.

He takes a slow sip, his eyes still locked on the fire, his thoughts drifting as he dreams of what's to come.

Part 13

Victor Gully
Saturday, 4 July, 2009

He was to meet her at the Samuel Sapphire Restaurant in Soho, 8 p.m. sharp.

Victor Gully took a couple of deep breaths as he stepped out of Victoria Station. Everything felt too busy for him. Finding a taxi in this chaos was going to be a mammoth task. Ten years ago, he would have revelled in the heat and the chaos, the semi-naked women, the pulse of the city. Now, all he felt was a faint distaste for the rush around him.

He was eager, but restless. After their last meeting, he'd convinced himself she would never return to his life. Maybe that year she'd spent in Sweden had changed her. Maybe it had flipped a switch in her head.

Finally, he managed to flag a passing taxi. The driver rolled his eyes when Gully gave him the address.

The traffic was thickening. Red lights baked under the evening heat. Tempers flared. But once they passed Buckingham Palace, the jams began to ease, loosening like a clenched fist.

The letter had arrived on Friday afternoon at the arts centre. A message, simply signed by her – no pleasantries, no small talk. Just her first name.

When the taxi pulled up outside the Samuel Sapphire, Gully suddenly felt out of his depth. The blue lighting blasted from the windows, giving the place the look of a glorified nightclub. He saw the suits going in, and immediately felt underdressed in his dusty brown jacket and jeans. He paid the driver and stepped out, trying to project as much confidence as he could.

Wow, this place was seriously posh. Young, rich couples streamed inside. Wait – wasn't that one of the actors considered for the abandoned film adaptation of *The Church in the Square*?

The restaurant's facade was smooth, featureless stone. The name "Samuel Sapphire" glowed in blue neon—six or seven times. Red rope and scarlet carpet lay before the entrance. Two burly security men, faces expressionless, waved people through. No wonder the cab driver had given him the silent earful.

Suddenly, a flurry of flashes blinded him. Three paparazzi were photographing a glamorous woman in a sparkly purple dress, her ultra-thin figure commanding attention. Gully made his way past as politely as he could.

The two security guards stopped him dead in his tracks.

"Sorry, sir," one of them said. "Invitation only."

"I have an invitation," Gully replied. "Name's Victor Gully."

The bouncers exchanged a glance. One pressed his earpiece. "We've got a Victor Gully here, says he has an invitation. Right, sir, I'll send him through." He lowered his hand, looked at his partner, then back at Gully. "Okay, Mr. Gully, you're good to go."

"Thanks."

They opened the thin glass doors, and he stepped inside. A woman in a dark blue dress greeted him. She approached him almost threateningly, her voice soft but completely humourless as she asked his name. Smiling as though she knew him, as though he were family, she said, "This way."

He followed her through the maze of tables and the cream of London society. Stares came his way – whether it was recognition or condemnation, he couldn't tell. Everyone here seemed to be dressed like they were hiding themselves. Even the restaurant, with its flickering blue lighting and soft music pulsing from the ceiling, felt like a shield.

She was sitting alone at a table in the back. At some point, she'd decided to keep her hair long, now flowing loosely around her bare shoulders. At another point, she'd evidently decided to wear dresses. The one she wore tonight, he remembered from an awards ceremony in 2001. She stood when he approached and waved away his escort.

"Long time, no see!" she whispered, pulling him into a tight hug.

"Yeah, it's been a few years!" he replied.

"Please, sit. I've ordered us a bottle of red," said Scarlet.

"How've you been?" he asked, settling into his chair.

"I've been okay," she replied as they sat down. "How's the writing?"

"It's stalled, like a lot of other things!"

"Well, you'll be pleased to know I've read everything you've written. To be honest, *The Church in the Square* was my favourite."

"That's what everyone says!" he chuckled.

Scarlet leaned forward and placed a soft hand on his shoulder. "Listen, before we eat, let me get straight to the point. I've been keeping an eye on what you've been doing near Canterbury. I know it's been tough, especially after that business with Jarrett. Awful stuff. I'm giving your arts organization a small cash injection."

"I really appreciate this, Scarlet; it means a lot to me. I'll be honest, I've been counting down the days until the end of summer."

A waiter approached with the bottle of wine, uncorked it. Scarlet raised a hand to stop him, indicating she'd pour it herself. She filled their glasses, hers first. Gully risked a quick glance at the bottle: a sixteen-year-old Argentinian malbec.

"To good health," she said, raising her glass.

Another waiter appeared, notepad in hand.

"Sorry, I didn't give you a chance to look at the menu properly," Scarlet said to Gully.

"It's okay," he replied, eyes darting over the expensive laminated items. "I'll have the soup for starters, and the salmon for mains."

"Never took you for a salmon person," she quipped. "I'll have the pate to start. For mains, I'll take the steak. And can you bring another bottle as well?"

"What projects do you have on the horizon?" he asked.

"Well, I've been thinking about a return to music – as a solo artist." Her eyes dropped. "Maybe an autobiography. Not sure. Mostly, I'm just trying to enjoy life. After Sweden... I've become a different person. I've even quit smoking. Exercise nearly every day. No takeaways, no spirits. Just good wine, good company."

"I think –"

"Hold on a second, there's something else I have for you. I've spoken to a friend of mine in the literary world and mentioned your name. You've got a slot at the Coldstream Book Festival next weekend."

"Thank you! How did you manage to swing that?"

"I persuaded them to add you as a last-minute addition to an author panel. You should get the details by email on Monday."

"Why are you doing this for me?" asked Gully.

"Because my last words to you weren't kind. I feel like I need to make it up to you."

"Honestly, you don't need to," said Gully. "That day in the café... I think it was emotional for both of us."

"Well, you've got a slot."

They left the restaurant together, both mildly drunk.

"My car should be here in a moment," she said.

A flash from a paparazzi camera enveloped them both. Scarlet shot the photographer a dark look, and he started backing away.

"I'll give you a lift to the station," she offered. "Actually, shit, it's nearly ten. What time does the last train leave?"

"I'm not sure."

"I've got three guest bedrooms for you to choose from. Why don't you stay the night?"

"I thought you still owned your parents' old house?" Gully asked. A trickle of saliva collected at the back of his throat, causing him to gag. He quickly muffled an apology.

"I do, but I've got a new apartment in Chelsea. Lovely penthouse. I think you'd like it."

"Okay, then."

"The car's here."

Though he wasn't sure if he'd ever been here, he recognized it immediately. As Scarlet thanked the driver, Gully tried to mouth a series of questions. Once the car had pulled away, she gave him a reassuring pat on the shoulder.

"Bloody hell!" he exclaimed. "How...?"

"It's a long story. Lots of negotiations. A few tears here and there, you get the picture. But, well, here we are..."

Scarlet led him around the back of the apartment block, where a rusty spiral staircase wound its way up to Roger Miser's old penthouse. As they climbed, flickers of memory came back. Maybe he had been here before, most likely drunk.

Inside, the apartment felt emptier than one would expect for someone of Scarlet's standing. Aside from two cream-colored sofas and a glass dining table, there was little in the way of furniture or decoration.

"I prefer to keep things simple," she said. "Well, with the exception of wine..." She gestured toward a large rack crammed with bottles.

"Thanks for this. I didn't fancy crawling through Canterbury in the early hours."

"Not a problem. Always happy to help when I can. You're a decent man, Victor. Just remember that."

"Thanks."

"Take a seat. I've got another bottle of that wine we had at the restaurant, if you'd like a glass."

"Yeah, I'd really like that."

He let himself fall onto one of the sofas, his eyelids growing heavy. The room was quiet, but his attention was drawn to the latest model of plasma television. Yet, it wasn't the flat screen that caught his eye – on its glass support stand sat a faded photograph. He leaned in closer.

"We had that taken in Glasgow," said Scarlet, approaching with two full glasses. "Nineteen-Ninety. On our way to our very first performance. Seems like a lifetime ago now. Well, it was."

A stab of sadness hit him. Susan's face – so young, so innocent, so perfect – brought a lump to his throat. He didn't care that his eyes were welling up. He didn't care.

"She was lucky that you came into her life," Scarlet said softly, handing him his glass. "She was really bloody lucky."

"Where is Coldstream?" Gully asked, breaking the silence.

"It's in Scotland, right on the border with England. Funny little place. But they're holding a big smash there this year. The Coleburn family is sponsoring it."

"The Coleburn family?"

"Oh, just some rich family who own a bunch of media outlets. Anyway, they're sponsoring the festival this year. I think you'll have a great time."

"I hope so."

Sunday, 5 July, 2009

He woke the next morning with a thumping headache. Sitting up in the unfamiliar bed, he reached for the glass of water and downed it in one go.

The guest bedroom was more barren and basic than the rest of the penthouse. The only redeeming feature was a giant photograph of a motorcyclist on an epic journey across a desert somewhere. He'd fallen asleep like a pin dropping into a well last night, so hadn't bothered to take it in. Now, feeling the effects of the hangover, he admired—and envied—the brave soul riding off into the sunset.

"Sleep well?" Scarlet stood in the doorway.

"I did, thanks," he replied, his voice still dry. "Think I had one too many of those glasses, though."

"We always used to do the same, back in the day." She snorted with laughter. "Listen, a quick breakfast, then I need to turf you out. I've got a couple of people coming over for a photoshoot. A magazine thing."

Waiting for his train, Gully thought about her. Over the years since that event in the café, he'd often imagined the conversations he wanted to have with Scarlet – dreaming and hoping for the day when the two of them would finally sit down and talk. Like it or not, Scarlet was the link to Susan, his chance to understand who she really was. And now that the reconnection had come and gone, there was so much he wished he had said.

Monday, 6 July, 2009 – Friday, 10 July, 2009

His week passed in a blur—emails and messages interrupted by written passages. During his lunch breaks, which often stretched into hours, he would go over the arrangements for his Saturday event. A bloody boring event on the future of journalism. His fellow guests were from the tabloids and broadsheets, no doubt eager to share their views.

He set off early on Friday. Despite good planning, the journey took several hours. He hadn't driven such a long distance in ages and, despite the satnav, got lost just south of Newcastle-Upon-Tyne. After one unnecessary and nerve-wracking mistake, he found himself stuck in city-centre traffic. When he finally emerged on the north side, he felt at least ten years older.

Upon reaching Coldstream, the satnav thankfully guided him straight to the hotel, which was just a short walk from the festival venue. It was clear that publishers and sponsors had booked the place out, judging by the packed car park.

The chain hotel, bathed in green, blue, and grey light, reminded him of the headquarters of the primary antagonist in the gangster novel he'd once dreamed of writing – a vision, thankfully, that never came true.

Checking in took nearly half an hour, thanks to an elderly couple asking the manager about every single thing the hotel had to offer – and then repeating their questions. By the time his turn finally came, he had transformed into that impatient twenty-year-old who'd written into the early hours – a man both exhausted and determined.

"Sorry for the delay," said the manager, looking just as bored and irritated as Gully.

"No worries. Checking in – Victor Gully."

"*The* Victor Gully? *The Church In The Square*?"

"Yeah, that's me."

"Such a great novel. How did you achieve so much success so young?"

"I truly don't know." Gully tried to laugh it off. "Sorry, it's been a long drive."

"Not a problem. Anyway, I should have you checked in momentarily."

"Thanks."

"Okay, here we go... Just a second... Alright, that's you." The manager handed him a keycard. "Get some rest, Mr. Gully. It's good to have you here."

Saturday, 11 July, 2009

It was the first event of the day, held in the main festival tent. The air was thick with humidity, the canvas of the tent sagging slightly under the weight of the morning sun. Sweating from the already warm day, Gully took his seat and sipped some water. The tent buzzed with the low murmur of anticipation, and the faint smell of fresh coffee mingled with the earthy scent of grass from outside.

The moderator shuffled through his papers as the applause died down, pushing his round glasses further into his face. "Well, good morning, everybody," he said, "and I'm pleased to welcome you to this event, *Journalism: A Future Worth Living For*. My name is Melville Braddock, and I'm a writer and journalist. I'm really thrilled to be chairing this event, and I'm privileged to have several distinguished individuals with me. On my far right is Tod Kingston. Tod is a journalist based in New York, writing for a variety of newspapers and magazines. His new book, *A Random Character: Why Journalism Is Losing Its Appeal*, is a bestseller in the U.K. and he was recently featured in a documentary series on corruption in the media. On my immediate right, Dominic Abel. He is a well-respected columnist at several major newspapers and was recently nominated for a string of awards for his exposé on the East Anglia Communist Movement. On my immediate left, Dionne Kersey. Dionne is well known for her crime reporting for several tabloid newspapers but has recently relaunched herself as a crime novelist. Her debut book, *Night Fire*, the first in the Inspector Ravenna Randall series, was published last month. Lastly, on my far left, is Victor Gully. Mr. Gully is perhaps best known for his debut novel, *The Church In The Square*, which launched him to international acclaim."

"Introductions done, let's get straight into it. Journalism is not in the greatest place right now. What are your thoughts on potential scaremongering over swine flu? Tod, why don't you start this off?"

"Of course. Well, what I'll say is that things have been… a little over the top." Tod Kingston spoke with absolute authority on the subject. You could sense it from the tone, the narrowing of his eyebrows, the way he refused to make eye contact with anyone. A clear sense of superiority.

Gully wasn't surprised that he barely got a word in during the event – and even more so when the others were cast into that sparkly silence. When the moderator finally brought the event to a close, the applause was all directed at Tod and his new book.

Afterwards, there was an opportunity to sign books in the festival's shop. Shelves upon shelves of the latest publications filled the tent, so much so that people were crammed together like sardines. Two staff members tried to keep order, but their tired faces betrayed their resignation.

Gully found himself seated between Tod Kingston and Dionne Kersey at a long table dedicated to signings. A poster behind him, peeling away from the tent fabric, declared: *Meet Your Favourite Authors*. Gully's first customer was a fresh-faced kid. He scribbled his signature on the page, not bothering to look up again.

As the signing drew to a close, Dionne began to look flustered. "That was a complete waste of time," she complained.

"Utter fucking waste of time. Three fucking readers." A cigarette appeared between her lips as she stormed toward the exit.

"I'm heading back to the hotel," Tod said. "It was great to meet you, Victor. Have a nice day."

"Great to meet you too." Gully checked his phone for messages, then looked up to see the tent nearly empty, except for an elderly, fairly chubby woman vacuuming the floor. Just as he was about to get up, the cleaner waddled over to him.

"Do you mind?" she asked, holding out a copy of *The Church In The Square*.

"Oh my word!" he exclaimed. "How did you get this? Bloody hell! Sorry…"

"It's quite okay," the woman said.

"I never thought I'd see another copy of the first edition. They only did a print run of a hundred. Oh, my, my, my…" He flicked his pen over the inside page. "Sorry, do you want a personal dedication?"

"If you please. For Sharmaine Bateson."

"No problem… Right, there you go!"

"Thank you so much. Can I just say, I'm a massive fan of yours? I've read everything you've done. Makes my life in Newcastle a bit more interesting!" Sharmaine gave a crooked grin.

"That makes a change. Normally it's the church book people care about. I've never figured out why it became such a bestseller, why people are so obsessed with it." He knew how desperate he sounded, but the mystery of it all hung over him like a hood.

"Well, I think you're a wonderful writer."

"Thank you."

"Right, no time to dally around!" The lady gave him a small grin. "Back to work!"

"See ya." But as he made for the exit, he stopped. "That's a hell of a commute you've got, isn't it? All the way from Newcastle?"

"Oh no, not quite!" The old lady's eyes lit up. Sapphires in a hailstorm. "No, I mainly work at Newcastle Airport as part of the cleaning team, but the company I'm with occasionally sends us to other venues. All part of our contract."

"Oh, right. Well, I'd better be off. It was nice to meet you, Sharmaine."

"Likewise."

He lay awake that night, tracing the patterns and swirls on the ceiling. Frustrated, bitter, annoyed, and jealous of Tod Bloody Kingston. What a fucking arrogant prick! A smack in the jaw would have come in handy.

"Why, oh why?" he muttered. "Why the fuck did I come up here?"

If Ellar Cameron had been there, well, that would've been a very different set of spanners. At least he would have dominated the session and given it some spirit!

After another small bottle of vodka, the rippling corners of sleep began to claim him. Flashes of his childhood, of memories of girls he once fancied running in pretty dresses, of forgotten words.

School bullies telling him in stern voices: *"You'll never be a writer, Victor. You're fucking shit. Post that piece of shit to*

Wormwood Scrubs. They'll jerk off over it after their morning porridge."

Yet, he did it. *The Church In The Square* turned his teenage years into international bravado.

Red bursts of light when he asked a girl to a Christmas dance. Green blinks as he landed in New York... as a kid... for the start of his book tour for *The Church In The Square*. White flashes as the media stuck him to every front page. Blue flashes as he woke up.

"What the...?"

The ceiling flickered and blinked in multiple shades. Sirens added to the mix.

He moved to the window, seeing the gathering of police cars. Screaming.

He dressed quickly, throwing on whatever he could. Bounding down the stairs like a rabbit, no time to wait for the lift that always seemed to take forever. The stairs were cold and unstable, but they led him down.

Police surrounded someone in the centre of the lobby. Some had batons out. Gully strained to see who it was, but they were drunk, judging by their slippery feet.

"My boy!" the person yelped. "My boy! My boy!"

"Things okay?" he asked, but his words didn't seem to matter.

"Calm down," one of the officers said to her. "Let's just calm down."

The woman's voice could pierce lead. Gully could sense her brokenness—something that simply couldn't be captured.

The cleaning lady. Sweet Sharmaine, now dishevelled, her uniform ripped, eyes leaking like taps. She held a bottle in her hand, sucking on it, summoning the last dregs.

"My boy!" she cried out. "My boy, gone!"

"Stand back, please, sir," one of the officers said to Gully.

"I know her!" Gully yelled.

"Don't care. After what she's just done – smashing a policewoman in the head with a bottle – she's spending the night in the cells. Please leave the area, sir."

Perhaps in a distant day, he might have taken a stand, but now, he stepped back. He noticed her glare of disgust, but he backed away, dipping his head. Even when she called his name, when she launched insults, when she mocked his little face, when she provoked him with Susan, he simply kept walking.

Part 14

R oger Miser
Tuesday, 17 June, 1980

There were no words to describe a girl who had simply gone. Patsy Monroe had made her decision. Roger Miser stared at the bed where he'd had his cuddles with her and shrugged his shoulders. Well, there was a new girl now anyway. Claudine, with her straw-coloured hair, gave him satisfaction on every level. Claudine Blackstein completed him, in the strangest way.

Dressed to his best, tie done up neatly, he set off.

As promised, Claudine had given him her number and address, and he'd phoned her yesterday. Dinner had been promptly arranged for tonight – with her father in attendance as well.

She lived a mile outside of town, to the northwest – far from the carnage and trauma that poor Charlie Petter had unleashed. Miser was expecting to be grilled tonight on that. He imagined her father as a stern fellow with narrow eyes and a military haircut.

He decided to walk rather than take a taxi and soon found himself outside the hub of musical bravado that St Pierre had mutated into. Finding the Blacksteins' house was surprisingly easy, even though the roads here were nameless and the dying, blistering heat distracted him constantly.

"What a dump," he remarked under his breath. A cottage smothered in overgrowth, its front garden begging for a cleanup. The windows were caked in spiderwebs and grime. A car, halfway to becoming a skeleton, rusted away on a driveway built from cracked paving slabs. Yet, despite the chaos, there was a strange sense of order – as if the decay had been purposefully arranged.

Concerned he'd got the address wrong, he approached the front door to double-check. Yep, Number 51. He raised his fist and hammered down.

"I'll get it!" a male voice shouted from inside.

The door opened. Not quite what Miser had imagined, except for the trimmed moustache. A man stood there in a white shirt and silver tie, hair combed and gelled into place. A brown leather-strapped watch hugged his wrist.

"You must be Roger Miser," he said. Not the slightest hint of friendliness. A very firm handshake was the only bridge between them. "I'm Miles Blackstein, Claudine's father. Please, come." His sharp American accent cut through the humid evening air.

Keeping his eyes low, Miser followed him inside. The gentle smell of gravy and mashed potatoes wrapped around him, making his stomach growl. Christ, he was ravenous.

The kitchen was crammed to the brim – half-prepared food, cutlery, crockery, cookbooks splitting at the spines – but the old mahogany table in the centre gleamed, as clean as a whistle. The father of the girl he – yes, he needed to bloody admit it – fancied, gazed at him like he wanted to devour him alive. There was hunger in this house.

"Please," said Miles. "Sit."

"Thank you."

Claudine stood at the stove, stirring a pot with a large wooden spoon. "Stew's almost ready. It's lamb. Hope you like it, Roger."

"So, the great Roger Miser then," said Miles. "I said, *please sit.*"

Miser sat, feeling suddenly small. Too humble. Too polite. Too bloody feeble.

"You found us okay?" asked Claudine.

"I did. Bit of a strain on the legs, but I got here without any bother."

"How are things going at the festival?"

"Very well. Well, except for the recent incident with Charlie Petter. Can't believe what happened. But things are moving forward."

"Let's hope so," said Miles, uncorking the wine with knuckles turning white.

Claudine glared at her father. She ladled out steaming stew into three bowls and tossed them down onto the table. She fetched a plate of bread from the sideboard. "Bon Appetit."

"What got you into the music industry, Roger?" asked Miles.

"Fancied something challenging."

"You certainly got it."

"Well, I'd hoped to make a splash, as they say. Things turned out... interesting. This summer is about my legacy, about getting the next generation ready. The decade ahead will be challenging, but rewarding. You've got to be ready to brace for the unpredictable –"

"And you're not." Miles let his spoon drop to the rim of his bowl, an ear-piercing clatter ripping through the kitchen.

"Well, I wouldn't put it like that. But I need to step away. I'm thinking of it as a handover, you could say. One hundred singers and bands are going to be selected. One hundred."

"Well, it's some party, I can say that for sure," said Miles. "You've raked up the whole goddamn town."

"It's had the full blessing of the mayor," said Miser. "My festival will put St Pierre on the map. Anyway, enough about me, tell me about yourself, Miles. I've noticed you've got a thick New York accent. Are you from there?"

"Yeah. Twenty years as a NYPD homicide detective. Retired two years ago, came out here. Actually, my last case involved two of your friends, Keith and Philip Leighton."

"Oh, Christ, I remember."

"The sons of bitches tried to take on the mob," said Miles, shaking his head. "Their lawyer was found at the bottom of the Hudson with his tongue cut out and fingers sliced off."

"Awful story. Philip told me all about it. Poor Keith – I know the effect the whole thing had on him. He's practically catatonic."

"Do you think I care?" Miles took a sip of his wine. "I know you're eager to go out with my daughter. Let's be clear about that."

"Yes, I do." Miser felt his neck grow hot. "She's beautiful. She's amazing. I really like her – I really like you, Claudine. Really, I do."

"You're a man with a string of marriages behind you. I don't trust you," Miles said, voice dropping to a dangerous quiet.

"It's for me to make the decision," said Claudine. Her stew seemed to drown her.

"But I'm your father," said Miles. His harsh accent tore through wood and metal alike. "You will do as you're damn-well told."

"What was it like being a cop in New York?" Miser said, desperately trying to steer the conversation away from disaster. Miles seemed like every strict father's nightmare. Christ, the man was *cunning*.

"It was okay, until I got flushed out," said Miles.

"I thought you said you retired?"

"Officially. When you're a cop in New York, they say don't trust anybody. I followed that rule my whole goddamn career. Slipped up once. That was enough."

"You must have some stories from your time there," said Miser, probing carefully.

"Shooting a lot of bad guys dead, you want to know what that's like? Is that what you're trying to get at?"

"Well, no –"

"I shot a lot of men. Mainly black guys causing trouble. Trust me, you don't want to know the horror stories. Stabbings, rapes, mutilations. Men, women... children. Lives changed forever. You don't want to know."

"And it's not something to be discussing over dinner," said Claudine sharply. "I propose a toast. What are we drinking to?"

"Whatever you want," said Miles. "Do I look like I care?"

After dinner, while Claudine was cleaning up, Miles took Miser out into the back garden. The tension seemed to have drained from the former cop – his breathing was steadier, and he even cracked a smile. He'd poured them both a whisky. As he handed Miser the glass, his forefinger pressed briefly into the crook of the younger man's elbow. Not hard. Just enough.

"Thanks for having me over," Miser said. "Your daughter, I really like her."

"I know you do. You've got my blessing."

"Thank you. That means a lot."

Miles nodded, then looked off across the yard. "She means the world to me. My wife's been gone ten years. Claudine's all I've got."

"I'll be good to her. Faithful. I promise. Well – I still need to ask her out first."

"Then do that. But listen to me." Miles turned, his eyes steady. "If you play games with her, if you lie to her, if you hurt her in any way – I'll bury you. You understand?" A pause. Then, softly, almost kindly: "Now go inside. Talk to her. Ask her out. And then fuck off back to your hotel."

She'd said yes. Relief, yes – but he wasn't celebrating. Truth was, something in her had dimmed. That shimmer he'd seen before? Gone. He gave her a light kiss on the cheek and left, saying he'd meet her tomorrow night at the hotel bar for that long-promised drink.

The day's heat had bled into the night sky. He paused, looking up at the stars. For a moment, he pictured himself up there – weightless, remote. He remembered the night Skylab fell. He'd stayed up for hours, watching the sky, hoping for even the faintest glint. A waste of time. Futile, like most of his hopes.

Roger Miser had spent most of his life among the stars, one way or another. Usually slumped in a chair, half a bottle of vodka in his left hand.

When he got back to the hotel bar, he found George sitting alone, a glass of whisky untouched in front of him.

"How'd it go, Roger?" George asked.

"Well, her father's a complete wanker. Apart from that, lovely evening."

"What did she say?"

"She's meeting me for a drink. Tomorrow."

"Congratulations." George slumped forward, voice low. "There's been another incident. A fight. Guy knocked his girlfriend out cold. Smashed all her teeth in."

"Christ. When?"

"You know that café we've been having lunch at? That couple we always see? It was them. He thought she was checking you out. They argued out in the street. He swung for her. Caught her square in the face." George mimed it – an ugly gesture, complete with a sloshing sound effect.

"Jesus, George. You're pissed. Go sleep it off." Miser put a hand on his shoulder. "We've got another full day tomorrow. This is our town, our summer. Goodnight."

Wednesday, 18 June, 1980

The hotel bar wasn't the greatest, sparkiest place for a first date – but it was quiet, at least. They sat in the corner by the window. Rain tapped gently at the glass, like a long, hesitant kiss. Between them, a solitary candle flickered, its flame beginning to shiver.

"Your father's an interesting man," Miser said. "He certainly tore into me."

"He means well. He really does."

"I can't believe you said yes. I was shitting myself, honestly."

She laughed – perfect teeth, all in line. He reached out, let his hands touch hers. She didn't pull away.

"What do you even see in me?" she asked. "I'm not a movie star. I'm just... common. A common girl. Hair tied back. Plain as bread. That's who I am. I'm not one of your festival highs and lows. Is that really what you're after, Roger? Really?"

"What's wrong with that?"

"You seriously think I'm okay as I am?"

"Claudine, I've spent years trying to be someone else. I'm done with that. This festival – it's my legacy, my soft landing. I'm just trying to be... a regular guy."

He could feel the effort in his throat as he spoke, like forcing soft words through clenched teeth. But sometimes that was the price.

"Well, you've got your work cut out for you."

"So, tell me about your background."

"It's more complicated than you think," he said.

"Believe me, I've heard complicated before. Try me."

"I'll have to tell you later," he said, nodding past her. "Your friends are here."

She turned. "Oh, sh –"

Bruce Ryall stood in the doorway, arms relaxed, one thumb resting casually near the small pistol strapped to his waist. On either side of him, Little Dave Perkins and Big Dave Rogers emerged, moving forward like shadows cast in sync. Claudine's eyes widened.

"Guys, can I help you?" Miser stammered. "Guys, please."

The trio split to the sides as Gary Holmes stepped through. The fat, affable brute glanced around, nodding as if approving a restaurant. "Lovely place," he muttered. "Yeah. Not bad."

"How can I help you?"

"Sorry to interrupt your evening, Rog," Holmes said, lighting up a cigar. "But there's been a bit of a situation. You need to come with me."

Smoke drifted lazily upward. He licked his lips, winced slightly. Heavy breathing filled the pause.

"Mr Holmes," said Miser, "I'm... on a date."

"And I'm sorry to ruin it. Truly. But this is urgent."

"Can't it wait?" Miser asked, keeping his voice flat.

"Rog, I wouldn't be here if it could. Sorry, darling," Holmes added to Claudine, "but your boyfriend's needed elsewhere."

Miser stroked her elbow. Her skin was warm beneath his fingers – soft, sure, and unknowable. Christ, was he in love?

"I'm really sorry about this," he said. "I mean it."

"It's fine," she said, coldly. "I'll just go back to my father and soak up more of his charming company. Wouldn't want to get in the way of you two lovebirds. I mean – who the fuck is he?" Her face twisted. "Well?!"

"His name's Gary Holmes," said Miser. The dread in his chest churned with embarrassment. "He's... an old associate."

Claudine shook her head. Her fingers dug into the table. He reached out again, but she pulled back, grabbed her coat. Heels clacked on tile as she shoved past the men.

Big Dave couldn't help himself. "Bloody hell, Mr Miser, she's a moody bit of meat!"

"You watch your hole!" Holmes snapped. "Or I'll button you up." He took a long drag on his cigar. "Right. Rog. Time to go."

Miser didn't argue. Nobody said no to Gary Holmes.

By the time the convoy arrived, night had fully collapsed. The rain had stopped, but the damp still clung to Roger Miser's ankles, cold and creeping.

Gary Holmes led the way through a sea of police cars. Blue lights burned holes in the dark. Miser didn't need to ask if they'd been paid off – it was blindingly obvious.

"Rog, I'm truly sorry," Holmes said, laying a heavy hand on his shoulder. "I mean it. I'm so sorry."

Patsy Monroe's body lay at the roadside. Her eyes stared blankly into nothing. Her face was pale, drained of every-thing. Arms flung wide like a fallen doll.

Beside her was a man, collapsed in a similar sprawl.

Miser knew him immediately. Serge Ferris.

"Tell me what happened," he said, the words sharp, brittle.

"Him," said Holmes. "It's him. He's making his move."

He turned to face Miser fully now. His voice dropped.

"Rog, mate – we need to finish this. Now."

Part 15

Victor Gully
Monday, 3 August, 2009

Since *The Church In The Square* had been published, Victor Gully hadn't just been ostracised by friends and family – he'd been shunned by other writers, too. Too young, they said, to join their elite little club. No rejections under his belt. Too famous, too fast.

But as the years passed, the resistance softened. Not into acceptance – he would never get that. He would always be the outsider. The little kid who never quite grew up.

His romantic life had been sparse, broken. The ones who rushed to his side left just as quickly. Only Susan had really stayed. The rest had been replaced with unsavoury comforts – escorts, discreet upper-class women who gave him the illusion of significance. A rented kind of affection. A performance of intimacy.

Still, the fake love hadn't filled the gap. And worse, the work had started to suffer. The more he wrote, the more the flaws showed. The more dissatisfied he became. His stories stuttered, lost their pulse. Started and stopped like broken engines.

Since Coldstream, though, he'd had time to reflect – on the path he was on, the man he wanted to become. That place had rattled him. The horror he'd seen in Sharmaine, the raw brutality of her loss, had left its mark. Something had to shift. It was time for a change. A fresh beginning.

This residency would soon be over. He'd be out of a job – not that he needed one. The Far East called to him: travel, escape, a new cast of characters. His life was always one fiction after another.

He closed his laptop, flexed his fingers, and paced the room – what had once been Henry Jarrett's apartment. Most of Jarrett's things were gone, but a few notebooks and oddments still lingered. A curse? Maybe. Was it an exaggeration to call the residency cursed?

Later, he wandered through the village and ducked into The Lake Arms for a quick drink. He didn't stay long. He could feel the eyes on him. The hush in the room. The unease.

The rain had started its dance again by the time he walked back. He stopped on the lane, gazing toward the darkening horizon, wondering if Susan might be out there, looking up at the same sky. He closed his eyes.

And the illusion vanished.

Part 16

L ake
January, 1970

He finishes his thoughts just as the first snowflakes start to fall.

A smile creeps across his face. He sets down the coffee cup and warms his hands by the hearth. It won't be long now, and he wants his guests to feel welcome. After all, isn't he such a gracious host?

No point denying it: his plan for revenge is in full swing. And frankly, he's amazed at how quickly it came together over Christmas. Just a few days, and everything snapped into place like it was waiting for him.

Nine o'clock. The chimes ring through the mansion – *his* mansion. He walks calmly to the front steps as two sets of headlights appear on the horizon. Right on time. He slips behind one of the grand stone pillars, watching them approach.

Both cars pull up. Doors open. Immediately, the shouting starts.

"What the hell are you doing here?" snaps one.

"Fuck you, that's my question!" barks the other.

Lake suppresses a laugh. It's like watching two teenagers argue over a mixtape. Pathetic.

He steps into view, waving breezily. "Hi, both! Quick life tip: when you get a letter in the post saying five million pounds is hidden in an abandoned house, maybe do a little background check first."

Morton Jerkov stumbles back. "Very funny. Is this your idea of a joke, Lake?"

Fabrice Ortelli – fatter, sweatier, and somehow even slimier – can't even form a word. Christ, the man's grown sideways. Lake feels his stomach turn.

"You know me," Lake says. "I don't joke. Borstal knocked that habit out of me."

"I'm done with this," Jerkov snaps, wrenching open the car door. "Clifford, you've no idea what kind of shit you're in. This time it won't be Borstal – it'll be a real prison, sunshine."

Lake moves fast. Down the steps and across the gravel in a blink. The kitchen knife plunges into Jerkov's throat. One deep strike, then again. And again. The old bastard finally topples, twitching, his breath cut short. Lake steps back, breathing hard, a grin curling up at one side of his face.

Ortelli's panicking. He's somehow wedged himself into the driver's seat, jabbing the key at the ignition like a child. Lake strolls over, whistling, and plucks the keys from his shaking hand.

"Mr. Ortelli," he says gently, "no need to panic. I'm just here to say thank you – for everything. Remember the cuddles you used to give me?" He leans in close. "Time to return the favour."

"Please, don't hurt me!"

"Oh, Fabrice. I wouldn't dream of it. Ah – here they are."

A black van appears on the road, coughing smoke. Lake lifts Ortelli from the seat and props him up like a broken mannequin.

"You're about to go off on a grand old adventure!" he says, cupping Ortelli's face and kissing him full on the lips. "All for you."

The van stops. Two men climb out, gloved hands ready. Lake steps aside like a magician revealing a trick.

"Here he is," he says. "Handle with care."

Ortelli flails. "What's going on?"

Lake leans in. "You're going to Asia. You'll be joy and pleasure for a very niche clientele. Sorry, too poetic? Let me be blunt: I've sold you into Asia's sex trade."

Ortelli nearly collapses. The men catch him.

"Take him away, boys."

"No! Please – don't – please!" he screams.

Lake gives a little wave as the van door slams.

"Your boss get the payment?" he asks the driver.

"All taken care of," comes the flat reply. "Thanks for your business."

"No problem at all. Be gentle with him. He's terribly sensitive."

Once the van disappears, Lake moves both cars to the garages. He douses Jerkov's body in petrol, strikes a match, and watches until there's nothing left but blackened ash. Then, methodically, he digs a grave and buries the remains.

By lunchtime, the bloody clothes have been burned. The driveway is spotless.

He pours himself a drink after dinner and settles by the hearth, staring into the flames.

Two more down.

"Two more down," he whispers.

January, 1971

A year has come and gone.

Clifford Lake stands in the kitchen, brewing yet another pot of coffee. The scent drifts through the quiet house – a house he's called home for over two years. But now, the end is near. A long week stretches ahead: packing, cleaning, saying goodbye.

The thought is almost surreal. A year has passed without another soul to talk to, and yet, here he is, still standing in the same spot, still breathing. He lets the moment settle in, his fingers tapping against the edge of the counter.

He carries the steaming cup to one of the top-floor living rooms. Through the expansive windows, he watches the snow fall relentlessly, each flake caught in the pale light. Flurry after flurry, each one as cold and indifferent as the last.

In one week, he'll be gone. A homeless traveller, drifting from place to place, his revenge slowly taking root. For now, though, he allows himself this moment of calm. He knows better than anyone: nothing lasts forever.

Part 17

R oger Miser
Tuesday, 24 June, 1980

Somehow, she'd forgiven him.

He was the legendary Roger Miser, after all. The man who made and broke people. The man who set things in motion and broke the wheel.

Yet he couldn't give his full self to the blooming relationship. When he should have been thinking about what flowers to buy her, he was watching the skulking figures of Big Dave Rogers and Little Dave Perkins. When a candlelit dinner should have been at the forefront of his mind, he was preoccupied with the next time Gary Holmes would summon him to a meeting to discuss "arrangements."

In truth, though he would never dare say it, he hated the gangster's influence. Since the day Holmes had lent him the dosh to launch his record label, Miser had been a caged bird. Of course, he would never speak out about it. He wouldn't even dare.

Since the incident a week ago, Gary Holmes had mostly left him alone. Miser knew the gangster was hunting for Clifford Lake. Holmes would turn over every inch of the town, rip up every stage, and eventually start smashing knuckles. That's what petrified Miser most. When Holmes and his firm went down that road, Miser's legacy would be in ruins. Every newspaper from the Wash to Washington would be on it. He imagined the headlines: Music Legend's Dirty Criminal Secret. Roger Miser's Shame. Roger Miser Flirts With Danger. But the most dreaded of all: Roger Miser – The Real Truth.

Holmes had made Miser into the man he was, but he was also a liability, to put it mildly. Holmes could bring him down. Since that first deal in the backroom of The Winking Turner in East Ham, Miser had been latched onto Holmes like a dog. Despite the fame, the glamorous parties, the countless girls, the marriages – Miser's life was a tinderbox.

And this Claudine had added an extra match to the mix.

It was just after two o'clock in the afternoon, and the two – dare he say it – lovers were sitting on the banks of a pond, the remains of a picnic scattered between them.

"So, busy day ahead?" she asked.

"Yeah, there's a competition between a few of the bands. Unofficial thing, but they're really keen to do it. George is overseeing it, but I need to keep an eye on things. You never know with these kids."

The sun bore down on them, its rays scorching their arms. Insects skimmed across the water, their dance blending into the hum of the thickets.

"So, are you going to tell me what's going on?" demanded Claudine. "Or shall I just keep trying to guess? I'm a bit scared, to be brutally honest. I'm worried about getting too close to you."

"Holmes and I go back a long way…"

He told her everything.

From setting off from Yardley Wood with five pounds in his pocket, cleaning public toilets in Bow, and overhearing a conversation that mentioned the name Gary Holmes, to approaching one of the gangster's henchmen and proposing a business deal. From there, he formed a record label that had impacted every corner of the globe.

But Claudine wasn't impressed. "Who the hell is Clifford Lake? You've mentioned him a couple of times."

"He was some stupid kid who got in the way. Made a bad decision. Messed around."

"Sounds pretty serious." She shot him a dark look.

"Claudine, Claudine, don't worry about anything." He touched her cheek gently. "Lake's nothing but trash. He's trying to look cool, stir people up, create havoc – but he's just a lonely waste of space."

"You're telling me the truth, right? After what happened last week, I was reluctant to give you a chance. But I'm a forgiving woman. My father's taught me about forgiveness and compassion. I'm giving you a chance. I'm trusting you. Now, are you telling me the truth?"

"I am. Clifford Lake is nothing. He's a piece of shit. He's come down here because he's pissed about the way things worked out for him, and he's jealous. That's all. He's just some little nobody."

"You're a decent man, Roger. I want you to know that." She picked up a sliver of apple and chewed it slowly between her lips. "You're such a good man. Just... just keep yourself at a healthy distance from Gary Holmes. I don't like him. I don't trust him."

"I'll be careful, I promise."

She fumbled through the pile of picnic detritus, quickly giving up on any attempt to find any remaining food or drink. Her eyes flickered with uncertainty, torn between the different places in her life. He knew that look – he'd seen it across a drug-fuelled afterparty.

"All I ask is that you do your best."

Wednesday, 25 June, 1980 – Friday, 27 June, 1980

When Roger Miser took a step away from things, the music world noticed. Everyone saw it. In 1972, he went on a holiday to some distant place in the world – a chance to breathe, to escape the strains of Gary Holmes and the suffocating grip of the music business. It took just two days before the newspapers swooned and swished! His four-week trip was swiftly shortened to a mere four days of worrying and panic before he returned to Britain. Music had trapped him like a vice gripping an egg, threatening to crack his fragile shell at any moment.

This festival was supposed to be his release from the bird-cage. But even then, he needed a short break.

He and Claudine left St Pierre in the early hours of Wednesday. In a Citroen SM Miser had bought (in cash) from a local penniless dealer, they drove toward the south coast. Did it matter that they never quite made it? They didn't need to make it anywhere. They spent aimless hours in the countryside, eventually giving up on their dream of sipping cocktails in Cannes and settling instead for a night at the side of the road, laughing at the sheer stupidity of their situation.

Miser would never admit to being in love. As far as he was concerned, love was nothing more than a concocted brew of opportunity and deceit. He saw it every day: proclamations of "I'll never leave you," promises, men on their knees in pathetic prayer. He was sure he'd never use the l-word in front of her.

They kissed and cuddled under the starlight, but no deep words were exchanged. In the years ahead, he would look back on that night, sometimes in a drunken haze, wondering if perhaps he should have said something.

When they returned to St Pierre on Friday afternoon, reality snapped them back. George Ashton was on them the second they pulled up in the hotel car park. He had an armful of paperwork, which he shoved straight into Miser's hands.

"You've got that heavy metal lot from Ontario to watch later," George's voice was rapid and panicked. "The mayor also wants to speak with you. The lead singer from that folk group – the one from Nebraska – was using cocaine in the grounds of the school."

"Is that such a big problem?"

"Well, considering that summer school programme begins next week, it absolutely bloody-well is!"

"Well, give the mayor my most sincere apologies and kick the band out of the festival." He could clearly see that George wasn't impressed. "Oh fine, tell him I'll make a donation to the summer school."

"I'll leave you two alone," said Claudine, putting on her sunshades and already starting to make tracks.

"No, it's not a problem." Miser, startled, rushed up to her and clutched her hands in his. "Hey, let's spend the rest of the day together. Why don't you come to a few performances with me tonight? You'll love it."

"I really should be heading home. My father will have a thousand questions for me. Oh dear, he'll probably check I wasn't taken advantage of."

"I'll see you tomorrow? Dinner?" Miser asked.

"Yeah."

They kissed, briefly, but in full view of passing musicians and the media. The papers would be talking about it soon.

After she'd left, Miser told George to make the appropriate arrangements with the mayor and started back to his room. In the lobby, he found Big Dave Rogers propped against a wall, a French tabloid in his hands.

"Ah, Roger, good to see you." Big Dave folded up the paper and dropped it in a nearby waste bin. "The boss has invited you to dinner tomorrow night. You'll be picked up at half-past six."

"Could I rearrange it? I've got dinner with my..." He wasn't sure which term to use. "I've got dinner with my girl-friend."

"He's invited both of you. And Claudine's father as well. Little Dave's been to see Miles and given him the information."

"If I can ask, is this about... Lake?"

"Clifford Lake's been run out of town. Happened yester-day. We found an empty farmhouse where he'd been hiding out. As soon as he saw us, he pegged it. Ran for the hills. Snivelling little bitch. We'll find him, don't you worry, but we've seized everything he has. He's not a threat anymore. The boss wants to celebrate tomorrow night. Make sure you're there, Miser. Don't disappoint Gary Holmes." Big Dave lit up a cigarette. "See you tomorrow. Mind how you go."

Saturday, 28 June, 1980

It was Little Dave Perkins who picked them up.

Miser felt relieved that Miles had dressed well. When dining with Gary Holmes, appearances mattered. Men wore suits and ties; women, dresses. Claudine didn't look comfortable in hers. Judging by the creases and stiff folds, it had probably been buried in a suitcase for years.

He sat between Claudine and her father, trapped and cramped.

"Miles, did you go to any of the performances today?" he asked.

"No."

"Dave, what about you? Catch any of the events?"

"Workin', mate. No time for fun and games," came the snappy reply.

Maybe it was best to stay quiet. Miser gave Claudine's hand a quick squeeze but stared straight ahead.

As they pulled into the driveway, Little Dave gave a nod to the two guards on duty. Miser heard the sickening crunch of gravel beneath the tyres.

"A bit secluded," Miles remarked.

Gary Holmes was waiting out front. His three-piece suit, scarlet tie, gold-plated watch, and polished leather shoes screamed wealth. As the guests stepped out, he strode over to Miles, hand extended.

"Mr Blackstein, it's a privilege," he said.

"Good to meet you, Mr Holmes. Thanks for the invitation."

"Not a problem, not a problem. Roger, good to see you looking sharp. And you must be Claudine. May I say, you look particularly lovely this evening. Please, come in."

A bottle of red wine had already been uncorked. Candles flickered. The table was neatly set. Holmes gave his thick square spectacles a quick polish and began pouring the wine.

"Drop of the French stuff – can't beat it," he said. "Please, be seated."

"It's a lovely little cottage you have, Mr Holmes." Miles offered a wry smile to his daughter.

"Thank you. Anyway, let's sit."

Holmes had a way of making everyone feel on edge, no matter the setting or company. Tonight was no different. The table was arranged to separate them: Holmes at the head, Miser at the foot, with Claudine and her father facing each other along the sides, framed by a forest of candle flames.

"I'd like to propose a toast," said Holmes, raising his glass. "To our future endeavours."

"Cheers," said Claudine.

They sipped.

"Future endeavours? Can I ask what you mean?" Miles said.

"Well, I'm a pragmatic man," said Holmes. "Always have been. I was born to nothing – not even a wooden spoon. But pragmatism built me an empire. As Roger Miser knows, I'm always looking for new ventures. What I've seen in St Pierre has me excited. I'm planning a major investment in the music business."

"I thought you were here to kill that guy harassing you and Roger," Claudine said bluntly. No one usually dared speak to Holmes like that.

"Yes, and he's been dealt with. That's why we're celebrating. But I'm staying on. I've seen a goldmine of potential. I'm setting up a music academy right here in St Pierre."

"We need to discuss this," Miser said, his gut twisting. If word of his connection with Holmes got out, it would ripple through the entire music industry. That could never happen.

Holmes nodded firmly. "And we will. I'll send through the paperwork. You and I, Rog, we're going to build a new empire. Now – first course: cream of mushroom soup."

Two of Holmes's men served the starter. Miser hated mushroom soup, but you never – never – refused Holmes's hospitality. A single bread roll with a knob of butter offered the only real substance.

"I really appreciate you all coming tonight," Holmes said. "Truly. It means a lot. Rog, you and Claudine make a lovely couple. I'm happy for you both. This is the beginning of something new – for all of us."

After dinner, Holmes led them into the living room. He threw on a purple smoking jacket, lit a cigar, and poured whisky for himself, Miser, and Miles. Claudine received a small sherry.

"It's been a lovely evening," he said. "Absolutely smashingly lovely."

Two extra armchairs had been added, forming a semicircle around the fireplace.

"Let's..." Holmes gestured at them – it didn't sound like a suggestion.

"So, you like St Pierre?" Claudine asked.

"Absolutely love it," Holmes said. "Got amazing ideas for the academy. That school in town – I could buy it, convert it. A starting point..."

"You have a lot of ideas, Mr Holmes," Miles said, voice sincere, lies swirling beneath the surface.

"Gary – please. You and I, Miles, we're the heads of this family. And I've got big plans. A music academy, sure, but more than that. I want to expand operations. With your law enforcement background, I know you can help. I'll pay well – mansion-level well."

"I'll think about it."

"I'm already putting the paperw –"

The lights went out.

"Nothing to worry about," Holmes said calmly. "Just a power cut. Used to get them all the time when I was young. I'll find –"

Two distant gunshots cracked through the night.

"Shit!" hissed Holmes. "Boys, secure the area!"

Chaos erupted – cries, shouts. Little Dave barked orders. Big Dave relayed them. Confusion mixed with discipline.

"Is it him?" Claudine stammered. Her fear was raw. Her father didn't reach for her – he just sat there. Coward.

"Don't worry, darling, you're safe." Holmes tore off his smoking jacket and reached beneath his chair, pulling out a double-barrelled sawn-off shotgun. "Had this since I was young. I call her Estella. My trusty little angel. Right – let's get this sorry sod."

Five armed men rushed in. Little Dave was among them.

"Boss," said the small man, "all the tyres are slashed."

"He's nothing but a dead man," said Holmes. "Rog, stay behind us. Keep the others with you."

"Can't we just hide?" Claudine asked, gripping her sherry glass tight.

"I'm not taking that chance," Holmes growled. "Right – move out."

Miser felt a hand on his wrist – Claudine's. She looked terrified.

"It'll be okay," he whispered. "Stay with me."

They stuck close behind the group. Miles was panting, irritable. As Miser stepped outside, he saw Holmes's men setting up defensive positions. The boss loaded cartridges into the shotgun and snapped it shut.

"Clifford Lake! I know you're out there!" Holmes bellowed. "I know why you're here! I know what you want! Come and get it!"

Silence.

"Come out here! Face me like a man, you little bag of shit!"

Something zipped through the air. A silent punch. Miser strained his eyes.

A thud.

Claudine screamed. He pulled her close, shielding her eyes.

"Fuck!" Big Dave hissed. "That bastard!"

It was the head of the young man who had waited on Miser and Holmes before – bleeding out in the dirt.

Another thump. Another head, bloodied and filthy, landed near Holmes's feet. He stepped back, inhaled sharply.

Gunfire erupted. Holmes fired, reloaded, fired again. Bullets rained into the trees.

No time to think. No time to even try. Miser gripped Claudine's hand.

"With me!" he shouted at Miles. He veered left, into the trees. "Keep going! Don't look back!"

Branches tore at their skin. Dust filled their mouths. Miser didn't care if Miles kept up – all that mattered was her.

The gunfire intensified behind them. Shouts. Panic. Holmes roared commands.

"Roger, slow down!" Claudine cried. "Please – I can't, not in this dress!"

"No chance! You stop, you die! Keep moving!"

"Wait!" Miles panted. "Roger, wait!"

"No! I'm –" But Miser stopped mid-sentence. The gunfire had ceased.

"Maybe we should go back?" Miles suggested.

"No. We keep moving. Back to St Pierre. Come on."

He'd always run. Always fled. Yardley Wood station flashed in his mind – alone, broke, and determined. But now, at least, he had a purpose – however mad it was. He held Claudine's hand as tight as he dared, and led her and her father deeper into the night.

Lake
Sunday, 29 June, 1980

He's waited years for this, planned everything out, what he'll say, how he'll say it, but words still catch in his mouth. Eventually, he clears his throat, calms himself, and gently slaps Gary Holmes's cheek.

"Wakey-wakey! Rise and shine!" Lake shouts.

Holmes jolts awake, sees him, tries to throw himself out of the armchair, but he's pushed firmly back down. His wrists and ankles are taped together. He bears his teeth. "You're think you're so funny, don't you?" Holmes tries to pull his wrists apart. "Come on, cut these away – I'll teach you a proper lesson, Sunshine. You and me, man to man, let's do it."

"You're forgetting, it's a Sunday. God's sacred day. No fighting. But I've prepared a nice Sunday roast for you!" shouts Lake

"Fuck you."

"Using that language on a Sunday?! Shocking!"

"What – where am I?"

"Here's a tip: make sure you check your weapons in future. I switched all your bullets for blanks. Infiltration. One of the many things I learnt in borstal."

"Get to the point, Lake. I'm telling you, you'd better release me. My boys will rip you to pieces if you don't."

"I'll take the chance. Look around you, Mr Holmes, look where we are."

The hotel room probably has the luxury that the Gary Holmes expects on his trips. Bed made to perfect precision, tea and coffee set laid out, car and home magazines. Silk curtains and a chandelier. So authentic. A wonderful, first-class hotel, but completely empty.

"We're twenty miles south of St Pierre," Lake explains. "Nice little golf resort in the middle of nowhere. You stayed here once, back in the early Seventies. Had a load of dignitaries and celebrities. Don't worry! I've bought it out for a whole two months, so no one will disturb us."

"Just tell me what you want," says Holmes. "A million in cash?"

Lake allowed himself to be emotional, just this once. "Nothing can buy the extreme misery you put me through, nothing! Two years eating rotting food, raped, molested, beaten up. Because of *you*. Believe me, you vicious cunt, you're going to pay for it dearly. Oh, I'm going to kill you, that's without question. But I'm doing to degrade you beforehand, humiliate you, and then you'll suffer in worse ways that you can possibly imagine. Right, shall we get started?" He pulls out a scalpel and a pair of pliers. "I'm going to turn you into a baby, Mr Holmes." He slashes at his clothes, rips them off in shreds. The fine designs, the New York logos, all turned to strips.

Holmes shivers in the chair, naked. A flabby body and a small cock are all that's left now.

"Right, Gary, you've got a choice. I can shave you first and then rip out your teeth, or I can rip out your teeth first and then shave you. What's your preference?"

"You're pathetic."

"Very well. I'll shave you first. I should warn you..." Lake pulls out a cutthroat razor. "I should warn you, it's a bit rusty and I don't have any shaving cream. Hope you're okay with that." He opens the razor up. It's all browned and blunt. A few specks of blood Patsy Monroe's blood are still on it. "Right, let's get you all pretty for the ladies!" He lunges forward and digs the blade into his scalp, starts peeling off the skin.

After an hour of kicking and screaming, Lake's work is finished. Holmes on the floor, in a custom-made nappy, on his hands and knees. His head and balls are drooling blood from where the skin has been ripped away.

"I've got something for you, Mr Holmes, a token of my thanks." He shoves a dummy between his lips. Blood seeps past. Lake's never exactly made much of a good dentist. Well, he yanked the teeth out lacking any care!

There's no bravado, no arrogance. All that's left is fear and blood. Holmes is crawling, without even being asked to. He's going for the door.

Lake's got a video recorder on him; everything's rolling. He calls out: "Goochy goochy goo! My big baby!"

Holmes pisses himself. Thankfully the extra-large nappy takes care of the mess!

"Big baby!" Lake shouts. "Make baby noises for me! Make cute little baby noises!"

The fat barrel of lard glugs. Elbows scrape on the carpet.

"Make some baby noises and I promise you that you'll be released!"

Holmes turns his head, tears in his eyes. He nods, starts baaing like a sheep.

"Not good enough! Again! Again!"

He manages it, briefly, a timid baby's cry, but spits out the dummy. Enraged, Lake shoves it back in.

"Think this is a joke?" he snaps. He turns off the video recorder. "This is deadly serious, Sunshine. I'm sending this tape to your London enemies and every mob boss in New York. You're a laughing stock now! Right, time for some fun." He brandishes the cloth and presses it against Holmes's face. When the chloroform has knocked him out, Lake whispers, "I've been looking forward to this."

When Gary Holmes opens his eyes, Lake is staring at him.

"How are you feeling?" he asks.

Holmes doesn't reply. He can't. A plastic tube is rammed down his throat; it's taped around the edges to his mouth. The fat baby's arms and legs are spread out, tied to the bed with thick cord. Straps cross his thighs and billowing belly, keeping him tight and snug to the bed. Lake checks everything, makes sure everything is fastened in place.

The tube leads from Holmes's stripped mouth up to the ceiling, where it snakes its way over to the wall and disappears behind a black curtain that hangs where the mirror once was. Lake does a final check on it, briefly looking behind the fabric where he ensures that the connection is tight. Everything in order, he waddles back over to Holmes.

"You see, Gazza, I know what it feels like to be petrified. I know how it feels to be alone, vulnerable and helpless. I know what it's like to have everything stripped away from you, your pride and dignity. You thought I was some kid to bump out the way. A favour to your mate, Rog. I saw and experienced things no one should have to. Getting poked by some fat slimy cunt. Beaten on a regular basis. Fed rotting food. Two whole years. My family? Gone, all gone. My innocence? Raped from my body."

Holmes isn't a gangster anymore. He's a big baby, crying. If not for the tube in his mouth, he'd be wailing. Trembling like jelly.

"Don't be sad!" mocks Lake. "You're in a nice hotel! And you're receiving first-class service. I've made something for you. Over the last few weeks, I've made a machine." He stands up and yanks away the curtain.

He imagines what Holmes sees. Of course, Lake has spent hours and long nights working on it, so he knows every inch of it, but he fantasizes about the horror as Holmes sees the long, black metal tube, with cogs and pistons sticking out. It's as wide as a man's arm span and runs the length of the hotel – Lake's knocked through all the rooms on this floor to accommodate it. Lights flash and blink on the various control panels.

"I know you're a man who loves his Sunday roast, so I've prepared a treat. You'll love what I've called this. Its name is... *Old Guvnor*. I've rammed it full of liquidised roast chicken, potatoes, carrots, cabbage, you name it. Gallons and gallons of the stuff. Oh, and it's not been kept cold. It's all putrid, rotting, festering. And you're going to have the lot of it! I'm gonna pump it right into your stomach!"

Gary Holmes is yanking on the straps. High-pitched whimpering and moaning.

"Oh, Gazza, don't be frightened!" Lake can't help himself laughing. "I made this especially for you! Old Guvnor, don't you like it? It's going to make sure you get a proper tuck-in. A proper filling. Don't be such a cry-baby! No one likes a cry-baby! You need to eat your roast dinner!"

Lake hits one of the buttons on the main control panel. Old Guvnor cranks into life. Pistons and steam. Fred Dibnah's worst nightmare.

"To think, you were once a feared mob boss. Now, you're a has-been in a big nappy. Now, I won't hear any complaining. You're a growing lad and you need to keep your strength up!"

Lake whistles the chorus of *Food Glorious Food* and presses the start switch.

"Enjoy your meal!"

Part 18

Victor Gully
Saturday, 15 August, 2009

Victor Gully had never considered speed dating. In fact, the very idea seemed as foreign to him as a quiet afternoon at home. But Victor was a man who believed in spontaneity, in shaking off the rut of routine. Life was too short not to dive into the unknown, right? This morning, he had been lecturing a group of senior citizens about the life and legacy of Robert Burns. By the afternoon, he'd booked himself a spot at a speed dating event in one of Westminster's finest hotels. The change was jarring, but exciting.

He adjusted his tie, feeling the cool fabric slide between his fingers, and swept his hair back, trying to regain his composure. The man in the mirror looked confident, prepared. Ready.

But then, as he stood at the entrance of the Hanne Sharplin Hotel, a flicker of doubt crept in. He stood frozen for a moment, staring at the grandeur of the hotel's marble exterior. Should he go in? Was he overdressed? Would he make a fool of himself?

And then, of course, there was Susan. He gritted his teeth, pushing her from his mind. He had no time for that tonight. *Focus, Victor. You are the one in control.*

With a sharp exhale, he squared his shoulders and climbed the marble steps, trying to shake off the unease that clung to him like static. He was here to dominate, to show them who Victor Gully really was.

Inside the hotel foyer, the polished marble gleamed under the soft lighting. The air was cool, almost sterile, the kind of space that made every footstep sound louder than it was. As he approached the woman standing at the entrance, her tight-fitting jacket emblazoned with the logo of the dating company, Victor stood tall. He was here for a reason.

"Victor Gully," he said firmly, with an air of authority that didn't quite mask the nerves beneath.

"Yes, I see you here," she replied, her tone clipped as she scanned the clipboard nestled in the crook of her arm. "Ah, yes… A last-minute addition. You'll want to head into the Butterworth Bar. We'll be starting in fifteen minutes."

"Thanks," he replied, glancing around at the room, intrigued by its odd name. "Strange name for a bar!"

The woman's lips tightened, her frown almost imperceptible. "It's named after William Butterworth. You've heard of him, right? A Cambridge academic. Died under… well, let's just say, awful circumstances."

Victor's smile faltered. Who? He hadn't been listening – his mind was somewhere else entirely. "Perhaps I read about him somewhere. Thanks!" He brushed off the conversation with a forced chuckle.

As he walked in, his mind cleared. He knew exactly what to do. There was no place for shyness here. Confidence is key. He stepped into the bar, where the chatter of mingling guests buzzed around him, and the sight of the crowd made his pulse quicken. This was the real Victor Gully: a writer at the peak of his career, a man who had everyone's attention. He was untouchable.

A cold beer was quickly in hand, and within moments, he was engaged in conversation with a striking blonde. This was where he thrived—he was the life of the party. Nothing could touch him.

Just then, the host, a sharp-looking man with thin spectacles and a groomed beard, stepped onto a small stage. "Ladies, take your places," he called, his voice smooth and practiced. "Gentlemen, check your scorecards. You'll have five minutes with each date. When the whistle blows, move to the next table, and so on..."

Victor checked his card: Number 12. His first stop was a brunette, her wide smile the first thing he noticed.

"Hi!" he said, his voice smooth, clear.

The Butterworth Bar was a battlefield for men like him, each table a small warzone of masculinity and pride. The marble tables gleamed under the lights, the brown leather stools polished and well-worn, all designed to exude success and power. This was his world, and no one was going to take it from him.

"Hello there," the brunette replied, her West Country accent unexpectedly charming. He usually found that kind of drawl a turn-off, but tonight, there was something different.

"I know it's not the norm at these events," Victor began, leaning in just slightly, "but can I offer you a drink?"

Before she could answer, a gruff voice sliced through the air like a blade.

"No, he won't!"

Victor's head snapped up, his chest tightening. Every conversation in the room stopped, the air suddenly thick with tension. Standing above them was a man who could only be described as an intruder. He was too old, too rough, and too out of place. His face was marred by grey stubble, the tan on his cheeks harsh and uneven. A coke leather jacket hung on him like it belonged to someone else, and his baggy jeans made him appear monstrous.

"Excuse me, who are you?" Victor asked, trying to keep his voice steady, though a thread of unease began to unravel in his gut.

"You need to come with me. Now."

The host appeared at their side, arms folded, an air of authority hanging in the way he carried himself. "Excuse me, this is a private event," he said sharply. "I must ask you to leave immediately."

The man's gaze flicked to the host, and in a heartbeat, his hand shot out, revealing a pistol from inside his jacket.

"Back the fuck off!" he snarled, the weapon now pointed directly at the host. "I swear to God, I'll fucking shoot!"

A low murmur spread through the crowd. Panic rippled through the room as people scrambled toward the exits, stumbling over each other in their haste.

"Oh my," Victor muttered under his breath, all of his bravado draining away like water.

The man's eyes locked on him now, cold and unwavering. "With me. Now!" He swung the barrel of the gun toward Victor, then back at the host. "Move it!"

Victor's knees weakened. He knew the weapon wasn't a bluff. He raised his hands slowly. "Your problem is with me; leave these people alone..."

"Shut your mouth!" The intruder snapped, his voice venomous. "Right. Out the front. Now!"

Victor felt the cold metal press against his back as the man shoved him toward the exit.

"Please, let's just take it easy," Victor whispered, though his voice wavered with fear.

"There's a car outside. We're going for a ride," the man said, his words clipped, dismissive.

Victor's mind raced. *Kidnapped? Why me?*

"I'm not kidnapping you," the man muttered, as though reading his mind. "Keep your voice down."

As they exited the building, the receptionist tried to approach, but one look at the gun stopped her cold. She backed away slowly, fear on her face. Guests huddled in groups, some whispering to each other, others frozen in place. A mother clutched her toddler, eyes wide with terror.

"No one think about calling the cops!" the man shouted, his voice raw with anger. "I'm armed! Now move!"

Victor swallowed hard. His heart raced, each beat a drum of panic in his chest. "Who the hell are you?" he demanded, his voice hoarse. "What is this? What the hell is going on?"

The man's eyes narrowed, and his lips curled into a sneer. "Name's Ivan Stratton. No easy way about this…"

They reached the stairs, and Victor's feet slipped on the wet marble. Down below, a small hatchback sat waiting. Ivan waved the weapon toward it.

"Move. Quickly," Ivan ordered, thrusting open the passenger door and shoving Victor inside.

Victor slammed into the seat, heart pounding in his throat. "I want to know what's going on! I demand an explanation!"

Ivan slammed the door behind him and climbed into the driver's seat, starting the car with a roar. The tires screeched as they peeled out of the parking lot. Ivan cursed loudly as he swerved past a cyclist.

"Sorry for doing this to you," Ivan muttered, his voice gruff. "But we're in the shit." He scratched at his stubbled chin and swore again. "Fuck's sake!"

Victor's grip tightened on the seat. His pulse hammered in his ears. "I want an explanation, now! You've fucking kidnapped me! Who the hell are you?"

Ivan's eyes flicked to him for a moment, his expression hardening. "I'm gonna tell you a story. We're heading to Canterbury. But on the way, you're gonna listen to what I've got to say."

Victor opened his mouth to protest, but Ivan cut him off. "Everyone you love is in danger. Friends, family, pets, high school crushes. Everyone."

Victor's stomach dropped.

"Listen, and I'll tell you why."

Part 19

Lake

His work complete, he sets off at the break of dawn.

One final glance at the house – he raises his left eyebrow, sniggers quietly, and quickens his pace. A man of organisation and precision (borstal drilled that into him), he refuses to be late for his train.

He reaches the station in good time. The fake moustache is slipping again. He presses it back into place, pushing hard this time – it sticks. This is his least favourite disguise. It's tight, itchy, and absurd. But Campbell Litner, the punctual watchmaker from Ruislip, must blend in.

Spotting the lights of the train, a smile creeps across his lips. As it pulls to a stop, he hoists his suitcase. Stepping on board, a gruff guard barks for his ticket – no hello, no bonjour.

"Certainly."

Lake hands it over. When the stub is punched, he imagines punching the guard to death.

His seat is in a crowded carriage full of young families, all heading to Paris for quaint little getaways. He sits alone, suitcase between his legs, eyes sweeping the carriage. A young couple at the far end catch his attention: she has thick black curls, he has a face full of freckles and the kind of innocence Lake finds irritating. He weighs up whether he should kill them.

By the time they reach Paris, he's decided to spare everyone.

He ducks into the gents as Campbell Litner and walks out as Craig Laws, a dishevelled photojournalist just back from assignment.

In baggy jeans, with a mop of unkempt hair and a stained anorak, he heads for the taxi rank.

When his plane touches down at Heathrow, he feels a stab of disappointment: summer is ending. Not even the image of Gary Holmes choking on rotting roast dinners is enough to lift his mood.

At passport control, he smirks at the sight of an African family being relentlessly questioned by a customs officer, who keeps repeating the same line: "What is your travel history?" They don't seem to understand.

At the newspaper stand in the arrivals hall, front pages are plastered with Thatcher's face. Two coppers patrol the concourse, stifling yawns. A toddler wails for his mum.

Outside, the heat is seasonable – cooler than the oppressive swelter of St Pierre, but it still drags up memories of summer in borstal. For him, everything leads back to that place.

He heads for the nearest taxi and tells the driver to take him to The Savoy. After all, he's Craig Laws – eminent photographer, shelves of awards and trophies to his name.

That night, he sits alone at the bar in The Savoy. The place glows with low amber light, all gleaming brass and polished wood. Bottles line the back wall like jewels in a case. Around him, the city's beautiful people gather – young power couples, minor celebrities, the whole curated swirl. He sits with his whisky, eyes drifting from face to face.

There was a time he was destined to be gorgeous, just like them. A time he was meant to be... something. If only he hadn't got lost that day. If only he hadn't wandered into that less glamorous clothing store. If only. But he had. And now, retribution is in full swing.

In the cheerful chaos around him, he sees the version of himself that never happened. He allows himself a fleeting moment of self-pity – then shakes it off. He rises, swirling the amber in his glass, and begins to mingle.

"Three months in Papua New Guinea photographing the wildlife," he says to anyone who'll listen. "Caught food poisoning a couple of times – but I pulled through."

He overplays it, of course – makes himself sound rugged, fascinating, the kind of man girls lean in toward. And they do. Soon, he's the centre of gravity in the room. A celebrity by sheer force of invention.

When he finally tells them he needs sleep, they practically cling to him, pleading for just one more story. He stays, drinking with them late into the night, spinning more tales of his travels across Europe. And for a while – just a while – he believes he really is Craig Laws.

He's up at five the next morning.

Pulling on his Campbell Litner disguise, he heads out into the pale hush of dawn. He has to move quickly. He's rehearsed this moment a hundred times in his mind, but carrying it out is something else entirely. Every word must land precisely. No room for error.

He walks to the address, package in hand. When he knocks, the door opens almost immediately. An elderly man stands there, a cigarette smouldering between his lips, eyes rimmed with tears that the cold hasn't quite frozen.

"Here," Lake says, handing over the package. "Now, remember what I told you. On the fifth of June each year, you post one of these letters. The address is on the front of each. Do not open them. Two days after sending one, you'll receive fifty thousand pounds. Do this every year until you run out of letters."

"What if I die?" the man asks, voice cracked and worn. "I'm a widower. No one to look after me."

"Don't."

Lake turns and walks away, back through the quiet streets to the hotel. He slips into his room unnoticed and sheds the disguise. Soon, he's Craig Laws again.

Downstairs, he joins the same crowd from the night before for breakfast. Polished silver, clinking cups, easy laughter. But eventually, the moment comes to make his exit.

"I'm off to Canada today – to photograph bears," he tells them with a grin. "It was great meeting you. Have a fantastic day, guys."

He's on the road again, this time behind the wheel. Leaving London, he stops at a service station to change into his next disguise – Crawley Loop now, a hopeless casual worker.

He's heading north. Far north. He plans to hide out there until the heat from the summer blows over.

Borstal taught him how to avoid sleep, how to stay sharp even in the most depraved circumstances. The farther north he drives, the more his mind lingers on William and Emily Butterworth, and the gnawing desire to kill them both again. The road stretches out ahead, growing lonelier with every passing mile. The journey takes three days, but not once does he feel tired. When he finally pulls into Aviemore, he allows himself to relax for the first time; even permits himself a yawn.

The address is on the north side of town. When he pulls up to the curb, she's already waiting for him.

"I'm not too late, am I?" he calls out.

"No, it's okay." The woman flicks her cigarette to the ground, mashing it out with a pink slipper.

She's older and greyer than he expected. There's depression in her eyes, sickness simmering under the surface. She's short, squat, with one side of her head shaved clean. Lake wonders if it's a new look. Should he get in the spirit of things?

He steps out and shakes her hand. "Good to meet you, Mandy. Got all my stuff with me. Not much – just a few odds and sods."

"Honestly, take your time. No rush."

"Thanks. I've got the first month's rent ready."

"Just pay when you're ready."

Once he's settled into the room, Lake takes a few moments to rest – then swiftly dives into his preparatory work for the year ahead. Every detail needs to be catalogued: hotel bookings, flight arrangements, the travel documents for his various disguises.

Mandy interrupts him, a knock at the door followed by her entry without waiting for permission.

"Everything okay with the room?" she asks, her presence an invasion.

"Fine, fine," he replies. "It's perfect."

"Would you like a glass of wine later?"

"Yes, please, that would be wonderful. Just the one, though – I'm starting early tomorrow."

"Not a problem. You seem like a nice guy. The nicest lodger I've had in a while."

"Thank you. That means a lot. No one usually tells me I'm a nice guy."

"I'll let you get on with your unpacking."

Lake watches her leave, and the second she's gone, he scans the house with disgust. It's a mess – soiled clothes strewn about, used cups, overflowing rubbish. Christ, the woman lives in a complete shithole. A filthy, depressing place, every surface soaked in a sense of despair. The feel of brokenness hangs in the air – an abusive ex-husband, a teenager who's cut all contact, and no prospects.

His room isn't much better: peeling wallpaper, mould creeping along the ceiling, crumbs scattered across the carpet. Ha, it's nothing compared to borstal. In fact, it's a slice of heaven, as far as he's concerned.

Once his files are in order, he heads downstairs. Mandy is slouched on the worn sofa, eyes glued to the cathode ray. Crushed beer cans, takeaway boxes, and cigarette burns make up the décor of her living room.

"You know what, I fancy that glass of wine now," he says.

Mandy doesn't look up, just pulls the ring off a can of cider. "There's a rack in the kitchen. Pick whatever you want. Help yourself."

"Thanks."

"Don't just stand there, you fucking wimp – go and get hammered."

"Your house is a bit of a shithole. Needs a spring-clean."

"You don't like it, you can go and fucking live somewhere else."

"I like it here." Without warning, Lake steps forward, his hands wrapping around her head in a swift, practiced motion. Her body goes limp, collapsing forward. The can of cider tumbles to the floor, spilling its sour contents.

"Sorry about that."

On the fifth of September, he sees it on the news: Roger Miser has returned to England, with his ever-faithful George Ashton trailing behind. News crews swarm them at Heathrow, barking questions, hungry for a headline. Both men hang their heads in shame – dreary, defeated, the picture of misery.

"You sorry sods," Lake mutters, lifting his whisky to his lips.

He's given the house a proper clean. Everything is now neat, orderly. He's actually taken to the place, oddly enough. Too bad he can't keep it.

"Now you're suffering, Roger," he whispers to the screen. "Now you know how it feels."

On the 15th of March, 1981, Lake is woken by furious banging on the front door. It's early – still dark outside. He pulls on Mandy's old dressing gown and stumbles downstairs, heart hammering. The knocking grows louder. Angry, deliberate fists.

"Mr Clifford Lake, open up!" a voice commands. "We have a warrant for your arrest!"

Through the distorted glass he sees them: television crews, flashbulbs popping, five police officers, and a pale, dishevelled Ceri Britton, supported by a slender woman – his new wife.

"Yeah, that's him!" Britton growls. "That's the piece of shit who had me kidnapped!"

A reporter whips around to face the camera. "We are here at the moment of confrontation – Ceri Britton face-to-face with the man who orchestrated his abduction in Colombia last year."

Two officers advance, cuffing Lake before he can even protest. "Right," says one of them, "get him inside. On the sofa."

"What the hell is this?" Lake spits. "Some kind of prank?"

"You're busted, mate!" shouts Britton.

Dragged into the house, Lake is dumped onto the filthy old sofa – the very spot where Mandy met her end. The irony isn't lost on him.

"Come on, there's been a misunderstanding…" His voice trembles with false innocence. He knows it won't work. The wheels are already in motion, and they're crushing him beneath them.

Cameras roll. Reporters lean in. Britton kisses his wife's forehead as a microphone is shoved beneath his chin.

"How do you feel?" asks one of the journalists.

"Nervous," Britton replies. "But Angelina – God bless her – she's been my rock. I'd be lost without her."

A chair is set up facing Lake. Britton lowers himself into it, visibly shaking, tears of rage in his eyes. His wife rests her hands gently on his shoulders.

Lake scans the room. Journalists cluster in the kitchen doorway, scribbling furiously. Cameras tighten their focus. The tension is electric.

Britton leans forward, voice cracking. "Why?" he asks. "Why the fuck did you do it?"

Lake's face darkens. "Why did you abuse me in borstal?"

"I'm the one asking the questions." Britton's voice hardens. "This incredible woman helped me escape the jungle. We were both prisoners, both violated. But we made it out. We married. That's something you'll never understand: love."

"You're pathetic," Lake sneers. "You've spent all this time playing detective? And now you've dragged half the world's media here?"

"This is part of a major documentary. We're going to expose you for what you are. I know what you did to William Butterworth and his wife."

Lake smirks. "I know, right? I still feel dirty from it."

Britton's fury is building. "You think you're clever? You think this is funny? You're going to rot in prison, you sick bastard."

"I've missed your awful accent," Lake says. "Did I ever tell you? I fucking hate Aussies. Vile fucking bunch."

"Calm," whispers Angelina, her hand tightening.

"I want answers," Britton snaps. "Why me?"

Lake shrugs. "You deserved it."

"No –"

"Yes, you did, you cheeky little shitbag." He winks.

Britton lets out a shaky laugh, disbelief and rage colliding. The cameras don't blink.

Angelina whispers, "Tell him what happened. Don't hold back."

Britton shudders. "I can't."

"Be strong, my love." She runs her fingers through his hair.

He breaks. "The nights at gunpoint... being force-fed insects... I can't go back there."

"Imagine how I felt," Lake booms. "Eating rotting food!"

"You liar! You were treated well – fresh veg, clean water. And this is how you repay me?"

"I'm still repaying you."

"We've caught you, Lake. Caught red-handed. You've no idea what's coming."

Lake leans in. "No, Ceri. You have no idea what's about to happen."

Britton scoffs, turning to the camera crew. "This guy's a joke, isn't he?"

"Oh, Ceri," Lake says softly. "I'm so very sorry. Because your hell... is just beginning."

Britton's smile fades.

"I'll tell you what's really going on," Lake continues. "How did you escape the jungle so easily? Found by rescue teams just hours after slipping away? Almost too easy, wasn't it?"

Britton glares. "Don't start. I know your games. I've seen your type before."

"Angelina helped, didn't she?" Lake's tone darkens. "Led you straight into the next trap."

"Your world of excuses..." Britton starts.

"Okay, guys," Lake says calmly, "it's time."

Suddenly, the air shifts. Reporters drop their notepads. Cameras fall away, replaced by guns, all aimed squarely at Britton's head.

His face drains of colour.

Angelina slips a knife from her belt and presses it against his throat.

"Thanks for helping out," Lake says to the policemen. "You'll be paid next week. Paperwork's all processed."

"Much appreciated," one of them mutters as they file out.

Britton stares after them, stunned. "You're insane."

Lake grins. "Did you really think you could win? Everything – Colombia, the rebels, your little rescue, this documentary – all of it was mine. I designed it. My contacts in the East Anglia Communist Movement pulled every string."

"You're bluffing," Britton whispers. But Lake sees the fear creeping in.

"The interviews were broadcast," Britton insists. "The world saw them."

"No one's coming," Lake replies. "Because you're never going to be seen again. I'm sending you to Ilha da Queimada Grande. Snake Island. Off the coast of Brazil. Thousands of venomous snakes. No people. No rescue."

Angelina swaps her knife for a pistol, presses it to the base of Britton's skull. "Thanks for the brief marriage," she whispers. "Lake's paying well."

A cameraman steps forward. "Helicopter's ready in Kingussie."

"Don't let me keep you," says Lake. He turns back to Britton, smug. "Enjoy your little trip. You'll be stripped naked and dumped on the coast. Let's see how long you last."

Angelina pulls him to his feet.

"You can't do this!" Britton screams.

"It's happening, mate!" Lake laughs. "Enjoy your holiday!"

A month later, he leaves Aviemore.

He drives off after lunch, slinging the keys out the window like they mean nothing. What he doesn't need, he discards. By the time anyone stumbles on Mandy's body, he'll be less than a rumour. A smudge of memory. A speck of dust in a city that forgets fast.

Winter in Aviemore had felt lonelier than the ghost-thick silence of Wool's mansion. That isolation, stretched over dark days and longer nights, clings to him like mould as he moves south. The further he drives, the more his mind dredges up those dead hours. By the time he hits the humming veins of central London, his hatred for that time pulses through him like fever.

He spends the night at The Savoy. Nothing's changed. The furniture stands stiff-backed and poised, untouched by time. The staff wear the same lacquered smiles, their voices a blend of well-trained warmth and careful disinterest.

He skulks through the bar, whisky in hand, eyeing the parade of youthful flesh – bare shoulders, tight skirts, heels like weapons. None of them give him a second look. Who would? He's sloppy Craig Laws now, out of step, out of season.

He checks out early, the dawn sky still bruised with sleep. Humming a couple of folk tunes he remembers from school – tuneless and eerie in the quiet lift – he hops into a black cab and heads to Heathrow.

The terminal is a storm of movement. Security gates chirp, intercoms rattle off flight numbers, and trolleys clatter over the tiled floor like impatient insects. The air tastes of jet fuel and stress, perfume and coffee.

He checks in at the first-class counter, smooth and confident in his latest skin.

"Enjoy your flight, Mr Laws," says the woman behind the desk, eyes flicking between his passport and the screen. Her smile is bright but forgettable.

"I hope you make use of our new lounge as well," she adds, almost automatically.

"Oh, I've no doubt I will," he replies, flashing her a grin that doesn't reach her eyes.

He moves off, the weight of his carry-on swinging like an afterthought. There's no hesitation in his steps now. After a wasted winter, he's earned some indulgence. Let New York be his playground this time.

After landing at JFK, he pauses for a bitter coffee in arrivals before hailing the first yellow cab he sees. The ride into Midtown is slow, the traffic thick with honking horns and twitching brake lights. He stares out the window, trying to summon memories of his last trip to the city – but there's nothing of substance. Just vague impressions: grey rain, too much bourbon, and a missed appointment that no longer matters.

His hotel is just a couple of blocks from the Empire State Building, a high-rise of glass and quiet opulence. In the lobby, he's greeted by another polished front-desk clerk—this one with fire-red lipstick and cool, piercing blue eyes.

"Mr Laws," he says smoothly. "Staying for three nights."

She taps at the keyboard. "Yes, we have you here. Room 650. Elevator's to your left." Her accent carries that rich, effortless California twang – Malibu by way of Beverly Hills.

"If you don't mind me saying," he adds, glancing around the subdued lobby, "it's a bit quiet – quieter than I expected."

She leans in slightly, lowering her voice with the air of someone passing on a secret. "Long story. You know the music guy, Roger Miser? He had this whole week booked out. Big party planned, entourage, the works. But last week, he just called it off. Something to do with what happened in France last summer."

He raises his eyebrows. "I think I remember. Wasn't he with some local girl who... topped herself?"

"Yeah. That's the one. Word is, he's gone off the rails a bit since then."

"Explains why my editor got the room for peanuts."

She gives a shrug, lips pressing into a faint smile. "Lucky you."

"Well, thanks," he says. "Better get some rest. Shooting tomorrow. Photos."

She nods and watches him go, her smile unwavering.

Just before midnight, he slips out of the hotel, dressed in his most elaborate disguise yet: Vikki Dixon. Excess makeup, dramatic eyeshadow, and a perfect pout transform his features into something almost unrecognizable. The backstory he's concocted for her is rich – Vikki is an academic, an investigator of student complaints against staff at prestigious universities, and she's recently joined Columbia University. On the side, she's a high-class escort, weaving her way through a world of intrigue and sophistication. Tonight, she's on a mission, fully embracing her alter ego.

Her attire is flawless, a testament to her calculated glamour and eccentricities. As she strides through the streets, her confidence is palpable. She's in the zone – completely in the mood, and in the moment. Two cops walk past, their heads turning slightly, their eyes lingering longer than they should. But Vikki, ever the professional, pays them no mind. She whistles sharply through her fingers, hailing a cab with the ease of a true New Yorker.

"Chrysler Building," she orders, her voice smooth, the edge of excitement barely contained. "As soon as possible."

The cabbie, eager to please, nods enthusiastically. "You got it, miss!"

As the taxi weaves through the dark streets, Vikki reflects on the evening ahead, but there's no nostalgia. No memories to cling to – just the thrill of the job, the pulse of the city, and the promise of what's to come. When they reach the towering structure of the Chrysler Building, she pays the driver double the fare without a second thought, exits with a practiced swish of her hips, and clicks her heels across the pavement, the echo of her steps amplified by the empty streets.

She approaches the front doors, but they're locked – exactly as she anticipated. Without breaking stride, she pulls out the wire she's kept hidden in her bag, twisting it expertly in the lock until it clicks open. A glance over her shoulder assures her she's alone. No one's watching. She steps inside, and the familiar hum of the city fades into the background.

The Bee Gees' *Stayin' Alive* blasts through the lobby, the disco beat filling the air. One lone figure – Disco Dave – shuffles awkwardly across the floor in a half-hearted attempt at dance. Dressed in the uniform of the building's night security guard, he's too lost in his movements to notice her approach.

"Stayin' alive, stayin' alive," he sings to himself, twirling and spinning in place. Then, with a start, he sees her. His eyes widen, and he gulps audibly.

"I'm a bit lost," Vikki says, her voice a velvet mix of sweetness and confidence. "Could you help me?"

His confusion turns to suspicion. "How did you get in here?"

Vikki can't help herself. "How do you think you suit that uniform?" She smirks, her eyes sparkling. The grey suit doesn't quite fit the man's awkward frame – she's noticed that the moment she laid eyes on him.

Disco Dave hesitates. "I'm calling the cops. Stay right there!"

But Vikki is already moving. In one fluid motion, she whips a piece of cheese wire around his neck, falling to the ground with him in tow. Her hands are quick, efficient, squeezing tighter and tighter, forcing his airways closed. Dave struggles, his hands desperately clawing at the wire, but it's no use. His body convulses, and with a final, sickening crack, his neck gives way. The wire severs his head in one sharp motion, and Vikki rises smoothly, staring down at the man whose dance moves would never see the light of day again.

"Thanks for the performance," she murmurs, her voice tinged with dark amusement.

She steps toward the elevator, unbothered by the gruesome scene she's just left behind. The building's luxurious interior seems more like a set than a living space, the art-deco details lost on her as she focuses on the mission at hand. The elevator dings, and the doors slide open. As she steps out onto the top floor, she's already in motion, heading left down the corridor toward Number 6.

Her knock is light – too light. Like dust falling on a surface. She doesn't need to be loud. She knows exactly how this will unfold.

"Who the hell is it?" a groggy voice calls from inside. "It's nearly one in the morning!"

"Vikki Dixon," she replies smoothly, a sultry edge to her tone. "Open up, darling. I'm here to entertain you."

The door creaks open, and there stands Jefferson Reed – older, fatter, and barefoot. His eyes narrow in confusion, then in disgust. "What the fuck are you? I didn't order a hooker. Fuck off. You sick-looking cunt. Fuck off."

Vikki laughs softly, stepping closer. "Oh, babe. Don't you remember me?"

"Should I?"

"Yes," she says, stepping into his personal space. She leans forward, an unspoken promise in her eyes as she touches him between the legs. His hesitation is short-lived.

"Well, I like that stuff," Reed stammers, glancing nervously behind him. "But... the wife's in. She's okay with me doing this stuff, but... not in front of her."

Before she can respond, a voice chimes in from the hallway. "Jefferson, who the fuck is this?"

The sight that greets her makes her stop for a moment, but not for long. Tracy Cox – draped in a silk dressing gown, cigarette dangling from her fingers – appears in the doorway.

The recognition is instant. Tracy hasn't changed much – still the same cocky, confident air, though time has etched its mark on her. But her appearance doesn't bother Vikki –

Lake, beneath the makeup and disguise, feels the thrill rise once more.

"Oh, babe, you are hot!" Vikki gushes, leaning in with practiced allure. Her voice is high-pitched, sweet, and just a little too perfect. "Do you work out?"

Tracy's eyes narrow, and she recoils slightly, eyes full of disgust. "Get this whore out of here, Jefferson."

Jefferson looks flustered, clearly unsure how to handle the situation. "Come on, love. Piss off. I'll give you fifty dollars for the trouble."

Vikki straightens, her smile vanishing in an instant. "Don't you want to catch up?" She steps forward, closing the door behind her with a soft click. Slowly, she starts removing the wig. "I mean… it's been fifteen years, give or take."

Recognition flashes across Tracy's face, and for the briefest moment, her eyes widen. "Fuck," she gasps, as Lake's transformation continues. The shrill voice is gone, replaced by something more dangerous.

"Remember me now, Tracy?" Lake asks, his voice low, thick with disdain. "I came into your shop once. A long time ago."

Before she can respond, Lake's fist flies, connecting with both their faces in rapid succession, knocking them out cold. It's messy, swift, and brutal. Just the way he likes it.

He's actually a little jealous of their apartment – just a little. The grand view of the Manhattan skyline, a state-of-the-art television and sound system, a kitchen crammed with top-end gadgets, and a bedroom fit for royalty. He loves it. While he waits for them to stir, he stands at the window, gazing out across the glittering metropolis. As a child, he used to dream about New York. His imagination would race through his veins like ice water.

From the bathroom, muffled murmurs drift through.

"I'm on my way," he calls.

Inside the tub, Tracy and Jefferson huddle together, naked, trembling, their bodies knotted in fear. They're stuck with nothing to look at but each other – and the creeping yellow stream of Jefferson's shame puddling toward the drain.

"How are we this evening?" says Lake, stepping in. "A little nippy, isn't it? I thought it was supposed to be warmer today."

He's anchored them to the ceramic with screws and metal bars. Neat, brutal efficiency. He checks the restraints again – everything tight, everything just so.

"Sorry about all this," he mutters absently. "I'll try not to drag things out. I just want to make sure... everything's perfect before your lovely bath."

"We're sorry!" Tracy sobs. "We heard about what happened... about you going to borstal! We didn't know –"

"You did fuck all about it!" Lake barks, slapping her lightly across the cheek. "How does it feel now? To be trapped? Confined? Terrified? You'll be screaming for this to stop soon."

"Please!" Jefferson thrashes his neck against the rim of the tub, hyperventilating, gasping, choking on panic.

"I love this bathroom," says Lake, running a finger down Tracy's tear-streaked cheek. "It's proper luxury. You've got a tub fit for a god. Not like the crap ones the working man gets stuck with. Sorry – am I boring you?"

"We've got money," Tracy blurts, scrambling for a strategy. "Cash. In the safe. Take it. Take all of it."

"Oh, I will." His voice is breezy, distant. "But first I want you both relaxed. That's what I'm here for. To pamper you."

He turns to the tap and starts running the water. Steam hisses up into the air. "A nice, hot bath. Plenty of bubbles. Just imagine it. Do you know what happens to a body left soaking for hours on end? Skin starts to wrinkle. Then blister. Then it breaks. Starts to peel off in sheets. Eventually, it rots."

He looks at Tracy, something almost tender in his expression. "Do you remember that day in the shop? When you seduced me? I do. I always will. Just like I'll never forget the rapes, the beatings, the torture in borstal. They're part of me now. Part of my soul. And now – now it's your turn."

Lake holds up two bottles of bubble bath. "Lavender or camomile? Which would you prefer?"

Lake's journey through the next two years is as much a physical test as it is an escape, a continual search for anonymity in a world that seems to constantly close in around him. The miles stretch on like a dull, endless blur – he walks, he rests, he walks again. His feet ache and his body protests, but the need for movement, for distance, keeps him going.

New York fades from memory, as do the echoes of his past, each step a bit further away from the life he's left behind. He walks through the grey, silent roads of Pennsylvania, through the unremarkable stretch of Ohio, and past the faded storefronts of Indiana. All of it bears the faint mark of his presence. He is nothing more than a shadow in these places – a fleeting figure, a passing stranger.

There are moments of quiet satisfaction, too. He hitches rides when he can, blending in with other drifters on the road, but walking feels purer, more in tune with his purpose. He is anonymous now. His appearance shifts constantly. A beard, a pair of glasses, a carefully cultivated disguise, and he becomes a different man every time. The legend of the mysterious man with a beard and glasses – creeping across university campuses and disappearing without a trace – grows, and Lake watches it from a distance, his presence never quite caught.

One evening, in a bar somewhere in Arkansas, he overhears a group of students mourning the disappearance of one of their own. Their tearful eyes, their raw grief, are as familiar to him as the jagged edges of his own dark past. He smiles, a brief flash of twisted satisfaction, as he listens to their voices crack with sorrow. He resists the urge to mock their accents, holding his composure. It's a dangerous game, after all, and he's come to understand the art of restraint.

By August 1983, the relentless road leads him to the sun-drenched beaches of Los Angeles. The warmth of the West Coast, the golden glow of Venice Beach, feels like a brief respite from the harshness of the world he's been fleeing. For a week, he soaks in the sun, watching people live their carefree lives, enjoying the kind of freedom that eludes him. But freedom, for him, is just another illusion, a fleeting thing that slips through his fingers no matter how far he runs.

With a soft chuckle to himself, he books a flight out of L.A., one that takes him south – toward Chile, where the horizon stretches even further, offering the promise of new possibilities.

Each place he visits is just a stepping stone, a part of his never-ending escape.

Carl Letterman begins his work at the Bellatrix Observatory, deep in the heart of the Atacama Desert, at some uncertain point in his life. No one knows exactly when he started – only that he's been there long enough to be well-liked by everyone. The astronomers, professors, post-docs, and PhD students all know him as the kindly cafeteria worker, always there with a warm greeting and a smile. He's the steady presence that helps the long, gruelling hours of star mapping and data analysis seem a little less tiresome. When they come in for their morning meal after working the late shift, Letterman is waiting to serve them, handing over whatever they desire, always attentive, always eager to listen.

He's a good listener, too – watching the scientists with an almost voyeuristic interest as they discuss their findings, their latest breakthroughs. There's this one Scottish professor, though, who really gets under his skin. Lake fantasizes about dragging him out to the middle of the vast, empty desert, cutting him open, and leaving him there to rot. But he can't be bothered. The thought passes as quickly as it comes. It's the monotony of the place that wears on him, more than anything.

The work starts to drain him after a while. After five months of early mornings and the same tedious routine, the novelty wears off. He's tired of the endless cups of coffee, the endless meals served, the endless conversations that circle back to the same trivialities. Most of the PhD students are rude too.

They file in each morning like a herd, swaggering past him without a word, without so much as a glance.

"Full breakfast," they demand with an air of entitlement. "Fresh coffee. Now."

One day, Lake can't take it anymore. He waits for his moment. He takes one of them – one of the rude, self-important ones – drives him out to the middle of nowhere in the desert, and spends hours drilling out his eardrums before finally silencing him with the chainsaw's roar. The body is left to bake under the desert sun, but when Lake returns to the observatory, no one is any wiser. The students are sad for a while, a few long faces linger, but like everything else, they move on quickly. They heal faster than expected.

Still, the routine gnaws at him. He finds himself thinking about the letters his contact in London was supposed to send out. It's the only thing that disturbs his thoughts, that shatters the monotony. The quiet desert stretches on around him, but beneath the stillness, something is bubbling, and it's all he can do not to focus on it.

Two months later, a new face appears: a post-doc from Colombia. When she arrives for breakfast, she greets him with a soft smile, her voice a delicate blend of warmth and beauty. Lake finds himself inexplicably drawn to her but quickly suppresses the feeling.

One morning, after the breakfast rush, as the cafeteria begins to empty, she stands up from her table and walks over to him. "How are you?" she asks, her English tinged with a gentle accent.

"I'm fine," he replies. "How did the night go? The stars?"

"Really well," she says. "I've got a lot of data to analyse before I head back home. Do you live nearby?"

"I stay in the observatory quarters, but I have an apartment in Santiago. What about you?"

"Same here!" she exclaims, clearly excited. She extends a hand to him. "Lisa."

"Carl."

"I can't believe those PhD students treat you like that," she continues, her brow furrowed in concern. "I've already filed a complaint."

"Oh, it's not necessary. I'm used to it," Lake answers, trying to brush it off.

"You're from England, right? I can hear it in your accent. So pronounced."

"That's right," he says, keeping his voice even. "Hampshire."

"How did you end up here?" she asks, genuinely curious.

"Ah, long story. Fell out with the wife – she cheated on me. Decided I needed a change. I've got a background in catering, so I packed up, left England, and ended up here."

"That's very brave of you," she says, her admiration clear in her eyes.

"It's just a job," he replies, dismissing the praise. "But anyway, I'll let you get back to your work. I think there's some coffee left if you want a refill."

"I'm good, thanks." She smiles again, this time even wider. "It was really nice to meet you, Carl."

Weeks pass, and Carl and Lisa grow closer. Each morning, after she finishes her breakfast, he brings them both coffee, and they talk. He learns that she's divorced and moved here to start anew. In some ways, he's doing the same – though his story is a tapestry of lies.

"I want to know more about you," she says one morning in October. "You're an intriguing person, Carl."

"Not as intriguing as you," he replies, the words slipping out before he can think better of it.

"What are you doing for Christmas?" she asks, her eyes warm with curiosity.

"No plans. Just keeping an eye on the place," he answers, shrugging.

"Spend it with me," she suggests.

"Would you want that?" He raises an eyebrow, though a part of him already knows the answer.

"Yes," she says with a smile that could melt glaciers. She leans across the table and kisses him softly. "I really would like it."

Lake feels a pang of something unfamiliar – a twinge of guilt. He's broken his most important rule. He has no desire to bring her into his dark world, but as she pulls away, he justifies it. She's becoming part of Carl Letterman's world, not Clifford Lake's. And that, for now, is enough.

Beneath a portrait of Augusto Pinochet, the new lovers plan their escape. On December 16th, when the observatory closes for Christmas, they'll drive south to Santiago, stopping wherever the road takes them.

October and November slip by in a quiet blur. The lovers fall deeper into their secret. Lake continues to make the breakfasts and manage the daily tasks, keeping to the background as always. Lisa does her research, writes her reports, and smiles at him with a tenderness that leaves him feeling unmoored. It's a gentle, unspoken bond that they share, one that no one else at the observatory knows about.

But in the stillness of the night, Lisa sneaks him to the telescope. The first time they go out there, Lake is taken aback by the sheer vastness of the universe, a spectacle so grand that it feels impossible to comprehend. Stars burn so brightly they could be gemstones scattered across the heavens. She teaches him the basics of astronomy, and he catches on quickly – supernovas, red giants, black holes. The mysteries of the cosmos reveal themselves to him, like ancient secrets whispered on the wind. He sees Andromeda in all its majesty, its sprawling arms reaching out across the void. The beauty is staggering, its magnitude almost humbling.

In these moments, the weight of the universe presses in on him. The vastness of space, the secrets it holds, are so much greater than anything he could ever comprehend. And yet, in his heart, he feels as though he belongs to it – just a small speck in a boundless, magnificent expanse.

It's the closest thing to peace he's felt in years.

By the time dawn breaks on the morning of the 16th of December, Lisa and Carl are well on their way south. The cool morning air seeps through the car windows as the landscape stretches endlessly before them. Carl's body relaxes, and so too does his mind. As Lisa's car races down the long, empty road that separates sand from civilisation, Carl feels a shift deep within him. For the first time in what feels like forever, he is the man he was born to be.

They take turns driving, each driving for three hours at a stretch. When Carl's hands grip the wheel, the sensation of freedom floods through him, the kind he's only dreamed of in fleeting moments before. The road, the solitude, the open spaces – everything feels right. His past seems a distant shadow, fading in the rearview mirror.

They stop overnight in La Serena and walk hand-in-hand along the beach. The salt air tingles his skin, and for a moment, he lets himself breathe freely, unburdened. But as they walk, his gaze falls on the military presence patrolling the shore, their eyes hard, their postures stiff. The soldiers watch them with an intensity that unnerves him, a reminder of the weight of history in this place. Lisa, ever calm, reassures him with a soft squeeze of his hand. "Don't worry," she says. "It's just the way things are here. They won't bother us."

After their stroll, they take dinner at the hotel, where the staff treats them like royalty. They're serenaded with gentle melodies, paraded through the lobby, and told how lucky they are to have found each other. The flattery is almost too much, but Carl takes it in stride. They're indulged as a couple in love, and for tonight, it's enough.

Their original plan to stay just one night in La Serena quickly dissolves. The connection between them is undeniable – bonded like wire, stronger with each passing moment. They fall deeper for each other, the emotional gulf between them widening like the crevasse of an untold secret, one that pulls them further from the lives they once lived. Beach walks, declarations of commitment over dinner, the whisper of a future together – these things fill their time. It feels like a dream, an escape from everything, and Carl lets himself drown in it.

The next morning, they leave La Serena, but neither of them speaks of turning back. They hesitate for a moment, unsure of what comes next, but Lisa is firm. "We need to push on," she says. And so, they continue.

Upon arriving in Santiago, the shift in atmosphere is immediate. The bustling city is teeming with life, yet everywhere they turn, the shadow of Augusto Pinochet's regime looms. Troops in fatigues are stationed at every corner. They are scrutinized closely at every checkpoint, their documents checked and rechecked. They're asked repeatedly who they are, why they're here, what their plans are. Carl, however, is unbothered. He's seen this before – the serious eyes, the bloodstained lips, the hungry hands ready to pull the trigger. It's nothing new. It reminds him of borstal, of the brutal authority that always threatened to strip away his sense of self.

Lisa's apartment is located in the eastern part of the city, tucked away in a cramped tenement block. The building is modest, with peeling paint and cracked windows. They make multiple trips to move their bags upstairs, and Carl insists on carrying his own – no exceptions. As they reach her apartment, he notices that it feels empty, almost sterile. There's nothing to make it personal, nothing to give it the warmth of a home.

"I'm still fixing it up," Lisa says, noticing his confusion as she looks around. "I'll have it sorted in no time."

Carl shrugs, indifferent. "It's not my house."

She smiles softly and turns toward the small kitchen. "I'll finish unpacking. There's a restaurant nearby – really good local cuisine. How about I book us a table?"

"That sounds lovely," Carl responds, his voice calm but with a hint of something else.

She begins to walk away, but Carl steps closer, his hand gently grazing the back of her head. His fingers slip into her hair, and he strokes it softly. "I love it when you do that," she murmurs, closing her eyes. "Don't stop."

Carl leans in, his voice low and steady. "No intention."

He expects something drab – a few plastic tables with stained covers thrown over them, a menu with only four items. But the place is five-star. Almost decent. Spanish music hums softly in the background, and candles cast a warm glow over the eatery, giving it an atmosphere that feels both inviting and intimate.

"You like it, don't you?" she asks, smiling as she looks at him.

"The food means nothing to me. You do," he replies, his voice low but sincere.

She laughs softly, eyes sparkling. "You're so cute! But you'll love the cazuela."

Their table is by the window, offering a view of the street below – one filled with relative poverty. A one-legged man stoops to pick up litter; two semi-naked boys wrestle over a deflated football; a beggar licks between his fingers. It's a stark contrast to the restaurant inside. The tables gleam with pristine white cloths; the wine selection is as varied as it is expensive; the staff moves with practiced precision, eager to please;

and then there's Lisa, radiant and all-consuming, filling Carl's world in a way that makes everything else seem distant.

"You look distracted," she says, eyeing him with a mix of amusement and concern.

"How can I not be?" he murmurs, his gaze never leaving her face.

On Christmas Eve, they head into the heart of Santiago for a concert – a solo violinist performing in Plaza de la Constitución. The audience sits on fragile wooden seats arranged in a circle around the concrete stage, watching intently. Soldiers stand guard, weapons ready for any disturbance.

"She's wonderful, isn't she?" whispers Lisa.

"She is," Carl responds, his voice soft.

"Can you believe she's only nineteen? Can you?" Lisa asks, her eyes wide with admiration.

"I can't," Carl replies.

The performer, blonde hair swishing as she pours herself into the music, captivates the crowd. Her eyes are closed, lost in the melody, her feet dancing as gracefully as the notes she plays. She's pretty. Lake feels a flicker of something dark, an impulse he fights to suppress.

His thoughts turn quickly. He imagines dragging her into the Andes, strapping her to a rock, leaving her there. Or maybe flaying her with a blunt razor. A fleeting fantasy, quickly buried.

He allows himself a brief moment of respite. Just for a second, he lets the music take over.

As the concert ends, Lisa tucks her arm into his, pulling him away from the thoughts that threaten to cloud his mind.

"I'm taking you home, right now," she says, a smile in her voice.

"Thought you'd never ask," Carl replies.

In the taxi ride back, Lisa starts laughing at something, her genuine mirth filling the space between them. Even the sight of soldiers roughly bundling a man into a car doesn't dampen her spirits. Rifle butts slam down on his neck as they force him in.

"Sorry, it's not funny," Lisa giggles, trying to hold herself together.

"What is it?" Carl asks, curious despite himself.

"It was a story in the news a couple of weeks ago," she says, still chuckling. "A corpse washed up on the coast of Brazil. Covered in snake bites. Terrible thing. I shouldn't laugh."

Carl gives her a look, the faintest trace of amusement in his eyes. "I think that's quite funny."

On Christmas Day, they don't rise until ten o'clock. Carl makes Lisa a traditional British fry-up. Her fridge is lacking eggs and mushrooms, no bacon in sight, but he improvises. He's a man who's learned how to think outside the box. Borstal taught him that.

Against all odds, he actually has a present for her – a notebook. He bought it from a visiting tradesman with an overhanging, oversized hat. The man had glanced at the observatory and remarked in broken English, "This is a bad place. Did the Captain General allow this to be built?"

When Carl gives it to Lisa, she's taken aback. Her usual stern, almost mocking demeanour cracks, and she throws her arms around him. "Carl, you are such a good man."

"I love you, Lisa."

"I love you too."

She gives him his gift as they clear away the remnants of their breakfast. He tears away the paper and finds a pocket watch inside.

"It's over a hundred years old," she says. "So old."

"Thank you. Oh, my love, thank you."

On New Year's Eve, they walk to Plaza de la Constitución. An opera is being performed – a once-in-a-lifetime event featuring some of Chile's most respected actors. The performance is set to begin at ten and will carry on through the first hours of the new year. Entry is tightly controlled. Augusto Pinochet himself is expected to attend.

"He's a dictator, isn't he?" Carl murmurs as they approach the security checkpoint.

"So?" says Lisa.

"Well—"

"Keep it down. We'll talk after."

They're ushered through. The other side is chaos dressed in elegance – a press of well-heeled guests jostling to reach their well-assigned seats. A director – short, flustered, half his scalp surrendered to baldness – pinwheels in frantic circles, barking in Spanish. Carl recognises the tone of the words even if he doesn't catch them all. Stress never needs translation.

"That's him," Lisa whispers, grabbing his arm. "It's him! Look!"

But Carl isn't looking at Pinochet.

He's locked on the man beside him: Gerard Peterson.

A name from another world. A man from another life. A high-ranking officer in the EACM – and the very one who helped coordinate Britton's paperwork all those years ago. Peterson was known for being clinical. Methodical. Lethal.

Carl's body goes rigid.

"Are you okay? Carl?"

What the hell is a communist doing here?

"Carl?"

How the hell did he get into the country?

"Baby, tell me what's going on!"

"We need to leave. Now."

Peterson is staring straight at him, his expression frozen, calculating. He's in full EACM dress: the black suit, red tie, and the unmistakable hammer-and-sickle armband.

Then, without warning –

Lisa crumples.

A gasp. A collapse. His arms catch her, but it's too late. Her body is soft, already losing tension. Blood spills from her abdomen, soaking into his shirt. He clamps his hand to the wound. It makes a wet, pulpy sound.

"Get him!" a voice roars – thick with an English accent, deep, undeniable.

Gunfire erupts. The air shatters. Wood, metal, and stone splinter and crack.

Lake runs.

There is no thought, no hesitation – only movement. He has no plan, no home, nothing left. Just instinct.

A soldier lunges at him, rifle raised. Lake pivots, grabs the barrel, jerks it away. A sickening crunch as the butt slams into the soldier's face. Blood sprays. The man drops like a stone.

More soldiers appear, shouting commands, weapons drawn. Civilians scream and scatter – elderly couples, tourists, children. Pandemonium.

Lake lifts the rifle and fires, dropping two, maybe three pursuers. The others hesitate. They're young, nervous, and untrained – he can tell from the way they flinch, the way none of them returns fire.

He breaks free of the square, ducks into a side street, tosses the rifle into a trash bin without breaking stride.

Ahead, a parade is rolling through the streets. Music, smoke, streamers – a wild, kaleidoscopic vision. Lake crashes into it without missing a beat. He grabs a glittery hat off a teenager's head and shoves it on. Someone shouts in protest, but it's drowned by the throb of music.

Sirens wail in the distance. Orders echo across the rooftops. Lake hears the boots on pavement, the shouting.

Too late. He's already gone. He's always been too fast for them.

Grief? Maybe. But if he sees Lisa's eyes again – blank, wide, unblinking – he knows he'll shatter. Better not to think. Better to move.

Fireworks burst overhead. Bright ribbons of light smear across the dark. The parade swells with noise and bodies. He dances among them, ducking, weaving, invisible.

Then he sees them: men in black suits, walking both sides of the parade. Not military. EACM. Communists. A few faces he recognises.

"He'll be in here somewhere," one of them mutters.

"Look sharp," says another.

And then: Gerard.

He's closer now, clearly exhausted. Jaw tight, eyes burning. "Don't fucking let this guy get away," he hisses. "We need him dead."

Lake drifts to the left, inch by inch, weaving through dancers and drummers and partygoers. No sudden moves. No tells.

Gerard steps too close to the parade.

Lake grabs him.

A hand snakes around Gerard's throat, dragging him off his feet. His eyes go wide with panic.

The crowd around them cheers, oblivious.

Lake hurls him to the pavement behind a moving float. No one sees. No one notices.

He slams Peterson's head into the ground. Once. Twice. A third time. There's a crunch. A twitch.

Then nothing.

Lake vanishes into the crowd.

Two days later, he's on the move again.

Over the next two years, he travels farther than he ever dared, sees more than he ever thought possible. Landscapes blur. Borders fade. Faces come and go. He shifts from one disguise to another, weaving new identities like a spider spins its web – calculated, instinctive. Every new story is a fresh skin he slips into without hesitation.

But beneath it all, he never forgets who he is. Or who he was. Clifford Lake remains intact, hidden beneath layers of invention. And yet, in his own way, he's utterly lost – untethered from everything he once believed.

Lisa becomes nothing more than a fragment of a fracture of a memory.

He tries, sometimes, to pass as one of them. The human race. But the effort is always doomed. He knows what he is. The things he's done – what he continues to do – have cast him out forever.

In mid-1989, he arrives in Papua New Guinea.

He becomes Carl Letterman once more – this time with a few refinements. No longer a man of catering, but a professor of astronomy. Word of a new observatory opening in the highlands had reached him during his travels. He puts a CV together. Polished. Mysterious. Welcome aboard.

From Port Moresby, he hitchhikes and walks the rest of the way. His boots fill with red clay as he climbs to the empty hilltop where the telescope, still reeking of fresh paint, stands ready to pierce the night sky. The researchers and scientists welcome him with open arms – eager, even star-struck, to meet the legendary Carl Letterman.

But within a year, the atmosphere sours.

It begins with whispers in the breakroom. Glances. Silence when he walks in. Then come the notes stuck to his office door.

Weirdo.

You don't belong here.

Go home.

Fuck off, you soppy cunt.

"You're a brilliant scientist," says Kerry Gibson, the head of the observatory, as they sip bitter coffee one morning on the veranda. "But, to be frank, you have no people skills."

"Let me prove myself," says Carl. "We have visiting students, don't we? Let me teach."

Kerry shrugs. "To be honest, I don't think that's going to fix anything."

Two weeks later, he's called into a meeting with Sandra Barford, Kerry's deputy. Plump, brisk, all-business – a girl from Hampshire. Her accent is the most English thing he's heard in months. There's a mountain of paperwork between them. Her voice is all kindness and ice.

"There are other opportunities for you out there, Professor Letterman. This place just doesn't seem the right fit. Now, I know what you're like. You'll worry. But don't. We're all here to support you."

A month passes.

Sweat-slicked from the rainforest and smelling faintly of mould and rust, he's summoned again. Sandra closes the door behind him, offers him a seat, hands him a letter. He begins to read:

Professor Letterman is highly passionate about his astronomy, but I am concerned about his professional ability. During a meeting with him last week, when I asked for clarification on the size of Betelgeuse compared to Rigel, the explanation he gave me did not make sense. I have conferred with colleagues here, who also raised concerns.

I am also alarmed at his general conduct. He is often short-tempered and aggressive, as well as –

He stops reading.

Hands the letter back to Sandra.

"I won't have this," he says, voice flat. "It's a pack of lies."

"You need to consider your position here, Mr Letterman."

And he does.

A few hours later, he starts executing each and every one of them. He doesn't plan it out in any great detail. He goes in with a machete and simply hacks away at them. Some try to flee, but he's locked the doors with extra-strong padlocks. They scream and yelp as they attempt to bulge out. Lake picks them off with solid, clean cuts. Sandra Barford and Kerry Gibson go down quickly – maybe too fast for his liking: no suffering involved.

Teagan Brown says nothing. Just glares at him as he decapitates her. Stupid little bitch. Always trying to put him down: *"You're not even a real professor!"*

Jennifer Shields, the annoying high-pitched Canadian technician, tries to splutter an apology, but Lake shoves the blade through her neck.

Lynn Jones-Davies, the fat bitch who runs the reception, Lake particularly enjoys picking off. Machete in her guts, ripping everything out.

Steve Russ. Lake hates him with an absolute passion. He finds him and his autistic son cowering in a stationary cupboard. He gives them a polite smile, then swipes.

Ralph Palmer, the personnel man, stumbles in the corridor, slips and falls onto his elbows. Lake stabs him through the base of the spine, twisting the blade.

"Go on, be reasonable now, you Irish cunt," says Lake, yanking the weapon out.

He saves Raj Nott for last, cornering him in the breakroom by the water fountain.

"So, still thinking about making a complaint against me?" he taunts. "Hmm? Let's see how you can write a grievance letter without any hands!"

Lake learns of the massacre a few days later, during his flight to South Korea. A child, stumbling upon the bodies, skin shredded, dumped on a hillside – he'll be scarred for life. Lake can't help but chuckle. He knows he shouldn't, but the absurdity of it makes him laugh.

In the seat pocket in front of him, there's a celebrity magazine. He flips through it idly, smirking when he sees Roger Miser's miserable mug plastered under the headline: *Roger Miser To Launch Several Girl Bands Next Year*.

The article details Miser's regrets over the summer of 1980.

"That love triangle... something I shouldn't have gotten involved with. Stupid, really. How was I to know how Claudine felt that way about Marie? How the hell was I to know?"

Lake chuckles again, the bitterness in the laughter unmistakable. Another gin and tonic slides down. A redhead stewardess passes by, her tight-fitting trousers accentuating her curves. She doesn't notice him, but he watches her.

For a moment, he's tempted. He could strike. Nothing would stop him. He could kill her, mutilate her, dump her body in the sea. No one would bat an eyelash. But he doesn't.

Instead, he turns back to the article, reading it again, then a third time. Miser's agony has been perfectly realized in this article. His revenge on Roger Miser is complete.

Lake has spent years killing, tearing through the lives of those who've wronged him: Ceri Britton, Gary Holmes, William Butterworth, so many others. A blood-soaked path behind him, each act more violent than the last. Yet, Roger Miser deserved something more.

Lake knows what Miser must have felt when he believed that he was free from him. The relief. The joy of thinking he was untouchable. Lake imagines Miser with Claudine, strolling through the French countryside, free from the past. Miser would have laughed, thrown his carefree weight around, strutting into a café each morning, eyeing women in skirts. He would've fallen for Claudine, only for her to fall for someone else – the teacher at that summer school. A messy love triangle would have crystallized, full of passion and heartbreak.

Lake knows the sharp sting Miser must've felt when he was pushed to the edge, unable to control the situation, desperate to force apart the lovers. Miser would've used his media connections, but it all would have backfired. Claudine and Marie would've taken their own lives in a desperate act, leaving Miser broken, consumed by guilt and shame.

He can picture Miser now, drinking alone, trying to salvage whatever fragments of himself are left, clinging to false redemption.

And this, Lake thinks, is his punishment: the slow agony of shame, the loss of everything, the realization that no matter what Miser does now, it will never be enough to atone.

Lake reclines back in his seat, a rare moment of peace. He can kill when he wants to—he does so now for pleasure, the power in his hands.

But there is, of course, one last thing to do.

His contact in London will have sent several letters by now, all carefully crafted to lead Miser's family to Lake's hometown on the last day of August, 2009. They'll be expecting a violent confrontation, expecting him to turn up guns blazing. But there will be nothing. Absolutely nothing. Instead, the media will feast on the story. Allegations of abuse at Milton Borstal, of Miser's involvement in Lake's wrongful imprisonment – Tracy Cox, Jefferson Reed, the entire nightmare will be laid bare. Stratton's descendants, the ones still clinging to power, will be left exposed, their names dragged through the mud, powerless to stop the press from devouring them.

Clifford Lake orders a whisky this time, stares through the window at the starlit sky, and waits.

Acknowledgements

Thanks to the following: family, Richard Selwyn-Barnett, Lynette Jackson-Edwards, Ray Evans, Raedan O'Dubhghaill, and members of the Oxford Writing Circle.

Front cover image designed using Canva.

www.ingramcontent.com/pod-product-compliance
Lightning Source LLC
Chambersburg PA
CBHW071129180726
48291CB00007B/2108